The Boy from
The Cloth

Also by Patrice Matchaba

Fiction
Deadly Profit
Like Anthills after the Rain

The Boy from The Cloth

Patrice Matchaba
Edited by
Michelle Galloway

Writers Club Press
San Jose New York Lincoln Shanghai

The Boy from The Cloth

Writers Club Press
an imprint of iUniverse.com, Inc.

For information address:
iUniverse.com, Inc.
5220 S 16th, Ste. 200
Lincoln, NE 68512
www.iuniverse.com

ISBN: 0-595-20340-X

Printed in the United States of America

To my family.

All of them, pure and wonderful creations of God.

Each a true original.

Each one, one of a kind!

Acknowledgements

Michelle Galloway for her outstanding gift.

And God for his kind mercy and wisdom.

Introduction

No Man Knoweth the Day and Hour

"But of that day and hour Knoweth no man, no, not the angels of heaven, but my father only. But as the days of Noah were, so shall also the coming of the Son of man be. For as in the days that were before the flood they were eating and drinking, marrying and giving in marriage, until the flood came. Until the day that Noah entered into the ark, knew not until the flood came, and took them all away; so shall also be the coming of the Son of man be...Watch therefore; for ye know not what hour your Lord doth come. Therefore be ye also ready: for in such an hour as ye think not the Son of man cometh

(**Mk.** *13: 22; Lk 17; 26-36; 34-36*)

Contents

One

January 1999, Wilt residence, Washington D C, USA.

"Well then Gentleman…Let's start the ball rolling! I'll inform you as soon as I get back from Europe and the first phase of the plan is complete," said Galvez.

"Fine. Let me remind you all that you must not, I repeat, not discuss this with anyone outside the Millennium Club (MC)!" Wilt was serious. They all nodded in agreement.

Galvez and his team of bodyguards were the first to leave, then Bell and the others. All with their escorts. Nicky was the only one who didn't have a private army with him. He left with his driver and bodyguard. As he sat in the back seat of his BMW seven series, his heart was racing with excitement as they left Wilt's country estate. This had been a wonderful day for him and he was going to celebrate. After all it was Saturday evening and being single, well, divorced three times, he decided to call Ms Genevieve from his car phone.

"Hey Genevieve…how you doing, it's Nicky?"

"Oh Nicky, what a surprise. I haven't heard from your for some time. You're ok darling?" she asked.

"Never better my dear. Listen Genevieve who do you have with you there?" Nicky was straight to the point.

"Well Samantha is available. I know you like Samantha!" she responded.

"Yeah I like Samantha, but I want her to bring a friend with her this time. Say an oriental, tall and slim…can you arrange that Genevieve?" asked Nicky.

"Not a problem, I've just the girl for you. Where will you be darling?"

"I'll be at the penthouse. Send them in at 21h00. You have my credit card details don't you Genevieve?"

"Consider it done, Samantha and her friend will be there and should I arrange it for the whole night?"

"You've got that right Genevieve darling!" Nicky put the phone down, he was in for some fun and just the thought of Samantha was enough to give him an erection. In his mind he had images, vivid ones of Samantha making love to her friend and him joining in.

"Sir we've arrived" Nicky's erotic thoughts were interrupted by his driver.

"Fine Johnny, you can knock off now. I won't be needing you tonight. Pick me up tomorrow at midday!"

"Yes Sir…and have a good evening Sir!"

"You too Johnny…and aye, here's two hundred dollars, paint the town red on me!"

"Thank you very much Sir!" John was taken aback but grateful by all this sudden generosity.

It was 21h00 on the dot and Nicky's buzzer went off.

"Yes?" asked a cocky Nicky. He was in his penthouse and had a dressing gown on only. He was already naked. He had 'New York Voices' singing 'Stolen Moments' in the background and to complete the atmosphere he had turned the lights down low and lit several candles that he had placed all around the apartment.

"Nicky honey, it's me Samantha and I've brought my friend along, open up!" Samantha's voice was sweet, soft and oh so tempting.

"Come on in!" Nicky replied. He smiled in eager anticipation. Before the girls arrived he dashed for the bathroom. He opened his drug cabinet and took out one of the containers. He looked at the blue pill and smiled before he popped it into his mouth. It was Viagra and he opted for the maximum dose, a 100 mg. He figured it was going to be a long night and he could do with all the help he needed. Handling Samantha and her friend was going to be demanding. But thanks to Pfizer, even a man his age could literally hold his own! "Bloody wonder drug if you ask me. An erection on demand!" Nicky thought to himself.

"Nicky, you haven't changed, not one bit!" Samantha was at her best, flattering Nicky as usual. She was tall, slim, blond and a gorgeous creature. Maybe she was at least twenty now. Who cares Nicky thought to himself?

"This is my friend…you like her?" asked Samantha teasingly. She was rubbing her Thai friend's breasts as she was talking. She was obviously from Bangkok. Her smile was dashing, her tits small and firm with nipples that stood out, piercing her see through silk shirt. She responded to Samantha's caressing by reaching out to Nicky and grabbed his left hand. She pulled a laughing Nicky towards her and placed his hand on her right breast, so that Nicky could feel her erect nipples. She went on to stick her tongue out for Samantha and Samantha responded by covering her tongue with her lips in a passionate kiss. Nicky felt Samantha grouping for his groin. She exclaimed as she felt Nick's hardness. It was as if he was a teenager again. She went down on him while her friend started licking Nicky's neck, then his hairy chest and nipples, sucking them.

"Hold on Ladies…there is no rush, we have the whole night to ourselves" said Nicky trying to slow things down. They had hardly moved from the entrance. "First things first, Samantha why don't you pour us all some drinks, you know where the liquor cabinet is. In the meantime, I'm going to get the Jacuzzi running and show your friend around".

"Alright Nicky darling, I'll be with you guys shortly," teased Samantha.

By the time Samantha got to the Jacuzzi, her friend was sitting on Nicky, riding him in a slow rhythmic movement. Nicky was groaning with pleasure. She joined in the water, took a gulp of some champagne and then kissed Nicky passionately, transferring some of the champagne from her mouth into his. She did the same to her friend who continued with the slow writhing movement, letting Nicky fill her up. Samantha continued to do this until she had finished the first bottle of Champagne.

After about five minutes Nicky gently pushed Samantha's friend off him and asked Samantha to make love to her while he watched. Samantha and her friend were lying next to the Jacuzzi, out of the water in the sixty-nine position and giving each other pleasure, teasing and caressing with their tongues. Nicky took some huge gulps of Champagne while his eyes feasted on the wet, naked, beautiful bodies in poetic motion, in front of him.

After a while, he couldn't take it any longer so he entered Samantha from behind. Her friend continued to use her tongue and hands, this time on Nicky and Samantha. Nicky screamed with pleasure and shuddered as he came into Samantha. Than he went back into the Jacuzzi, smiling and exhausted. His heart was pounding. He pulled Samantha and her friend, who were all giggling into the water. They continued to caress and kiss each other. Realising that the first bottle of champagne was empty, Samantha went back to the kitchen and brought another bottle. She opened it while she was still in the kitchen and took a swing of it while she was there.

"Samantha my dear, don't take too long with the champagne!" shouted an excited Nicky." And while you're there bring some cigars and grapes with you."

Samantha came back with the champagne, cigars and the grapes. They were all hungry after having worked up an appetite. When they had almost devoured the grapes, Nicky lit the cigars for all of them and for the next twenty or so minutes they relaxed in the water, smoking cigars while the bubbles massaged their naked bodies and listened to Mike Jagger and the Stones playing 'I can't get no satisfaction!'

Soon they were at each other again. This time Samantha went for Nicky and used her tongue to harden him. Nicky rose to the occasion. Thanks to the wonder blue pill. When he was nice and hard, she sat at the edge of the Jacuzzi and opened her legs, guiding Nicky into her. Her friend in the meantime was sucking Samantha's breasts and massaging Nicky's back.

When she realised that Nicky was about to come, she stopped him gently, smiled and then pushed him out of her. She held him by his waist and guided him to her friend who was now also sitting on the edge of the Jacuzzi, opposite Samantha and Nicky. Nicky obliged and entered her. Samantha clung to him from behind and when she felt him shudder, she grabbed the two of them tightly and the three kissed each other passionately.

When Nicky finished coming, he suddenly felt tired and dizzy. He clambered out of the Jacuzzi and just about managed to drag himself to the bedroom. He could feel his heart pounding in his rib cage and he felt exhausted. Having drunk almost a full bottle of champagne didn't help. So with the girls following behind him, giggling, he slumped onto the queen-sized bed and within a few minutes he was in a deep post-orgasmic sleep.

Nicky remembered waking up sometime at night, with a crushing pain in his chest. The pain was excruciating, as if he had a severe case of heart-burn. But what worried him was that the pain radiated into his left arm. He tried calling for Samantha, but he could hardly open his mouth. He didn't have the energy to say a word. He was sweating profusely and could hardly move now. His fingers tried in vain to reach out for Samantha but they refused to obey his wish. Suddenly the room became lighter and lighter, until it was so bright that Nicky felt that he had to close his eyes. Then everything became dark and distant. He felt himself leave his body. It was a weird sensation at first. The pain had gone and he could actually see himself in bed with Samantha and her friend, the three of them lying in a tight, innocent, naked embrace. Strange enough though, he still couldn't wake himself up and Nicky really didn't want to be woken up this time.

Samantha was the first to wake up. She moved her naked body towards Nicky, brushing her breasts on his right shoulder as she tried to kiss his mouth. Nicky didn't even make a sound in response. Samantha screamed. Nicky's body was limp but still warm. It rolled over towards her so that he was facing the ceiling. His lips were blue and there was froth spewing from the corner of his open mouth. His eyes were closed as if he was asleep and there was a sickening smile on his face. She immediately knew he was dead. Samantha's screaming woke up her friend.

"What's wrong Samantha?" she asked innocently with her cute oriental accent.

"He's dead. Nicky is dead!" Samantha shouted back, her hands covering her mouth.

'Oh God no…what to do now?" asked her friend, jumping out of the bed, wanting to be as far away from death as possible.

"Genevieve, I'll call Genevieve," replied Samantha. Cleverly she used her own cell phone instead of Nicky's phone.

'Ms Genevieve, it's Samantha, I know it's five in the morning, but Nicky is dead! We just woke up and he was dead, he must have had a heart attack or something," she added sobbing hysterically. She was now also standing as far from the bed as possible.

"Now listen Samantha, I want you to keep calm and follow my instructions. Ok…are you listening Sam?" commanded a composed Genevieve.

"Yes, yes. What must we do?" asked Samantha.

"Take a cloth and wipe all your prints off everything that you guys touched, everything!" replied Genevieve. She had been through this routine with her girls, so they knew what to do in a case like this." And Samantha, don't forget the door handles as well!"

"Ok Ms Genevieve." Samantha and her friend cleared up their belongings and any trace of their presence. When they were through it was 05h45. Then they slipped out of the penthouse, unnoticed. Nicky saw them leave. But then again there was nothing he could do for himself or them from above. He had to face it now, he was dead!

The post-mortem report from the coroner's office read as a cause of death; "Myocardial infarct due to an overdose of nitrates and Viagra!"

Bell shook his head in disbelief and shock. He had known Nicky since Vietnam and he never not once heard him talk about heart problems. He even checked with his physician and he also confirmed that Nicky was not on any anti-hypertensive medication, let alone nitrates. Fair enough he had prescribed the Viagra for Nicky, but that was after a thorough medical and Nicky was fine. The doctor was adamant that Nicky was not on any medication.

Bell then read the detailed notes from the forensic laboratory. They found large quantities of nitrates in the champagne bottles. Nicky had been murdered!

Two

"Doesn't that man know when to quit? I've just about had it with him. The bloody jerk thinks he can walk into this town and proclaim himself king…Well we'll see about that!"

"I agree with you High Priest, that man must take us for nuts if he thinks he can get away with all that crap!" The chief priests and scribes were milling around the dining hall. There was plenty of food on the table as the Passover feast had begun. The atmosphere around the table was acrid, full of deceit, cunning and vengeance. Their agenda was totally unholy and on their lips, murder was the word. Their minds were preoccupied with the gory thoughts of how they could murder that man. Various scenarios of how to torture him then snuff the life out of him were examined and meticulously analysed. They debated at length the pros and cons of taking that man's life. He simply had to die.

The previous day, that man had run rampant in the Temple, chasing away the merchants and turning all the tables upside down. He went on to warn his followers about them; the chief priests and the scribes.

"This man, how dare he question our authority and destroy our Temple?" asked one of the scribes.

"I say we kill him," responded another.

"Yeah, yeah, yeah!" was the resounding echo in agreement amongst these men. These men of the cloth.

"But how do we trap him, how do we take him away, isolate him from his followers?" asked another. There was an obvious tremble of fear and hate that echoed in his voice. The thought of confronting this man alone evoked emotions of fear in all of them. This man wasn't to be taken lightly. Many followed him, many believed that he was the Christ, the Son of the Blessed.

"That man is blasphemous, he must die!" repeated another of the scribes.

"Die he will!" the chief priest said.

He got up from the table, with a mug of wine in his hand. The liquid from the grapes was now getting to his head, warming it, filling it with rage, cunning and courage. They were all like a pack of hyenas moving in on the spoils of a kill, trying to wrest the carcass from a male lion. None had the courage to do it alone, out of fear of the possible, vicious retaliatory mauling. So they advanced as a group, giggling like the little devils that they really were and waiting for the opportune time, circling and attacking from different flanks.

"I know one of them who's prepared to betray him!" the chief priest murmured. He gazed across the room, looking above the rest of his hyena pack.

"One of the Disciples has agreed to join us today!"

"Which one of the twelve?" was the response from the corner of the room.

"Judas Iscariot! Judas will betray this man they call Jesus and then we'll kill him!" added the chief priest with disdain. His voice was now quivering with anger. His saliva had accumulated and frothed as white cakes at the corners of his mouth. He'd been talking for so long and with such passion that he had no time to swallow!

As Jesus walked through the rubble that he'd caused in the Temple, John, Peter, Andrew and James followed behind him. They were all quiet and afraid. They all thought that perhaps he'd gone too far this time. None of them ever conceived that any one man would have the courage to destroy the Temple and defy the chief priests and the scribes. Andrew was the most concerned as the previous evening Jesus had warned them about his eminent death. He had a sleepless night after that, so he wanted to know more. He needed the reassurance from Jesus.

"Master what will the signs of the End be?" he asked with genuine concern and fear. "How will we know the sign when all these things you talk about shall be fulfilled?"

Jesus took his time. He'd now managed to catch his breath, after the adrenaline rush that had raced through his veins as he chased the merchants that were selling in his house of prayer, his father's house! He bent down to open the last cage of pigeons that were meant for death that evening. When the last one flew out and spread its wings, tasting the freedom that it had so nearly lost forever, he looked at his disciples and shook his head in despondency.

"Take heed lest any man deceive you: for many shall come in my name, saying, I am Christ: and they shall deceive many!" Jesus then sat upon the Mount of Olives, over against the Temple. Peter and the others could sense that the time of his death was near. They sensed that Jesus already knew of the gory events that were yet to be played out in the days to come. There was a change in the manner in which he looked at them and the way he spoke. There was finality in his voice and a sense of urgency. It was as if he was trying to teach them as much as he could in the short time that he had left with them on Earth before he joined his Father in Heaven. They sensed that he was trying to give them strength, courage and faith, so that they could continue to spread his word even after man had murdered him. So Jesus went on.

"And when you shall hear of wars and rumours of wars, be you not troubled; for such things must needs be; but the end shall not be yet!"

There were sighs of relief amongst Peter and his friends. Deep down, some of them had thought that with the departure of Jesus, the world as they knew it would end. Little did they know then that they had their work cut out for them. Jesus went on to caution them.

"For nation shall rise against nation and kingdom against kingdom; and there shall be earthquakes in the diverse places and there shall be famines and troubles. These are the beginnings of sorrow!"

"We will always be at your side Master!" one of them said. It was more to comfort their own souls than to comfort Jesus. He ignored them and continued with his counsel to them.

"Take heed to yourselves for they shall deliver you up to the councils and in the synagogues you shall be beaten. You shall be brought before rulers and kings for my sake, for testimony against them."

"Master we will not betray you!" they responded almost in unison. "No Master, we'll never betray you or leave your side!"

But Jesus knew better.

"The brother shall betray the brother to death and the father the son; and children will rise up against their parents and shall cause them to be put to death! And you…" Jesus looked down at the four of them, and then continued, "you shall be hated by all men for my name's sake, but he that shall endure unto the end, he will be saved!"

With that Jesus left the Temple that he had laid waste. At the exit he kicked a vase that was full of wine that was still standing. It went crashing down the floor, spewing the intoxicating red liquid from the grape onto the marble floor of the Temple. He then turned around at the exit and looked at the mess in the Temple and shook his head in anger.

"How dare they use the house of prayer for profit and deceit?" he cursed quietly to himself. Peter, James, John and Andrew followed close behind, with their heads bowed in shame and sorrow.

Judas walked into the dinning room where the priests and scribes had gathered.

"Come in Judas, please come in and join us at the table…you are amongst friends!" the chief priest said as he rose to meet Judas and guided him to an empty chair placed at the centre of the table. The chief priest smiled. The others were making squeaky noises and utterances like the hyenas they really were, all in unison, all following the leader!

"Go on help yourself to some of the bread and wine…go on Judas, you really are amongst friends here. Don't be afraid!" the chief priest was using all the skills of cunning that he had mastered as he climbed the ladder of corruption in Jerusalem's corridors of power. Judas was nervous at first. He was torn between his greed for the money they'd promised him in exchange for his betrayal of Jesus and his love for Christ. But by the time he was on his second glass of wine, greed and betrayal had won against loyalty and honesty.

"How much do you want in exchange for the favour we ask of you?" asked the chief priest. Judas hesitated; he didn't know how he could price the life of the Son of Man.

"Twelve pieces of silver. I want twelve pieces of silver!" When he repeated his demand for the second time, his voice went up a decibel or two, trying to sound confident. The wine had helped. Little did he know that the scribes had offered him the juice from the grapes, knowing full well that he would then agree to betray his Master easily for much less than he was really worth.

"Twelve pieces of silver it will be!" echoed the chief priest in agreement. It was more in amazement that Judas had agreed to betray the Son of Man for so little. "The things man will do for money!" the priest thought to himself.

"How will we know that it's him in the crowd. How will you identify the Son of Man to us?" asked one of the scribes who was sitting at the end of the table. Judas turned to face him and added.

"I will kiss him!"

"Judas Iscariot…you're the man!" responded one of the pack from around the table.

The chief priest took out a bag, and threw the twelve pieces of silver onto the table. As the coins rolled onto the table towards Judas, the others laughed as Judas scrambled after the coins. Some had fallen on to the floor, under the table and he had to go down on his hands and knees to retrieve them. This caused the squeaky, hyena-like laughter to increase. Judas, at that moment knew, that as Jesus his Master had warned them before, one of them was going to betray him and lead him to his death. He now knew that he was the one. As he collected the last coin and put it into his sheep leather pouch, the sense of guilt and shame he felt began to overwhelm him.

But it was too late now. He had sold the Son of Man. They'd given him the twelve pieces of silver as he'd requested and now the ball was in his court. So as the hyena he had now become, he cowered out of the room of the elders and scribes, with his tail well tucked between his legs.

You could almost touch the tension around the room as Jesus and his twelve disciples ate the Passover in the guest chamber that had been prepared for them. Jesus asked them for their attention. Judas knew what was coming and his heart was racing in a panic with fear and guilt.

"Verily I say unto you" Jesus started out "one of you which eateth with me shall betray me!"

The Disciples gasped and again swore that they'd never betray him. Some fearful of the weakness of their conviction, started asking Jesus whether it would be them. They were after all only human. Jesus didn't answer their queries directly but added.

"Woe to that man that the Son of Man is betrayed! Good were it for that man if he'd never been born!"

Judas didn't know were to look, so he looked straight ahead, pretending he didn't know what Jesus was talking about. But deep down his heart ached. He felt ashamed of himself and was now a sad and depressed man.

Jesus took some bread, blessed it and gave them all a piece, for them to eat and added. "Take this bread, eat it; this is my body!"

Hungrily they all chewed on the bread and ate it. The fasting of Passover was now complete and they were all famished. But Judas found it hard to swallow the bread, because for him this ceremony had a different meaning. He was the only one amongst the disciples who really understood the significance of the ceremony and Jesus' words. Jesus then took the cup with the fruit of the vine that was before him. He lifted it up in thanks to his Father and again he blessed it and then asked that they all drink from the cup.

'This is my blood, drink it!" Jesus commanded them. Again Judas hesitated as he drank the wine. This betrayal to death of his Master, had now began to be played out in slow motion, guised as a ceremony of the Passover feast. He knew that there was little to celebrate but plenty to weep for. He felt powerless and he wished he could reverse the hands of time, but it was too late. He had played his role. Jesus was going to die; Jesus knew it and Judas more than anyone else knew it too. The other disciples were spared the emotional trauma that Judas was going through, for they knew not how the events of the following day would unfold. By the time the dinner was over, Judas had become silent and was now in a catatonic depressed state.

Jesus, however, went on to tell them more bad tidings. This time he was addressing Peter in particular.

"Verily I say unto thee, that this day, even in this night, before the cock crows twice, thou shall deny me thrice!"

Again all of them responded by promising Jesus that they'd never deny or forsake him. But Judas knew that the clock was already ticking and that the path that would lead to the murder of Jesus had already been cleared. His only solace was that there was another amongst his colleagues that would let Jesus down in his time of need. It comforted him to know that he would not be the only one to do so, although he now understood that his sin would be the greatest them all.

Later that evening Jesus took Peter, James and John and went up to the Mountain of Getsemane to pray. In fact he went to plead with his Father, to ask that he alter the events that were to come in the following days. His heart was wary and the thought of death filled it with sorrow. When he was alone he fell to the ground, positioned himself on to his hands and knees and asked his father to change his mind.

"Father, if it were possible, I know that you could make this dreadful hour pass?" Jesus didn't want to die.

"Abba, Father, all things are possible unto thee; take away this cup from me!" he prayed. For although his spirit was ready, his flesh was not. After asking his Father three times, Jesus knew that he couldn't change the chain of events that awaited him. So he returned to his three disciples who had fallen asleep and told them the truth.

"The hour has come; Behold the Son of Man is betrayed into the hand of sinners. Rise and let us go, he that betrayeth me is at hand!" and then they descended down the Mountain.

That evening as Jesus and his disciples were walking down the streets of Jerusalem, a crowd led by the priests, the scribes, their soldiers and Judas Iscariot, confronted them. Judas' and Jesus' eyes met for a fleeting second, then Judas' eyes escaped the glare. Judas couldn't look Jesus in the eye any longer so his eyes shifted to Jesus feet. Then he approached Jesus, with his head bowed in shame, his heart pounding in his chest and he embraced him. After embracing Jesus, Judas kissed Jesus on the forehead and then he stepped back.

During that second before the soldiers arrested Jesus, their eyes met for the last time. The tears had welled in Judas Iscariot's eyes; for twelve pieces of silver, he had signed the death warrant of his own Father. Jesus didn't resist the arrest. Instead he asked the scribes.

"Have you come out with swords to take me as if I were a thief?" He looked around at them, but none answered. They hid behind the noises of the mob, the false courage of the many and insisted that they take him to the palace of the high priest. Peter took out his sword in anger and took a swipe at the ear of one of the soldiers that had manhandled Jesus

"I will have nothing of that. Put your sword away!" Jesus shouted at him. In a sense Peter was relieved for he knew that they couldn't fight the whole mob alone.

So Peter followed behind the crowd as they led Jesus to the palace. He was torn between defending Jesus and saving his own skin. He was so frightened for his life that he decided to follow at a distance and when he got to the palace, he went to sit in one of the side rooms that housed the domestic servants of the high priest. There in the cloak of darkness, with the log fire to keep him warm and sitting amongst the chief priest's servants, he peeped into the room that Jesus had been bundled into. The hyena-like pack of priests and scribes were baying for his blood, tormenting him. They accused him of various crimes, but Jesus refused to answer them. He knew that the kangaroo court had already concluded that he was guilty and there was nothing he could say or do to change his fate.

"Aren't you one of his twelve disciples?" It was one of the maids who felt sure in her mind that even in the dim light she'd recognised Peter.

"I know not and neither do I understand what you are saying!" Peter responded rather sheepishly at first. The fat lady gave him a long stare and moved closer to him so that she could focus her gaze on his face. Peter was alarmed and instinctively moved aside, away from the fat female servant. She had foul breath and the look of revenge in her eyes and on her face frightened Peter

In the main room where Jesus was being cross-examined, the process was becoming a sham as one witness after the other contradicted each other and Jesus refused to answer the accusations. The high priest was losing his patience, so he decided to be direct.

"Art though the Christ, the Son of the Blessed?" he asked with obvious intent. There was a hushed silence in the fire-lit room. Jesus answered this time.

"I am!" he said calmly.

"Blasphemy! Blasphemy! Blasphemy!" was the angry chorus from the hanging jury that had assembled before him. Peter had buried his hands in his face when he heard the high priest ask that question. In his weak mind, being human, he wanted Jesus to deny that he was the Christ. But he knew that Jesus wouldn't deny it. He also knew that, it meant the death penalty for Jesus. As the crowd was shouting obscenities at Jesus, Jesus remained calm and motioned them with his right hand that he wanted to add something. Peter prayed in his heart that he would use this opportunity to retract his statement. Instead Jesus went on to add.

"I am Christ the Son of the Blessed and you shall see me the Son of Man, sitting on the right hand of power, coming in the clouds of heaven!"

"You have all heard that? You've all heard the blasphemy?" screamed the chief priest. "There is no need for more witnesses. This man deserves to die!"

"He must die! He is guilty!" was the chorus now. The chief priest smiled, he'd succeeded in getting what he wanted. His authority and power would not be challenged and threatened by Jesus again.

"You are surely one of them!" It was the fat lady, with the bad breath again, talking to Peter. She had moved closer to him without him noticing, as he'd been absorbed in watching the judgement and humiliation of his Master.

"Go away. I don't know this man!" Peter angrily responded and decided it was time to flee.

Outside the palace, the fat woman had now collected some of her workmates.

"I know you must be one of them! Even your accent is that of a Galilean!" She raised her voice this time, trying to attract attention. She was trying to incite the mob against Peter. Peter was shit scared!

"I told you that I know not of this man of whom you speak!"

Peter had again denied Jesus for the third time in a row. And when he was on his way out of the palace, almost at a trot now, he heard one of the cocks in the yard crow for the second time. Peter felt that thick, emotional lump developing in his throat and then the tears rolled down his cheeks. He remembered then that the previous night, Jesus had warned him that he would deny him three times before the cock crowed twice. And he'd done just that.

The following morning the chief priest and his pack woke up Jesus tied his hands tightly with rope until he bled like a common thief, and then took him to Pontius Pilate. Pilate was willing to listen to Jesus. He knew that the priests had an ulterior motive.

"Art thou the King of the Jews?" he asked. Jesus was quiet at first.

"Art thou the King of the Jews?" he repeated.

"Thou sayest it!" Jesus responded. The priests were getting impatient and worried.

"He said it himself last night!" the chief priest shouted. The others again concurred in unison. They were anxious that perhaps Pilate would find Jesus not guilty. And it being Passover, set him free!

"This man is not guilty of anything!" Pilate responded to the priests as he shifted nervously in his chair.

"He's guilty, he's guilty!" the crowd chanted to Pilate.

"Damn!" Pilate thought to himself. "I have to appease these idiots or else I'll have them being a civil nuisance!"

Pilate had picked up the slightest hint of a Galilean accent when Jesus had spoken.

"Isn't this man from Galilee?" he asked the priests.

"Well yes, but he has been inciting and insulting you saying that he has no respect for Caesar and that he is King…" Pilate motioned the high priest to be quite.

"Then he must be tried by Herod! He falls under the jurisdiction of Herod of Antipas, he is the governor there!" Pilate was keen to pass the buck to Herod, for he could find no wrong that Jesus had committed.

King Herod was not impressed with what Pilate had done. He too didn't want the blood of Jesus on his hands, so he quickly dispatched Jesus back to Pilate and told Pilate that this man was not guilty of any crime.

So the ball was back into Pilate's court again.

"Answer me please, Art though the King of the Jews?" he asked again. Pilate was almost pleading with Jesus. He wanted him to deny it so that he could let him go. But Jesus stood his ground and refused to answer. Pilate thought to himself "this man must have a death wish!"

"Don't you see that these men want you dead? Say something so that I can save you!" pleaded Pilate. Jesus maintained his silence. So reluctantly Pilate turned to the priests and scribes for their advice.

"Ok!" said Pilate in resignation. "What will you then say that I do unto him whom you call the King of the Jews?" he asked, turning to the priests and the unruly crowd of sinners that had gathered.

"Crucify him! Crucify him! Crucify him!" they all responded in a satanic frenzy. The venom in their response shocked Pilate. But seeing that this man had said or done nothing wrong, he asked the priests again.

"Why? What evil hath he done?"

"Crucify him! Crucify him!" was the response, only this time with more anger. The crowd was becoming agitated.

"So you say that you would rather see this murderer Barabas go free, then let Jesus be?" he asked for the last time.

"Yes! Crucify him!"

Pilate knew that he could not have it his way this time. "After all" he thought to himself this man they call the King of the Jews, had made no attempt to deny or defend himself. "I've tried all that I could to save him!"

Pilate stood up and motioned with both his hands for silence.

"You can have this man Jesus!" he said.

"Yeah! Crucify him! Crucify him!" the chant went on. Pilate left in a hurry, not wanting to part take any longer in this sham of a trial, this bloodthirsty orgy of hate and deceit. He knew that the priests wanted to have this man killed so that their own positions would not be threatened. But alas, there was nothing more that he could do. This man, the man they called the King of the Jews was going to die whether he wished it or not.

"Damn idiots" Pilate grumbled to himself as he walked into his private chambers, throwing a side glance at the priests and scribes who, like the hyena pack they had metamorphosised into, were smiling sheepishly in victory and bowing their heads to him as he passed by.

Judas now realised the gravity of his betrayal as the soldiers led Jesus to his death.

"Surely you guys don't intend to kill this innocent man!" he pleaded to one of the priests.

"Die he will!" was the response.

"But you'll be killing an innocent man…and I'll have his blood on my hands!" Judas pleaded. His pleas fell on deaf ears. The mob had been worked into a frenzy and they wanted to see this man butchered.

"Oh God! What have I done? What have I done?" Judas whispered to himself. Although the tears were flowing down his cheeks, he made no attempt to wipe them off. As the crowd dragged and beat Jesus up like an animal, leading him to the slaughter, Judas went in the opposite direction. He went up to a small hill were he used to play as a little boy.

There was a tree that he liked there. It was now tall and its branches were strong. Even if he sat on the main branch, it could withstand his weight. When he found his favourite branch, he sat on it. He took the belt slowly from around his waist. Trembling and with his tears now mixed with the slimy secretions that were running down his nose, into his mouth and over his chin falling like rain drops on to the ground below, he made the first knot. And for good measure he made the second knot.

When Judas jumped to the ground, the rope around his neck burnt his skin at first. Then it crushed his vocal chords. His eyes became congested, his blue tongue protruded from his gaping mouth, searching for air. He felt his rectum give in and open up, messing his undergarments. But Judas didn't give a damn anymore. It was too late. The light in his eye faded and in a distance, he heard his neck snap as he went down.

Judas felt a pair of hands pulling him up. At first he was relieved thinking that perhaps all this betrayal, this self-mutilation was a dream. But when he looked back to see who was pulling him up, he recognised the face. Then he knew it was all really over. It was Lucifer! He'd come to collect and thank him personally for the job well done!

"What are you writing there?" asked one of the centurions.

"The King Of The Jews" he replied. The crowd that had gathered to witness the murder of God's only Son laughed in response. He was inscribing the title on the top of Jesus' cross. Jesus hardly noticed them as he'd now become too weak and dehydrated after having dragged the cross through the city until they arrived at the place they called Golgotha. It was also known as the place of the skull. He was mentally and physically exhausted.

"You knock in the nails into his right hand while I knock in the ones on the left!" the two centurions agreed amongst themselves after they had tied his hands and feet to the cross.

As one of the centurions lifted the hammer high into the sky and brought it down with brute force, Jesus closed his eyes and prayed to his Father for strength. And when the right nail pierced his delicate and sensitive skin, crushing the small bones of his hand, Jesus let out a shriek in pain. He glanced at his mother, Mary, and as their eyes met, Mary felt a rush of emotions and the tears that had filled her eyes ran down her cheeks. She let out a scream when she heard the thud of the hammer as it crushed her Son's bones. Jesus felt for his mother. He felt that no mother should ever have to see her child being butchered like an animal and left powerless to intervene! He tried to tell her that it would be ok, that she shouldn't hurt because he would be born again, but the words failed to come out from his mouth.

"Damn it! Come on you lazy bunch…hold him down!" the centurion shouted to his colleagues who had suddenly decided to step back, flinching as they heard the crunching of the bones and saw Jesus body shudder in desperate agony.

"Hold him down! You guys thought it was an easy, clean job…well it's no different to slaughtering a bloody beast! So I want all of you to pin him down while we knock the nails into him OK!" added the centurion, with a hint of anger in his voice.

So the others did as they'd been told and held him down. Jesus had refused the mixture of wine and vinegar that would've helped to sedate him and maybe ease the pain. With each knock, the crowd and the priests cheered, while Jesus groaned with pain. Some spate at him and others hurled verbal insults at him.

When they had nailed his hands firmly to the cross, they then went to work on his legs. This was even more traumatic, more painful as the bones of the legs are bigger. So the centurion took out a bigger hammer and swung it down with all his might. Jesus screamed in agony as his bones were shattered.

"Shit!" screamed one of the centurions that was holding and pressing Jesus legs down as some blood squirted into his eyes.

"If you let go I'll have you whipped!" was the quick response of the centurion who was in charge of all this butchery. He was keen to get them job done with. So he sent the large hammer down again into Jesus ankles, driving the thick nail through his bones; then it happened again and again and again.

The blood was now spurting from the vessels from his hands and feet. This and the excruciating pain made him feel faint and slowly he started to lose consciousness. When they'd finished nailing him to the cross, they raised the cross up and anchored it into the ground. Having already lost a lot of blood, this made the flow of blood to his brain even more difficult. The skies were beginning to darken and he felt the palpitations in his chest as his heart was racing, trying to supply his oxygen-starved brain with some blood. It was proving to be more and more difficult as he lost more blood. The end was now near now he went into shock and his heart began to fail.

A young centurion, who had been watching all this satanic butchery of a helpless man unfolding before him, decided to end Jesus' misery. He took his spear and thrust it with all his might into Jesus' chest, aiming for his failing heart. There was a sickening noise as the blade first cut through the ribs then entered the soft muscle of the heart. Jesus shrieked and shuddered violently as the blood splashed out like an open tap all over his body, down to his legs and on to the ground. Perhaps the young centurion did this out of spite and hate, but perhaps too, he thought that he'd seen enough of this barbaric madness and he'd ease Jesus' pain and hasten his death. When the spear went into Jesus chest he screamed with all the strength that was still left in him to his Father. With the little air that was still left in his lungs, he just about managed, almost inaudibly to let his Father know his pain and anguish.

"My God, my God, why hast though forsaken me?"

Then as the young centurion pulled the spear out, it created a sucking noise as the air rushed into Jesus chest through the hole the spear had carved through his flesh and ribs.

Then all went blank. Even the sun hid away, refusing to witness and partake in this devilish slaughter of the Son of Man. The skies turned pitch black. Jesus the Son of Man was now dead.

In the background, Mary, his mother, had watched helplessly as they systematically and slowly butchered her son. She cried quietly at first and then it all became too much for her to bear. So she started sobbing hysterically and she had to be supported by Mary of Magdalene, who also was in tears. Even Mary Magdalene, though not a mother herself, felt that every mother should forever be protected from ever going through what Mary the mother of God had just witnessed. The child she had carried in her womb and nurtured for nine months, feeling his gentle kicks as they developed a bond only mothers and their children are privy to, was now no more!

His burial was a simple one. Once the centurions had informed Pilate that indeed Jesus was dead, Pilate agreed that Joseph could take him for burial. Joseph of Arimathea was an honourable counsellor and Pilate had no problems with his request.

So Joseph went in to the town and bought some reels of fine linen cloth. With the help of some of his friends they lowered the cross, with Jesus still on it, to the ground. Then Joseph started the gruesome task of slowly removing the nails that had pinned Jesus' hands and legs to the cross. His body had just begun to undergo the slow process of rigor mortis. So when they removed Jesus battered body from the cross, Joseph had to force Jesus' stiffened hands towards his chest. Then he wrapped him in the linen cloth.

Joseph, Jesus' mother and Mary Magdalene with the help of some of the disciples then carried Jesus' cold corpse down the hill and laid him in a sepulchre, which was hewn out of rock and then rolled a stone over the door of the sepulchre. Joseph, Mary Magdalene and Mary, the mother of Jesus, saw where the Lord Jesus had been laid to rest!

God then took his Son's spirit and Jesus sat on his Father's right hand side in heaven; watching over man and all that God had given to man on earth.

"But in those days, after that tribulation, the sun shall be darkened, and the moon shall not give her light, and the stars of heaven shall fall, and the powers that are in heaven shall be shaken. And then shall they see the Son of Man coming in the clouds with great power and glory. And then shall he send his angels, and shall gather together his elect from the four winds, from the uttermost part of the earth to the uttermost part of heaven."

(MK.13: 22; LK 17; 26-36; 34-36)

Patricia Oppenheimer wiped the tears that had welled in her eyes. She knew that reading about the death of Jesus Christ always brought out these painful emotions in her. She wondered how anyone could be so cruel, so uncaring and heartless. She took some tissue paper and blew her nose and decided it was time to find her friend Father Khumalo. He always managed to cheer her up and that's what she needed right now; cheering up!

"Father Khumalo, could we talk?" she asked.

"Why my angel, you seem to be in tears. Please come in and I'll make some tea for you!" Father Khumalo was in his residence in Stellenbosch, a town a few kilometres from Cape Town, South Africa. The winter chill had all but gone now. It was early September 1998.

Three

21st September 1998, Cape Town, South Africa.

"Patricia can you quote the verse about the Burial of Jesus Christ according to Luke?" Father James was a strict but caring priest. He had watched with admiration as Patricia had grown from birth, through Sunday school and now she was a tender young woman. She was in her early twenties and was loved by everyone in the small town of Stellenbosch, in the Western Cape of South Africa. Stellenbosch was about sixty kilometres from Cape Town, the 'Mother City'. It was known for its temperate climate, fine wines and fruit farms.

"Yes Father" Patricia responded.

"Then go ahead and recite it my child," replied Father James.

Patricia was hesitant at first but having been brought up in a family that read the bible daily; it came easily to her.

"And, behold, there was a man named Joseph, a counsellor; and he was a good man, and just. This man went unto Pilate, and begged the body of Jesus. And he took it down, and wrapped it linen, and laid it in a sepulchre that was hewn in stone, wherein never man before was laid. And that day was the preparation, and Sabbath drew on. And the women also, which came with him from Galilee, followed after, and beheld the sepulchre, and how his body was laid. And as they returned, and prepared spices and ointments; and rested the Sabbath day according to the commandment"

"Well done, Patricia!" said Father James.

"But what is a sepulchre Father?" Patricia knew the answer but she liked to tease Father James.

He was now nearing sixty-five and she felt that his memory was becoming a little suspect. She'd noticed how over the years he'd aged from being the strong, sharp and athletic man to the more gentle, slim and greying priest he now was. He even had a classical 'Friar Tuck-Shakespearean' baldhead.

She, on the other hand, was at her mental peak and loved to intellectually spar with Father James. For all the ageing though, Father James loved the mind games that Patricia played with him. And because of his wisdom, he played along with the memory loss act. He would tell the class that he had a strong family history of Alzeihemers disease and so the class should forgive him if he tended to forget things, now and again. Sometimes, for his own convenience, he would stretch this game too far and pretend that he'd forgotten one or two of the students' names. He never forgot Patricia's name though. Never ever. She was special to him. He realised very early on in her childhood that great things were to come from her.

"Ok Patricia, please take me and the rest of the class out of our misery and tell us what a sepulchre is!" he said pretending to be ignorant, playing along with the "I have forgotten" game.

"Well it means a tomb or burial vault. But not just any kind, it's usually cut in the rock or a cave. It can also be built from stone or bricks as a burial vault." Patricia explained.

"Thank you Patricia for coming to our rescue" Father James added.

Patricia was the third in a family of five of the Oppenheimer family. She was twenty years old and had been born in Boston, Massachusetts in the United States. Her father was on sabbatical then. So that allowed her to retain her American citizenship. She also had an American passport. Fortunately for her, dual citizenship was legal in South Africa. She had long dark hair that she tied it at the back into a ponytail. Her blue eyes complemented her beauty and the African sun had bronzed her skin beautifully.

She had since been to the States on several occasions and had stayed with friends of the family in Boston, New York and Baltimore. Her father's best friend was a Senator in Washington and she stayed with the Bell's whenever she was in Washington. Now that she'd graduated from high school, she decided to take the year off and help Father James at the local church with the scripture classes. She planned to leave for the States in 1999, to study theology and philosophy at Harvard. Well at least that was before she met Jos Leon. Since then her priorities had changed.

Father Khumalo was praying in the church that evening. It was a cool evening although it was summer in the Western Cape of South Africa. He was now living with Father James. Although everyone said that he was understudying Father James at the local Church, he knew they'd sent him to Stellenbosch to recuperate. He suspected that they all thought that he was still psychotic. He knew that he needed Father James' spiritual guidance and support. He admired and respected Father James as a mentor, colleague and a friend. His forty-seventh birthday had just passed and although he was physically strong, his heart needed solace and spiritual guidance. What he'd been through in Rwanda and in the Natal Midlands of the KwaZulu province of South Africa had taken its toll.

As he prayed that evening, on his knees, he thanked God that he was still alive and well. He thanked him also for the food that he ate daily and the abundant fresh drinking water. Father John Khumalo knew that although most people took these things for granted, many poor souls around the world were denied these basic necessities. He'd witnessed many who had been denied the most basic of human rights; that of the right to life.

Although he was off the medication prescribed by his psychiatrist in Cape Town, he knew that he was still not quite the same man he had been before. Dr Carl Matthew had been very good to him. He had listened patiently as he recounted the horrors of the massacres in Rwanda.

He remembered his time in Kigali. He could still smell the sweet sticky smell of death. That smell he'd tried so desperately to scrub off. The memories he'd tried so hard to block out. Every time he thought of the terrible fate so many had suffered, a wave of emotion broke over him, tightening the muscles around his throat and his eyes would fill with tears. He would shed tears of empathy almost every day for those who still mourned the loss of innocent children, parents and loved ones.

Father John Khumalo recalled the irony of seeing some 'crisis tourists' with backpacks in what was left of the city centre, waiting impatiently for passes to visit the mountain gorillas–Rwanda's last remaining attraction or asset. Although he himself appreciated the tragic loss and threat of extinction of the "Gorillas in the Mist", he couldn't help but notice that these tourists seemed to care more about their distant Darwinian cousins, than their fellow humans being massacred daily everywhere around him. A whole nation was in the process of being systematically exterminated and yet all they were concerned with was the extinction of the gorillas.

The officials at the DFNA (National Ministry of Forestry and Nature) often made them wait for days and sometimes even weeks for access permits. They too had no real care for their own. To them it was a game of control and patience. As large amounts of money and big egos were often at stake the travellers would succumb to the whims of the gatekeepers and cough up the precious green bucks, the mighty dollar. It was a case of 'you help us and we'll help you'. It was all such a masked façade and you never really knew who was thinking what. An official you were dealing with at the time was a friend until someone of higher standing could help you. And so it went on with each collecting his cut, capitalising on the manmade and programmed genetic extinction of a great species.

Father Khumalo thought of how ruthless and insensitive some of the journalists he'd met were. This hurt him most, because it was to them that the greater society and the weak entrusted their fate. It was their responsibility to sell the Rwanda story to the rest of the world. It was through them that the truth of the massacres could reach a world that was fast globalising despite the people of Rwanda. Instead they'd demand to see the highest officials to justify sound bites and the most brutal descriptions involving the highest number of victims. Reports of ten or twelve dead at a time, as in KwaZulu Natal, South Africa, was no need to rush off and leave their whiskeys at the bar, nor did it provoke an adrenaline rush.

They were looking for a story that would sell at home, that would put the Royal sex scandals on the second page. No one cared about looking for the real truth and the cause of this devilish orgy of human madness that had its roots so deeply embedded in the history of Central Africa and its colonisers.

One news crew after the next would enter the overcrowded Central prison, which was bursting at its seams to accommodate the hundreds of men and young boy killers in pink pyjamas. They'd mingle with the murderers, take a few good shots to use as fillers or cutaways, interview the meanest looking bastards and then only a few hours later be visiting the refugee camps sprawled out around Lake Kivu harbouring the refugee orphans of the carnage, victims and perpetrators alike.

It was clear to Father Khumalo that most of the journalists didn't clearly understand the situation themselves. What tore his heart most was that he felt they could have done more, acted earlier and brought the truth to the world sooner rather than later.

If only they'd taken the time to listen, they would have also heard the silent, piercing screams from helpless children and women as they were surgically disembowelled with machetes, or as their skulls were spilt open to expose the white flesh of the brain.

Wasn't it after all their duty as journalists, if not to mankind, then at least to themselves, to act as a voice for those poor bewildered children and the women who had to endure being repeatedly raped before being hacked to death? And what about their emasculated men, who hid frozen in shock and listened from the attic or watched from hideaways in the mountains running for their lives with the mountain 'gorillas of the mist'?

Father Khumalo was so emotional one day during his counselling session that he decided to read a statement from the African Rights report to his psychiatrist. He so much wanted him to realise that he wasn't insane and that what went on in Rwanda could only have been done through the hand of Lucifer himself. He felt that if his doctor could hear and understand what he'd gone through, he would be able to relate to his depression and anger. So he read this paragraph of the African Rights report to him;

"The response to the aftermath of the genocide was almost as shocking as the response to the genocide itself…The survivors of the genocide are not the beneficiaries of national and international compassion and support, rather they are almost wholly forgotten, while displaced people and refugees receive massive and indiscriminate assistance…it was the refusal to face reality of what is one of the very worst crimes against humanity since the foundation of the United Nations."

Dr Carl Mathew was genuinely moved by what the father had told him. Being a middle class white in South Africa, he found it difficult to comprehend what went on in the rest of 'Black Africa'. To be honest, initially, he really didn't care what went on up North in 'Africa'. He confused Hutu for Tutsi and visa versa. But somehow this story touched him. Perhaps in all this he realised how privileged he had been as a white man born into a racially segregated South Africa. He was also touched that a fellow countryman of his, and a black man at that, had made it his personal crusade to go and help those less fortunate in Rwanda. He went on to ask father Khumalo.

"Father were these massacres, these terrible crimes against humanity driven by tribalism only?"

Father Khumalo was touched that at least someone in South Africa was eager to hear the truth. So he tried to explain what he believed went on.

"Well doctor, the journalists' naivety made them gullible to the MRND party line that the killings were 'tribal' in nature. They were caught up a campaign of misinformation and by portraying the genocide as 'tribalism' they were, in fact, providing a smokescreen of confusion, which allowed the killers to proceed with their premeditated plans. It was so well planned that it actually remained hidden from international journalists for a good three weeks as the first democratic elections in South Africa became the central focus for the world's attention on Africa".

It was obvious to Dr Carl Matthew's that Father John Khumalo was a well-read and philosophical man. A man with a searching and questioning mind a man who had not lost touch with humanity. It was also clear from their third consultation why this experience and that of his home province, KwaZulu Natal in Richmond, South Africa had taken its toll on him. His retreating into an emotional sanctuary was the only way he thought he could handle and comprehend it all. It was a coping mechanism that Father Khumalo had opted for when he realised that the rest of his world didn't seem to care. They couldn't see that these were bad signs, devilish omens. At times he was convinced that the Devil himself had descended on earth and that perhaps Lucifer had finally won the war against Gabriel and God's other good Angels!

Dr Matthew's job was to encourage him to ventilate and discuss his fears openly. This, in his experience and teaching, was the best way to help father deal with his anger and depression. So he continued to prod and ask more questions.

"So, who decided who should die? I mean was it easy to tell who was Hutu and who was Tutsi?" Father Khumalo looked straight at Dr Mathew, but, in fact, his focus went past him. His mind was back in Rwanda.

"Those spared were fortunate enough to look more Hutu than Tutsi. In fact, I remember one man I met down at the local market. He showed me how he had taken a razor and scratched away the ink classifying him as a Tutsi on his identity card and he survived to tell the tale!" Father Khumalo managed a smile when he recounted this incident. He smiled because this one at least had a happy ending. But he also smiled out of pity that humans had to hide their own unique cultural identity given to them by God, in order to remain alive.

It reminded him of the extermination of the Jews by the Nazis, the ethnic cleansing of the Croats and Muslims by the Serbs. He added as a side thought; "Essentially two millenniums after Jesus sacrificed himself for us, mankind has still not evolved beyond the laws of the jungle, where the fittest survive". He shook his head in dismay and resignation.

Then, as had happened before during the previous consultations, tears would roll down onto his cheeks, past his mouth and chin and drip down onto his shirt. He made no attempt to wipe them or hide his emotions. His pride was of very little consequence in the face of all the human tragedy that he'd witnessed. He felt that the fact that he was still able to express and feel sadness and pain was a blessing. For he had witnessed people in Rwanda and Richmond who had been so traumatised and abused that they were no longer able to cry. Their tear buds were like empty wells in the hot Kalahari Desert, showing no pity for the animals in the wild that walked hundreds of kilometres in search of water, only to find the well empty. They would simply stare blankly, their eyes darting from place to place, trying to avoid making contact with the certain death that awaited them. Perhaps, Father Khumalo thought to himself, at least they still felt afraid. Fear it seemed was the only luxury they'd left from the enormous bank of emotions once bestowed on them by God.

Besides what Father Khumalo had experienced as a priest in Rwanda, he had listened to many painful stories. These stories were still vivid enough to cause him nightmares and on occasion he would experience auditory and visual hallucinations. He had become a truly disturbed man.

"What you are suffering from Father Khumalo, is not uncommon for someone who has been through what you have been through. It's called post traumatic stress disorder (PTSD). However, it can be managed.

Here, this Prozac will help with the depression and with a few more counselling sessions, you should be well on your way to recovery. I know that you come from a very supportive background. You have others in your congregation who can give you spiritual and emotional guidance. Perhaps some of them have also been through similar traumatic experiences!" added Dr Matthews.

"I know I'll be ok soon doctor, and I really appreciate your listening to me. I'm already feeling a little better. At least the nightmares are less frequent now," replied Father Khumalo.

"What helps most, however, is that whenever I meet someone who was there at the time, I feel an inevitable bond with them, a bond of common understanding or maybe misunderstanding of having witnessed accounts of the cruellest form of human suffering".

His last consultation had been the day before. Today he was looking forward to evening mass. He loved evening mass and he really liked working with Father James and Patricia.

As he knelt in the church in Stellenbosch, he imagined himself in Rwanda, at the pulpit. Even to this day, as he stood at the pulpit on Sundays, he would ask himself so many questions which his congregation in Stellenbosch and those in Kwa Zulu Natal, also needed answers to. "Where was God when all this madness erupted? He remembered Jesus Christ's last cries as He hung on the Cross-, "Eli, Eli, Iama sabachthani? (My God, my God, why hast Thou forsaken me?)"

"If he'd forsaken his own Son in His hour of need how on earth can I explain what has happened in Rwanda and KwaZulu Natal? How could He have let it happen?" he asked himself.

"What can I tell these poor souls?" It was not that Khumalo had lost all faith in God, it was just that being human and weak, he needed support and guidance. He needed answers to this insanity. He needed to know whether the ending of the millennium was heralding the coming, not of the Son of God, but of the devil himself. The God whom he'd got to know was merciful, loving and kind. It was difficult for him to understand how what had happened in Rwanda and was happening in KwaZulu Natal and Kosovo, could have been sanctioned by the very same God he knew.

As a learned man, he had read all he could to understand the carnival of murder and evil that befell the Rwandese. It also helped that he had obtained a Bachelors degree in History and Philosophy at the University of Natal, in Durban, South Africa. He was often asked by people who knew what he'd been through, how much the people of Rwanda were to blame? Father Khumalo felt that some of the colonial powers were to blame to a large extent. France's role for example, he thought should not have gone unnoticed. He recalled and repeated to others what Dr Jean Hervé Bradol of MSF-France said at the time;

"the people carrying out the massacres today, who are putting this planned policy of extermination into effect, are financed, trained and armed by France."

It was common knowledge that the French trained the Presidential Guard (GP), which in turn trained the "Interahamwe", the 'killers' themselves.

In fact, since the first world war, it was Father Khumalo's lament that the French and English had not fostered common understanding and now even on foreign soils they acted out their animosity. He thought that this was an important underlying argument because the Tutsi were driven out of Rwanda many years ago and lived in camps in Uganda where they spoke English. According to the French were only protecting their interests in Francophone Africa. The role of the US government in the crisis was also less than honourable-delaying and obstructing aid to the RPF (Rwandese Patriotic Front-predominantly Tutsi) areas, while sending relief funds and aircraft without hesitation to Hutu-occupied refugee camps in Goma, then called Zaire.

His mind raced back again to the killing fields of Rwanda, as he knelt down in prayer. Many thoughts were rushing through his mind. It was a classical case of things going horribly wrong. On the one hand, he saw the total depravity of man and on the other, the total failure of man's attempted solutions. The United Nations (UN), the people entrusted with caring for the victims, at times also proved part of the problem, not the solution. All in all, Father Khumalo wondered at times, what on earth could have made him think of the UN as the reincarnated Saviour? Only Jesus could have saved the people of Rwanda. Only the Messiah could now save the people of Kosovo and his own people in Richmond, Natal.

In his humble mind, the experience in Rwanda and Natal had convinced him that man was inherently evil. That he was not evolving and improving. Mankind had fallen into the deepest sin against itself; each man was prepared to take the other's life. He reasoned that, this was the reason why we needed laws, armed citizens to restrain the evil within men's hearts. If Jesus is the resurrection and the life and if His church is unshakeable, unstoppable and unbeatable, how come so many people were slaughtered while seeking refuge in the churches? These were the same questions he had while he was kneeling outside the church at Gitarama afraid to enter in the event that the writhing sea of maggots would mistake him for dead. Whenever he closed his eyes he could see the fear and hear the screaming as people huddled together in the corners hoping to be spared from the blunt blade of the machetes that had up to now not known the taste of human flesh. And as each body succumbed to terrible blows and sunk lifelessly onto the floor, the blood from their veins and arteries would squirt onto the Church's floor, overflow, then dry up as it coagulated and seeped into the dust outside.

What disturbed father most was that this happened, all in the full view of the Lord Jesus Christ.

The horror of the massacres still rang out to him whenever a church bell chimed its tune. He remembers the 2800 Tutsi believers who had gathered in church, seeking shelter and protection, only to be slaughtered by Hutu mobs at Cyahinda. At Kibeho, another 4000 were massacred in the church. In the church in Mibirizi, 2000 were killed and in the Shangi church, 4000 were murdered, while at Rukara, 500 were killed. In just a 100 days of this devilish orgy of murder, almost a million of God's people were systematically slaughtered with machetes, machine guns, grenades and rockets.

"Where was the world? Where were the Organisation of African Unity (OAU) and the UN? Where were you God?" he asked in a hushed voice.

Father Khumalo felt the tears again gliding down his eyes. He wondered how he as a priest, was supposed to carry on believing. He whispered to himself in prayer.

"Dear God…why did you allow this to happen right in front of your eyes? All of them had seeked sanctuary in your house, yet all of them died in your home, the church. I know that though art strong and I am weak, but please give me a sign, any sign so that I can believe that all that death was not in vain. I want to believe that you have not forgotten us, your children in Africa!"

He wiped the tears from his face and stood up from where he had been kneeling. He was still alone in the church. As he faced the altar and Jesus on the cross, he raised his right hand slowly to shoulder height and clenched it into a fist. Then Father Khumalo started singing in Zulu, "Nkosi Sikelele I Africa"(God Bless Africa) out aloud. At first his voice was trembling and hoarse with emotion. But by the time he got to the second verse, he was singing loudly and with melody.

When he had reached the third verse he sensed that someone had joined him and was singing as a soprano. He turned around and it was Patricia. She had slipped into the church and was now also singing with him in Zulu, God Bless Africa. She walked towards him until she was standing next to his left shoulder. She took her right hand and grasped his left hand, until they fitted into each other like a glove. She gave him a warm supportive squeeze. As their eyes met, she smiled and with her left hand she wiped a tear that had refused to dry up on his left cheek. Than they both looked forward and continued to sing "Nkosi Sikelele I Africa", God Bless Africa. After the song had finished they both knelt again and said a prayer. Then they left the church around midnight.

Four

"*Honduras is mortally wounded, but not about to expire. We will get back on our feet...may the Lord illuminate us and give us all strength. Our capacity for suffering and pain was never before put to such a hard test.*"
President Carlos Flore-Honduras, October 1998.

On October 30 1998, Lucifer blew his foul breath and spewed his bile over the Atlantic towards Central America and its inhabitants. He sent a ruthless aquatic force called Hurricane Mitch. For one full week, he wreaked havoc on the innocent people of Honduras and its neighbours. Reaching speeds of up to 180 miles per hour, he spared nothing and no one. Dams burst at their seams, sending tons of mud and water to the villages and towns below. The mudslides formed their own 'highways', kilometres long and kilometres wide and choked all life forms beneath them. Lakes and dams joined hands, submerging humans, their live-stock and once fertile land. All the good things that God and man had created over centuries were demolished in that one week of gay, satanic delinquency.

Mitch left an orgy of destruction and in the process demolished almost all the bridges and the roads. One suspects he did this almost out of spite. It was as if he wanted to make sure that when he was done, the hand of the Lord would find it difficult to reach the needy. And they were many who needed help. Thousands of poor souls were stranded on rooftops. Mothers tied their children on treetops for days to prevent them from falling into the evil, churning, muddy currents below. It was as if the devil was eagerly waiting for their hungry and weak bodies to fall into the belly of the aquatic beast that he had formed below and then crush them with disdain. They were the lucky ones.

Lucifer's breath and vomit drowned over 8000 people, 2 to 3 million were injured and millions more made homeless. Even the cows, pigs and the chickens were destroyed. Crops were simply uprooted and washed away. During the last days of October 1998, Hurricane Mitch reigned supreme in Central America and hell in all its fiendish gore had truly descended on her. It was as if the last days of Pompeii were being relived; only the burning larva and fire had been replaced by water, wind and mud slides.

The choking screams for help can still be heard today; gurgling, groaning as their oxygen-starved lungs filled with muddy water. Drowning, dying a painful, slow and agonising death. The Pacific Rim and Central America had never seen such horror and suffering. Families and clans were made genetically extinct as villages were submerged under the thick, brown mud. After Mitch had gone, water-borne diseases added their share to the unprecedented misery. Injuries sustained during the hurricane and the ensuing hunger also took their toll. Mitch then bid farewell to the Islands and returned to only the devil knows where.

Manuel Diaz recalled going through the ruins of his muddy village, looking for his family. Dead or alive, the sight of any member of the family would have been a blessing. Just one relative would have been enough to put some hope into his heart. But the mud was so thick that it had caked into moulds, hardening in the midday sun. The stench of rotting human flesh, coupled with that of the pigs, dogs and cows was too much to bear. Although Manuel had been through medical school, this was different. It was a scene taken from Lucifer's diary. A scene straight from hell. Nothing could have prepared him for this.

He knew that he was at the right spot, because the hill that he used to climb as a kid, with his brothers and sisters, was just about visible rising above in the background. His home village was situated just below the hill, so he had to be at the right place. The scarf around his nose and mouth helped to keep the sickening smell of death to a bearable level. He had no choice anyway. Using a stick, he moved the mud away from the mangled human forms sprawled all around, buried at different levels within the mud. He desperately looked for any sign of life, a familiar face or even a piece of clothing that he could identify.

The corpses that were on the surface were in different states of decomposition. Their abdomens were bloated and distended, ready to burst at the slightest accidental prod, and their skins, a dusky mortuary grey, already beginning to peal off, exposing the pink flesh below. The maggots had by then started their work in earnest and the vultures kept circling above, waiting to complete the cycle and journey called life on earth. As he rolled some of the victims over, the maggots would scatter away, dashing from eye sockets, nostrils and every bodily orifice. He could hardly recognise any of the people from his village. Some of them had only one hand or leg, some had been decapitated. Dogs were helping themselves on the abundant human flesh, easing their hunger. At times it was even difficult to decide if the bodies were male or female. Almost all were naked, their clothes having been ripped off by the brute force of the muddy avalanches.

He must have searched for his relatives for at least two days, until he realised the futility of it all. They had all perished, probably washed away to sites kilometres away. They were now either being bathed by the torrential rain or buried in the makeshift graves created by the mudslides. It dawned on Manuel, that he was now the only surviving member of the Diaz clan.

When the reality sunk in, Manuel was sitting in a hotel room in Tegucigalpa, the capital city of Honduras. The city itself had not been completely spared, as some of its neighbourhoods were decimated. The power supply had been cut off and there was no running piped water. There was panic, despair and despondency everywhere. One could almost touch the shock, anger and pain. Manuel did what he could do to help at the local hospital. There was so much suffering, so much hunger and death in its peaceful finality abounded. It was a time for dying.

They ran out of drugs and blood within the first day of Mitch's visit. It was dreadful. Here were these poor souls who had escaped Mitch's bile, only to succumb because there were not enough drugs, intravenous fluids and blood to go around. Only his national pride and love for his country kept him going, not crying or breaking down. Sleep was a luxury for those that survived as they struggled to save those who were still knocking on heavens' door, desperately trying to deny Lucifer absolute victory. Manuel recalled how weak and emotionally drained he felt then. He felt that God had betrayed him and his people.

He remembered vividly that he didn't even have the energy to cry. The extent of the tragedy that had befallen his country and his family was so devastating that he was left totally numb and devoid of any personal or individual human emotion. It was as if the whole country was in a state of shock and collective amnesia.

Lucifer had been ruthless and clinical. It wasn't enough that he had killed his entire family and thousands of his countrymen and women. The devil's disciple had also destroyed everything they held dear about their land and everything they'd worked for generations past. But to add insult to injury, Hurricane Mitch had also stolen their collective emotions when he left, leaving them dazed, powerless and paralysed as a nation. For a time Mitch had systematically, cerebrally decortified and disembowelled all of Central America with the precision of a laser-guided surgical blade. It was as if the whole nation needed one massive combined dose of electro-convulsive therapy, to get them out of their catatonic depressive state.

From a coping point of view, perhaps it was better that way. How else could one have mourned the passing of all thirty six relatives? How could one have mourned for a father, a mother, brothers and sisters, uncles and aunts, and childhood friends, all at the same time and do justice to their loving memories and lives? How in God's name could one have even begun to comprehend the death of thousands in a single week, with more queuing up to join them? So many were maimed and disfigured by the injuries sustained during Mitch's adulterous fling with the Islands and the ensuing rampant hunger, added to the misery and death toll. And because of the breakdown in essential services, there was very little they could do to help their own. It was a painful sight, which left him emasculated. When he saw the injured and sick, Manuel felt that perhaps he was lucky and that he should be grateful to God. Although he was angry with the Lord for having left them at the mercy of Mitch, he with held his anger and thanked the Lord for having spared him. He couldn't help but ask God why it had to be them and why with such ferocity? Why a country already impoverished, could be further burdened with so much. But he soon realised that it was a futile exercise and logic told him to abandon that line of questioning. God owed him no answers and he accepted that. So being the faithful Catholic that he was, he asked God to forgive his anger.

Since he was in Honolulu when Hurricane Mitch had made his evil rounds, he survived its wrath. In that way the genes from his family would continue to populate the earth and maybe one day again the people of Tegucigalpa would reclaim their land and happiness. As a trade-off for having escaped death's jaws, Mitch had left them with the emotional burden and vision of the pain and havoc he had inflicted on their loved ones with impunity. That was theirs to keep. Something only death could erase. The memory of the suffering and death of his relatives, his loved ones and his fellow countrymen was now his sole inheritance, a burden to torment him forever. But fortunately as his President had said, though the wonderful people of Honduras were mortally wounded, they were not about to expire.

"Manuel have you looked at the cell cultures' yet?" said Dr John Marks, a colleague and friend. He startled Manuel. He was back in Honolulu, Hawaii, at the fertility research laboratory.

"No, not yet John, the cells aren't ready…think in another hour or so, they'll be ready."

"How about a cup of coffee at the cafeteria then Manuel?" asked John.

"Sure thing!" replied Manuel.

Manuel had been the only member of his family who had managed to get a tertiary education. His rural village was proud of him, as he had excelled by all standards. He won a scholarship to study Medicine at Harvard, where he did his postgraduate work in molecular biology and gene manipulation. When he completed his resident specialist training, he couldn't exactly work in Honduras; he was too qualified in his field. He also loved the challenge of research and working at the Millennium International Research Centre (MIRC) was the best offer he got that kept him reasonably close to his village and country. He loved visiting his village in Honduras whenever he was on leave. He never broke that umbilical cord with his family, even though he'd been to the best medical schools and hospitals in the world. In fact, he could have easily had his pick, job wise, anywhere in the world in his line of work. For a peasant boy, who had looked after goats and cows during the better part of his youth, he had done exceedingly well.

It was now December 1998 and the devastation Mitch had left behind was now being repaired. People from all around the world had pitched in to help. President Clinton of America had offered over US$ 300 million in direct disaster relief aid, via the United States Agency for International Development (USAID), the Department of Defence and the Department of Agriculture. This allowed for the immediate disaster relief in the form of food, drugs, helicopters, shelter and logistics support. This had been co-ordinated by the Disaster Assistance Response Team (DART). Individuals from around the Globe, NGOs and other organisations all contributed. Doctors without borders (Medicins sans frontiers) sent staff, people sent clothes, food and money. The World Bank and the International Monetary Fund (IMF) had also come to the rescue in December by implementing a debt relief scheme for all the countries in Central America, that had been devastated by Hurricane Mitch. So besides the painful memories of the agonising death that his family experienced, Manuel had settled down to his work and things were going along just fine.

"Have you looked at your pay check this month?" John asked with a smile on his face, as he took another sip of his coffee.

"No I haven't yet, John. Why, did they put some condoms into the envelopes again?" Manuel asked with a chuckle. December 1st had been World AIDS Day, and as a reminder the previous year, the personnel department had included three condoms in each of all the employees' salary advice slips.

"No" replied John. "Our bonuses have been included this month. I must say it is a windfall. A welcome one at that. They have virtually given us an extra three months pay!"

"Gee that's great," responded Manuel, trying to sound excited. It wasn't as if he didn't give a damn about the money. It was just that the death of his family was still very fresh in his mind.

Also lately, in the last few months he started to wonder where all the money for their research was coming from and how the Millennium Research Council was making a profit out of the research work they were doing. Although they were getting fantastic results, the company had refused to have the data published in any of the scientific journals. He recalled that when he joined the MRC eighteen months ago, as part of his contract, he found it rather strange that he had to sign an oath of secrecy and he was never quite convinced that Professor Hans Schmidt was indeed a molecular biologist. He'd never seen any of his work published in the peer-reviewed journals. In fact, he'd never heard of Hans before. Hans was always serious and there was something cagey and secretive about him. He insisted on keeping all the scientific data and results. All requests for equipment and laboratory supplies had to go through him and him alone.

Occasionally a few wealthy looking south Americans would fly into Honolulu and meet with Hans at the MRC. Manuel and John were never invited to these meetings or introduced to these gentlemen, if one could call them that. They all looked as if they came from shady backgrounds. They dressed in expensive designer suits, wore shades all the time and never smiled. They always seemed to be accompanied by young, skimpily dressed women. The bulges in the pockets of their jackets, hinted at the presence of metallic equipment. They were definitely not molecular biologists.

Manuel had brought this up with John, but John wasn't interested. He was happy making good money and as far as he was concerned they were doing genuine molecular scientific research. There was nothing illegal about what they were doing and all their research so far had been on granulosa cells from Chimpanzees. They obtained these cells from the female Chimps' ovaries. They hadn't handled any human tissue so far, so surely there was nothing sinister about their work.

But Manuel was still concerned about all that money they were being paid. He was concerned about the dubious looking characters that Hans kept meeting with. Also the fact that though, they were having excellent results with the Chimpanzees, there was no attempt whatsoever to have the work published, despite it being groundbreaking research. Each time finding no answers to his questions, he would conclude that maybe he was unnecessarily concerned about these issues. After all he and his country were still mourning the death and destruction caused by Hurricane Mitch.

"If you don't want the money you can always deposit it in my Swiss account!" added John with a laugh.

"Over my dead body John," replied Manuel.

"Look it's Friday today, what say we meet at the Club for a few drinks, then if we get lucky, who knows maybe we can go dancing with some fine ladies later," added Manuel. He had coaxed his mind out of all those depressive thoughts. He was determined to start enjoying life again.

"Way to go!" responded John with boyish enthusiasm. "Let's behave like the real thirty-something, well-educated and rich bachelors that we really are. For speaking out loud, we are the cream of the crop of this town!"

"Ok, I'll pick you up from your place tonight, say around 19h30" added Manuel "and don't forget to bring the blue pill with you!"

"What blue pill?" asked a surprised John

"Viagra…I've seen you popping it into your mouth whenever you get lucky at the club" Manuel added, laughing. He couldn't resist taking a swipe at John.

"Bullshit Manuel, I don't need that stuff" John responded.

"That's not what I heard," said Manuel.

"Fuck you Manuel!" John answered with a grin on his face.

As Manuel and John were about to leave the cafeteria, Hans walked in, serious as usual, with his bow tie smartly placed around his neck. His fine blond hair was neatly pressed backwards and his eyes, a pure Aryan blue. He always wore a suit and suspenders to hold up his pants. He was at least six feet tall and had an athletic body. He was forty-five years old. He headed straight for their table.

"Can I see both of you in my office in ten minutes please?" It was an order, not a request.

"Fine" replied Manuel. He was more senior to John, so it made sense that he should respond to the order. John would do whatever he was told, so Hans didn't even acknowledge John's head nodding to the affirmative.

Hans still had a touch of the German accent although he'd spent most of his adult life in the United States, Baltimore in the State of Maryland, to be exact. His childhood was spent in the town of Oberammergau, in Germany. He grew up and finished his high schooling there. He still visited that town once every year, at the same time of the year without fail. He never talked much about his family or anything else for that matter. He was, however, a religious man and he considered himself a devout Christian. That's what confused Manuel most, because the men that came to visit Hans periodically looked like anything but devout Christians. Anyway, Manuel reminded himself again that it was none of his business. So he filed those questions away into some other corner of his brain. There was work to be done in the laboratory and that's what he was paid for.

"I have to leave for Baltimore tonight. I will be back in three weeks time on the 12th of January, next year. So you guys keep the fort while I'm away," said Hans.

"Sure" replied Manuel. John again nodded to the affirmative. They were both taken aback by the announcement. Manuel was tempted to ask him why he was going to Baltimore for three weeks, but decided to let it pass.

"And you guys have a merry Christmas!" Hans added with an uncharacteristic friendliness.

This was really not like the Hans they'd both come to know. He seemed too relaxed and was obviously pleased about something. Just what it was, neither had a clue.

"Well, you two should have a wonderful Christmas, Hans!" John had mastered the courage to add. He was relieved that Hans' prying eyes and ever-looming presence in the laboratory, would be absent for the next three weeks. That surely made him feel relaxed. It occurred to him that he was actually afraid of Hans.

"Manuel I want you to have the other laboratory completely sterilised in the meantime". Hans was now very serious.

"I will be returning with some very delicate cells. In fact this tissue is the reason why we have been perfecting our technique so far. So I want the culture media and everything else ready!" added Hans, locking his eyes with Manuel's.

"Sure Hans, everything will be ready. If I may ask, what sort of tissue can we expect?" asked Manuel, although he knew that he was unlikely to get the answer.

"Nothing must go wrong, we have only one shot at this!" Hans had ignored Manuel's question and Manuel decided not to press the issue any further. He knew when to persist with Hans and this was not the right time. Anyway it really didn't make much of a difference because they had perfected their technique and had an almost ninety per cent success rate. He felt that they were up to it and his scientific mind was actually looking forward to anything that was considered a challenge.

"Don't worry Hans, everything is ready and off you go to Baltimore. Make sure you have one on us on Christmas day!" Manuel had decided to decrease the obvious tension level that was beginning to build up. Hans had actually come to respect Manuel quite a bit. The personal loss and tragedy that had happened to his family in Honduras also touched him. Although he was a serious man, Hans admired hard work, honesty and emotional strength. Manuel had shown all these characteristics after the tragedy of Hurricane Mitch had struck him, his family and his country.

With that, Hans left that Friday evening. Manuel was still a bit concerned that Hans was going to be absent for that long and would return with tissue that he was not prepared to divulge the nature of. He felt that somehow his life was going to change dramatically soon. It was nothing specific that gave him that premonition, just a whole bunch of things that didn't fit lately.

"Well I'm off Manuel, see you later tonight, mate."

"Yeah!" Manuel responded.

Manuel admired John's carefree attitude. Perhaps it was because they came from totally different backgrounds. Although they were both in their thirties and had specialised in similar fields, John came from an extremely privileged background. He was English, born and bred in London. The only other time that he left London was to spend his post-graduate years at Cambridge University. There he did his doctorate in the genetics department, made famous by the Noble Laureates, Watson and Crick. They were the first to decipher the DNA code. DNA is the material in every human cell, that is responsible for determining who we are, how we live, what diseases we are going to get and so on. In fact, it is fair to say that the DNA genetic material was the sole basis for differentiating us humans from other animals and for differentiating each human from the next. So John came from a very sound academic pedigree. He was good at his work and Manuel was of the opinion that he was the best in the world in molecular genetics and disease. John was recruited, in fact rather; head hunted for this job by Hans himself. John being the easygoing fellow he was, was more than eager to spend some time in the warm sun and beaches of Hawaii. That was in stark contrast to the damp, grey conditions in Cambridge and London.

Besides that, he loved a good drink and he could handle his beer quite well. And, of course, he loved the women that were the trademark of sunny Hawaii. The fact that it was a tourist centre and hence a lot of the population was transitory suited him fine. He was not about to settle down. Weekends were literally spent on the beach or in the club. Manuel enjoyed his company as they had a lot in common besides their social upbringing. He too loved the life in Honolulu.

Five

January 8th 1999. Washington, DC. USA

Senator David Bell Jnr was sitting in his office suite at Capitol Hill, Washington, DC. It had been a torrid year for his party. It all started around 1992 when the Independent counsel, called Starr, started to investigate the Chief Executive of the country, the President of America. What started as an investigation into some land deal, ended up as a personal investigation into the President's sex life, five to six years later and about $US40 million or so having been spent. That was besides the media torturing the American and international public with endless details about the impeachment process. And oh…to crown it all, his friend Nicky had been murdered under mysterious circumstances the previous week.

Senator Bell was still dumbfounded about how Bill had managed to escape impeachment and come out of it, probably as the most popular American President of this century. This really pissed him off. He'd spent a lot of his time, energy and more importantly money, trying to see this President out. Instead the President came out smoking and hell,

Senator Bell thought to himself, "Now Hilary was even thinking of running for the Senate seat in New York!"

"What a real fuck up" he muttered to himself. "Next thing she'll be running for President…and that would mean Bill would be there again for another two terms. And this time with no reason not to openly gloat and string up a beat or two on his Senegalise African drums and sax! Damn!"

Senator Bell wasn't about to let this issue go that lightly. If he couldn't get his way via the ballot or the special prosecutor, he would continue with the plan he and Paulo Galvez and the rest of the Millennium Club (MC) had been working on. This was a long-term plan that was going to restore his control over the White House forever.

"Senator Bell, your wife is on the line, should I put her through?" asked Louise his secretary.

"Sure" Bell grunted.

"David darling, will you make it for dinner at the Wilt's tonight at eight?" she asked. In fact she was reminding him of the dinner.

"Oh yeah, honey. I'll meet you there. I have a business appointment at 18h00, but I'll make it for the dinner.

"Fine darling, please don't delay tonight, you know that the Wilt's have always contributed generously to your campaign fund!" she replied.

"Don't worry Grace, I won't miss the dinner for anything!" and he meant that.

As he put the portable phone down, he stood up and walked to his bar. He took out a bottle of Jack Daniels and poured himself a double. He took it down in one gulp. He poured himself another double and took out his gold pocket watch from his right waistcoat pocket, it was 16h30. He still had some time to kill before his meeting with Paulo Galvez.

Senator David Bell Jnr then gazed at the pictures on the wall opposite his table. There were pictures of him, his wife Grace and their two sons, John and Peter. He was proud of his family, particularly his boys. John was doing well on Wall Street as a partner in one of the major brokerage firms and Peter was now working as a plastic surgeon in Los Angeles. Both had graduated from Harvard, just like him and his father David Bell Snr before him. He was now 65 years old and he and Grace had been together for 35 years. "Fine woman" he thought to himself as he stroked Grace's portrait with his stubby fingers. He kissed her picture and hung it back on the wall.

He then lifted his favourite picture. Held it slightly at a distance from his spectacled eyes, so that he could see all the guys on it. His eyesight wasn't as good as it used to be. The picture was taken as his platoon was leaving Vietnam. Well what was left of it. That picture took centrestage on the wall. He was proud of his contribution to the military in Vietnam, to the American cause, even though their exit wasn't so graceful.

He made a lot of friends' there in Nam and also lost some. But he rationalised to himself that it was a just and religious war. He hated Communism with a passion and he was proud that he'd done his part to keep it in check. Andrew Wilt was his best buddy then and still was today. He polished the glass covering the picture with his handkerchief and muttered softly "The bastards didn't even give Nixon a chance. At least he had the balls to resign"; he was back to his futile anti-Bill mood again. Vietnam had brought back memories of the way Richard Nixon was unceremoniously bundled out of the White House. Well, it depends from whose viewpoint you look at it. Bell was of the opinion that Nixon gave the Democrats the finger, rather than allow them to humiliate him. Nixon was his idol in those days.

Wilt had gone into investment banking on his return from Nam and was now a multimillionaire. That's not to say that Bell was poor. The Bell's owned a lot of property in New York and Baltimore. This had been accumulated by the past three generations of his family. They'd also invested outside the States. They had apartments in Paris and Rome. But their prized investment was a three hundred-acre wine farm in the prime vineyards of Franshoek near Cape Town, in South Africa. Not only did they believe it to be the most beautiful place on earth with its rolling hills, imposing mountains and fine Mediterranean weather, it was a place the family went to, to escape the bitter winters of Washington.

It also paid them handsomely from the noble wines produced on the farm and now exported throughout the world. Since the farm was bought in 1986, he had managed to get it at a bargain, because of the then isolated Apartheid government's desperate need for foreign currency. There was also a two-tier foreign currency exchange mechanism, the so-called financial rand, which was a scheme designed to attract foreign currency. This made anyone who had dollars to spare an instant South African Rand millionaire

The Bell's tried to spend at least one week together every year, in Cape Town. Bell had bought the wine farm in 1986, during the peak of the apartheid regimes terror and international isolation. He had opposed the Robinson Bill and American sanctions against the National Party government of PW Botha of South Africa. He was convinced then that PW Botha's government was the last bastion of Christianity in Africa. They, after all, had been fighting a communist trained and equipped terrorist army, mainly the African National Congress and the Pan African Congress. Fair enough, things seemed to have worked out well with Nelson Mandela. But he still didn't quite trust the ANC as the new government in South Africa, particularly the heir apparent, Thabo. He was even more distrustful of the special binational relationship between the US and South Africa, meetings initiated by Al and Bill on the one hand and Thabo Mbeki primarily on the South African side. His right wing mind went on the attack again. He couldn't help it. The mere thought of Bill always triggered the release of pretty violent neuro-transmitters in his brain. This issue literally gave him a headache.

"Damn, to think that the guy dogged the draft and still managed to become the 42nd President of this great country…what a mockery!" Bell had returned to the futile personal war he had against the President. He didn't realise that it was only chewing him up, destroying his soul. He didn't have the sublime compartmentalisation skills Bill had patented. Whereas Bill grew from adversity, became stronger and smarter, Bell simply became a bitter, disappointed and vindictive old man.

Bell failed to appreciate that for all the weakness that Bill had, the American people still loved him and so did his family. They loved him because he put the common person on the street first. He cared about welfare, education, blacks and Hispanics, homosexuals and women's rights. He was human. What the Senator failed to grasp was that all these people made up the greatest country of the 20th Century, called America. Bill and Al were part of this new America. Bell and his colleagues had missed the boat. After all these years, his kind still failed to realise that "it's the economy stupid" that mattered most to the American public, not who gave whom a blowjob.

"It sure isn't the America I had in mind when I fought in Nam" he grimaced to himself. Perhaps Bell could be described as a conservative. There was nothing un-American about that, but even in his own Republican Party, he was branded as belonging to the extreme-religious right. His group was now tacking all the flack for the failed impeachment drive, which not only led to the party's loss of popularity, but also to the unprecedented soaring popularity of Bill. Now Al was waiting in the wings, perched high up perfectly like an eagle with a panoramic view of the terrain and the competition. Just in time for the year 2000 elections!

"The guy even inhaled the stuff…and the electorate didn't give a shit! Fuck the opinion polls, what do they understand anyway about sacrifice, honour and Christian family values?" Bell went on to himself. It never occurred to him that perhaps most young American voters, particularly the baby boomers, had actually inhaled and that oral sex was no big deal. The Editor of the "Journal of the American Medical Association"(JAMA) in 1998 was wise when he published a study that showed that the average American College student didn't think much of a blow job. It got him fired though by the Republican controlled top brass of JAMA.

"Sir, I'll be knocking off now, is there anything else you want me to do before I leave?" interrupted Louise through the speakerphone.

"No, you can leave Louise, I'll lock up later. See you on Monday." Bell responded.

It was Friday the 8th of January 1999.

Bell took his 100-kilogram mass and sat on his leather chair. He massaged his balding scalp and sighed deeply. It was now 17h15, so he cleared his desk of as much paper work as he could. Then he went to his bathroom, took a leak and opened his wardrobe. He took off his old shirt, put a fresh one on and a different tie.

It was time to meet Galvez. He never met Galvez in his office. He was well aware of Galvez's criminal activity and dubious sources of income. His connections in the Central Intelligence Organisation (CIO) had kept him well informed. He had all the information he required to keep Galvez under his control indefinitely…well at least that's what he thought. They were going to meet at a restaurant in downtown Washington. He was going to travel with his two trusted bodyguards. Even though he'd known Galvez for the last five years, he still didn't trust his type. He made for the door and switched off the lights. He was feeling warm and confident after the double Jack Daniels.

As they cruised in his Buick to the restaurant, Bell decided to call Wilt from his car phone.

"Wilt, Bell here!" he declared with confidence to his buddy.

"Hey Bell, don't tell me you taking a rain cheque on my dinner party?" asked Wilt.

"Come on Wilt, I wouldn't miss it even if you didn't send me an invite. I have to meet with Galvez just to finalise the arrangements we made the last time we met at your place" replied Bell.

"Is Galvez back in town?" asked Wilt sounding rather surprised.

"Yes. He came in from London today and he said that he had to meet me urgently. He says that it's all systems go and that we need to make the final arrangements for Maria" added Bell. There was a long pause from Wilt's end. He was taken by surprise.

"Bell…is this it now, is this the real thing?" Bell could sense the excitement in Wilt's voice.

"Look Wilt, I'll brief you to night, but it seems like it's all systems go now" said Bell.

He went on to add. "If it's all systems go, maybe we should call a meeting with the rest of the guys for tomorrow?"

"Well, let's wait and hear what Galvez has to say" replied Wilt.

"See you at eight then buddy!" Bell put his phone down and decided that although the last few months had been difficult, things were about to change. He was going to make sure that all those that mocked him and his strict adherence to his pure Christian values would not laugh at him much longer. He had lost the impeachment battle in February, but the smell of victory in war was near. At times he felt that God had let him and his friends down. He thought that a quite little prayer was now appropriate to re-affirm his subservience and loyalty to God.

"O Lord, thou hast deceived me, and I was deceived:
thou art stronger than I, and hast prevailed:
I am in derision daily, every one mocketh me.
For since I spake, I cried out, I cried violence and spoil;
Because the word of the Lord was made reproach unto me,
And a derision daily…
But your word was
in mine heart as a burning fire shut up in my bones.

But the Lord is with me as a mighty terrible one:
Therefore my prosecutors shall stumble,
and they shall not prevail
They shall be greatly ashamed; for they shall not prosper:
Their everlasting confusion shall never be forgotten. Amen."

It was the prayer from Jeremiah's lament with God. Bell had obviously taken his defeat over the impeachment personally and to a spiritual level.

"Sir we've arrived. Do you want us to come along or should we wait for you outside?" asked Henry his bodyguard. They'd parked outside the Japanese restaurant.

"Henry you come along with me. You can sit at the bar and watch my back. Jack you stay in the car!" ordered Senator Bell. Jack was the driver. He wasn't exactly impressed about the idea of staying in the car, as the winter chill hung in the air.

Galvez was sitting at the table in the corner, with one of his body-guards. They were both facing the door so that they could see who was entering.

"Reservation for Mr Galvez please?" asked the Senator's bodyguard as they were approached by a waiter at the entrance.

"Yes Mr Galvez is waiting for you, please follow me," said the waiter as he bowed gently as a sign of respect in keeping with Japanese tradition.

"Senator Bell, what a pleasure to see you!" Galvez said standing up to meet Bell.

"The pleasure today is all ours I believe" responded Bell as they gave each other a firm handshake. With that Bell nodded to his bodyguard, who then left to sit at the bar. Galvez's shadow did likewise.

"Dom Perignon?" Galvez asked and without waiting for Bell's response he filled up the champagne glasses.

"That special an occasion is it?" asked Bell with a grin on his face, his eyes searching Galvez's' for a hint as to the importance of the occasion.

"Beyond your dreams" responded Galvez. "But before I give you the good news amigo, let's order some food, I'm starving".

"Oh you go ahead Paulo, I have another dinner appointment tonight with Wilt, and you know how he is when he's entertaining" said Bell.

"Ok, but have a little sushi and caviar, it's the best in town…then you can wash it down with the champagne. Waiter!" The waiter hurried along to the table. Galvez was a regular here whenever he was in Washington. They also knew that he was a very powerful and rich man. He grumbled a lot about the service, but he always tipped handsomely.

"I'll have the sea food platter!" Galvez ordered and he was already in the process of tucking his napkin on, covering his considerable belly.

"It will be ready in a minute Sir" replied the waiter. They had pre-pared the platter ten minutes before Galvez had arrived. He always ordered the same food and the drink was either Remy Martin cognac or Dom Perignon champagne.

Bell took a gulp of the champagne. They were both big men with big appetites and were not in the habit of eating or drinking slowly. His eyes met Galvez's and they both grinned; he in eager anticipation of the news and Galvez because he was enjoying having Bell's undivided attention. Galvez nodded slowly and said.

"We wait until my food arrives. A man should never discuss business on an empty stomach." He was really soaking up the attention that Bell was according him.

"Here Mr Galvez, please enjoy" said the waiter as he put the huge platter in front of Galvez and gave another subtle bow as he was moving away. Galvez started with the crayfish and when he had a chunk of the tasty flesh in his mouth, he took a sip of the champagne. He wiped the moisture left by the champagne from his moustache, and then he began his story.

"I have a piece of the cloth".

"What?" asked Bell, showing his shock, disbelief and joy, all at the same time. For a moment his mouth remained open.

"Yes, I have it. It's in a secure place here in Washington and I'll be sending it to Hawaii, to the research Laboratory" added Galvez with an obvious air of victory. He was oozing with confidence and pride. He went on.

"It was in London for the past century or more as my sources had said all along. I approached the seller and gave him an offer he couldn't refuse. $US 200 million and 5% of the shares we hold in Microsoft and Amazon.com. Of course I informed them that if this deal ever leaked or if they'd given me a fake, I would kill them and their family!" Galvez meant every word he was saying. He was now going through the prawns sucking the juices out as he searched for the delicate flesh.

"How do you...I mean how do we know it's real?" asked a stunned Bell.

"My contact's word is good enough for now. He has never in the last twenty years been wrong. Anyway we will test it at the Millennium International Research Centre (MIRC) laboratory in Hawaii."

"We have put a lot of money into this..."Bell went on hesitatingly, but was interrupted by Galvez.

"Believe me it's the real thing. Don't forget that I have also put in quite a lot of my money into this. No one double-crosses me. It's the real thing". Galvez was now trying to break the crab up, so that he could eviscerate the crustacean.

"This is to the you, the Millennium Club and to the Cloth!" Bell was standing up as a sign of respect, toasting with the glass in his right hand. Galvez also stood up to join in the toast. He went on to praise the Lord for what they had accomplished so far. They both felt the incredible intensity of the occasion. They now knew that it was their destiny to accomplish so much for the Lord, as the century was about to change. Galvez added his favourite prayer from the bible.

"The steps of the good men are ordered by the Lord:
and he delighteth in their ways;
The Lord knoweth the day of the upright:
and their inheritance shall be forever.

They shall not be ashamed in the evil time:
And in the days of famine they shall be satisfied"

"I'll drink to that Galvez...waiter, more champagne please and bring us the best Havana's in the house!" ordered Bell, laughing with joy and excitement. They both felt that God had chosen them, the Millennium club, to fulfil his promise to bring back the Son of man.

"What say you come by Wilt's place tomorrow, so that we can all celebrate and discuss our preparations" suggested Bell.

"I'll be there at 10h15. There is so much we need to discuss. Inform the rest of the club tonight, even if it means they have to fly back from wherever, they must make it." Galvez was back to his serious tone again. He lit his cigar and then waited while Bell Jnr lit his too. Galvez drew a big puff from his cigar and blew the thick smoke into the air, towards the ceiling. He went on.

"No one except the members of the Millennium Club must know about this now, not even family! "He paused for a while then added. "Particularly the wives, they must not know."

"That's fine with me and I'm sure that the rest of the Club will not find fault in that" added the Senator.

"Good, I'll fill you guys in on all the details tomorrow!" concluded Galvez. The waiter was taking his plate away. He had finished the whole platter.

"Get me a double Remy Martin champagne cognac please" he said to the waiter.

"Yes sir…" The waiter was interrupted by the Senator. "Get Mr Galvez a double KWV brandy, the twenty-year-old one. You do have it?" he asked.

"Yes sir" and the waiter looked at Galvez, waiting for his approval.

"Comeon Galvez, try something different, you'll be pleasantly surprised" Bell said convincingly.

"Ok, KWV it's going to be then!" Galvez said, looking at the waiter who was clearly intimidated by the presence of these two powerful men.

Galvez took a cautious sip of the KWV brandy, swirled the liquid in his mouth and then smiled. "Real fine…smooth. Where the hell is this from? Asked a surprised Galvez.

"From Cape Town, South Africa…I have a wine farm there and we have shares in the company, KWV that makes it. In fact, the company has just listed on the Johannesburg Stock Exchange and is doing well!" Bell was obviously very proud of his fine investment.

"You old devil, why didn't you tell me about this…Cape Town huh?" asked Galvez as he now took a confident gulp of the twenty-year-old brandy.

"Don't worry, I'll give you a case of the stuff tomorrow. Give some of them to your colleagues down there in Colombia" he added with a smile.

"Gracias amigo…But I'm not sure if I'm going to give any of this stuff away" laughed Galvez.

It was 19h35 and Bell announced that he had to leave to catch up with his wife at Wilt's dinner party. They gave each other bear hugs and agreed to meet the following day at Wilt's place as planned.

The Senator stood up and his bodyguard quickly pulled his chair out of the way from behind him. They made for the exit. Henry, his bodyguard, led the way as they approached the Senator's Buick across the street. By the time they were halfway across the street, Henry was beginning to feel a creeping sense of panic. Security protocol was that, David his colleague should have started the motor running. The car's lights were still off by the time they arrived at the car. Instinctively he pulled out his 9-mm pistol from his left shoulder halter and told the Senator to stay back. He approached the driver's side with the gun pointing in readiness and shouted.

"David…David!" There was no answer. He cocked the gun and when he was a few feet from David's door, he noticed the blood that had dried up on the ground. Some of it was still dripping from the beneath the door.

"Shit!" Henry shouted out and pulled the door open. David's body lay slumped on the steering wheel, a bullet wound at the back of his head. Henry felt his neck for a pulse; he was dead.

"What the hell is going on?" asked a visibly shaken Bell standing a few paces behind.

"He's been shot sir, more like executed…shit!" responded Henry. He took out his phone and as he was dialling, Bell grabbed the phone from him.

"Who are you calling Henry?" asked Bell.

"The FBI sir, that's the protocol!" Henry responded with a surprised look on his face.

"No FBI!" shouted Bell. "We'll handle this matter internally. It could have been a personal thing or a simple mugging. No FBI! Am I clear enough Henry?"

"Yes sir!" said a bewildered Henry.

"Now move his body to the back and let's get the hell out of here!" instructed the Senator. A bewildered Henry did as he was told. He grabbed David by his arms while Senator Bell lifted his feet. His limp life-less body was still warm. They dumped him into the boot with a thud.

"Shit" cursed Henry as he looked at his white shirt. It was all soggy and messed up with the typical dark red clotted blood and he had to wipe away pieces of David's' brain." What a fucking way to go!" he added and spat onto the ground.

The site of the big hole in David's skull, that had turned his skull to mash, made him nauseous. Spitting helped him to discard the saliva that had accumulated in his mouth. Senator Bell took out a cigarette and lit it. He took a long drag and then passed it on to Henry. Henry was actually trembling. He inhaled deeply. This eased him a little and certainly helped with the nausea.

"Let's get the hell out of here!" Bell shouted. His mind was working overtime. Was this a professional hit, was it a random act of violence, what should he do now? All these questions sped through his brain like an adrenaline rush. He had to make decisions quickly. "Fine let's head for the nearest police station!" he ordered Henry, who had already started the car.

"Yes Sir!". Henry's mind was also in a spin of its own. Who could have done this and why didn't the Senator want the FBI to be involved? He decided to shelve his questions and concentrate on the situation. His duty was to protect the Senator. So he sped off since he wasn't sure if they were still in danger. He needed to get to a more secure place. Then maybe the police might make sense of all this. So he headed for the police station as instructed. As he twisted and turned negotiating the corners at high speed, there was a constant dull, thudding noise from the boot. It was David's body as it rolled from side to side, oblivious to pain or any other sensation for that matter.

The Senator in the meanwhile had called the Chief of Police in Washington and gave him the facts of the story. That they had to leave in a hurry because they felt insecure, and they couldn't leave David's body behind and so on. The Police Chief didn't argue too much and instructed him to head to the police morgue instead and he would handle it from then on. Bell Jnr sighed in relief when he switched his phone off. He had averted a full-scale FBI investigation on the scene. He couldn't have them or the press knowing that he was having dinner with Paulo Galvez.

"The meeting with Galvez never happened" Bell said looking at Henry.
"Yes Sir! You can trust me Sir!" Henry had been minding the Senator for years now. He liked him and they'd developed a special friendship.
"I'll remember that," said a grateful Bell.

Six

27th November 1095. French city of Clermont-Ferrand.
The First Crusade.

"The Muslim Seljuks have plundered Palestine and Jerusalem! They have desecrated our Holy Land and laid waste to our places of pilgrimage. I say unto you all, that it is Gods' wish that we free Palestine and Jerusalem! God has come to me in a vision. He has instructed me that I organise noble men, men of faith and character, Christian men; to go on a Crusade to free Jerusalem and Palestine". Pope Urban-II was speaking to his subjects in a field outside the walls of the city of Clermont. Every man stood in attention, awe and fear. For the Pope was more than the head of the Church, he was the State. He decided when and if on all matters in these lands!

You could feel the sense of religious duty, of a calling beyond nationalism and all men, both nobleman and peasantry alike felt it was their duty and destiny to free the 'Holy Land'.

"Who amongst you men is willing to join this holy Crusade to free Jerusalem and Palestine from the Seljuks?" the Pope shouted, working the crowd into frenzy.

"Aye, Aye, Aye" was the enthusiastic chorus response from the thousands of men, all inhabitants of the City of Clermont. Some were ordinary peasants that lived off the land around the city. Land that belonged to Pope Urban-II.

"Who amongst you men is willing to die for the freedom of Jerusalem and Palestine?" Pope Urban-II asked. The crowd was now eating out of his hand as they all responded eagerly. With God on their side, none of them even considered the possibility of death. He had them exactly were he wanted them; under his total control. Their minds were his to play with, their souls to torment and their bodies, to do battle; in order that his power and wealth may reach far beyond the confines of Europe. He wanted Jerusalem back in Christian hands. Whoever controlled the town, the Son of Man was born in controlled the world. Pope Urban-II wanted to control the whole world!

The invasion of Jerusalem and Palestine by the Muslim Seljuks had angered Pope Urban-II. Jerusalem was now under the control of the Egyptians. He'd sworn to his God that he would liberate the 'Holy Land' even if it meant sending several armies to Palestine. Jerusalem to him was sacred. It was the place of the birth of Son of Man Jesus, and he felt it was his duty to ensure that it remained in Christian hands.

Little did he know then that this would be the first of another five Crusades to come. Little did he know also that even in the New Millennium, the control of Jerusalem would continue to haunt and destroy mankind in the form of one war or another. This struggle would continue into the next Millennium refusing to go away, hanging around like a sore on a foot that refuses to heal, only to reveal itself as a cancer. This cancer of man against man, father against son, and brother against brother, all in the name of God would continue to cause untold pain and suffering for generations to come.

Godfrey of Bouillon, who was Duke of Lower Lorraine, had been in the crowd when the Pope spoke to his people on that fateful day. The powerful oratory of his Pope moved him. He too felt the calling. It was like a deep-seated, uncontrollable genetic urge that called for the blood of the Egyptians. Before the Crusade that he was about to undertake, he'd never met an Egyptian or a Muslim. But somehow the Popes' vermin struck a deep chord in his heart. A chord that was as primitive as time itself, that of anger, vengefulness and greed. He couldn't explain why that was so deep rooted in his mind. Neither I suppose would the Kosovo Muslims understand the extreme hate and disdain that drove young Christian Serbs to annihilate them off the Earth. Serb men, who were not there during Godfrey of Bouillon's time, but still felt the same innate, genetic anger and evil.

So being of Noble upbringing, Godfrey felt duty bound to lead one of the armies to free Jerusalem from the Egyptians. So when he and a handful of other Nobles met in the Pope's courtyard, he'd already thought out a military strategy. He led the discussion from then on.

"We should form at least five Crusading armies. We leave by August 1096 and meet in the Byzantine capital, Constantinople (now Istanbul in Turkey). The Byzantine emperor, Alexius I Comnenus, has given us his word that he'll fight along with us! He's after all one of us, a Christian and a child of God!"

"What about Jerusalem...when do we free Jerusalem?" asked an impatient Bishop of the Pope's court. Godfrey of Bouillon remained calm and went on to explain.

"Once we have freed Anotolia from the Seljuks, we will attack the Muslims in Syria and Palestine. Then Bishop, only then will we be able to free Jerusalem!" Godfrey had the support of the majority of the Bishops and Noblemen there. Even Peter the Hermit, a preacher and a common man who had managed to raise his army of common men was in agreement.

21 October 1097; The Battle for The City of ANATAKYA, Turkey.

"The Turks have barricaded the City well Duke Godfrey of Bouillon," shouted one of his Captains.

"I can see that! I don't care if it takes us a year to take the city, but take it we will! Throw more boulders with the catapults. After that send in the foot soldiers, followed by the Calvary again!"

"Yes my Lord" the Captain responded.

The Turks responded to the charge of the foot soldiers by throwing hot oil and chunks of hot ash down on to them from the tops of their barricaded walls surrounding the city. Try as they did to protect themselves from the oil and hot coals by using their shields as a blanket, the oil seeped through, peeling off their skins as the oil cooked the flesh below. The screams were unbearable as some of the soldiers caught fire and were roasted until their bones were exposed. The more they charged the walls of the city, the more brutal was the defence. It was a hopeless situation.

"Stop the charge" Godfrey ordered. He realised the futility of the charge. He needed to reserve his man for the final battle, that of the holy City of Jerusalem.

"We'll wait and starve them to death. They can't have too much food and supplies with them!" Lord Godfrey added.

And wait it out they did. They camped the army around the city, blocking all exits. No one was allowed to enter or leave the city. It was only a matter of time before they knew that the Seljuks would starve to death. But being worthy opponents, they held on until the 3rd of June of the following year-1098. Only then did the city of Antakya fall.

Most of the inhabitants had starved to death and those that had survived were too weak to fight back. When the end came to the Turks inside the city, it was massacre. The Crusaders ransacked the city, murdered all the men, women and children. Next Godfrey of Bouillon left for Jerusalem in late November 1098.

When he arrived in Jerusalem, the Egyptians had fortified the city well. But Godfrey knew that the Lord was with him. On July 15 1099, before Godfrey of Bouillon stormed Jerusalem with all the military might at his disposal, he knelt down in prayer in his tent. He took out the Bible and read Jeremiah 20-22; The Destruction of Jerusalem Foretold. He felt sure that the Lord was working through him to cleanse the Holy City. A city that had through the decades been subjected to one violent take over after another.

"Thus saith the Lord God of Israel;
Behold, I will turn back the weapons of war
that are in your hands, wherewith ye fight against the King of Babylon,
and against the Chalede'ans…
I myself will fight against you with an outstretched
hand and with a strong arm, even in anger, and in fury, and in great
wrath.
And I will smite the inhabitants of this city, both man and beast:
they shall die of the great pestilence.
I will deliver Zedeki'ah King of Judah and his people into the hand of
their enemies, and into the hand of those that seek their life:
and he shall smite them with the edge of the sword; he shall not spare
them,
neither have pity, nor have mercy. Amen."

After he had said his prayer to God, Godfrey of Bouillon put on his armour and went on to attack the Holy City of Jerusalem. His army of

Crusaders fought as if they were possessed with the spirit. They were merciless, slaughtering the men, then the women and the children. Even the beasts were not spared. The Egyptians put up a brave defence but they couldn't withstand the continuous onslaught. Eventually they gave up. And as in the battle of Antakya the year before, and as the Lord of Israel had promised Jeremiah, every Egyptian in the city was murdered; supposedly to purify the 'Holy City'. Godfrey and the Crusaders had succeeded in returning the most 'holy' city back to Western Christian control.

"Find me the Cloth and the piece of the True Cross!" Godfrey of Bouillon ordered his men.

After a frantic search, the Cloth and a metre or so of the remaining part of the True Cross were brought to Godfrey. He knelt down in front of the Cloth and the True Cross and prayed to God.

"I need to be alone!" he commanded his Generals.

"Yes my Lord!" they responded in unison.

Again he read the Bible, this time from Jeremiah 32-33.

"Thus saith the Lord, the God of Israel,
Behold, I will bring it health and cure,
And I will cure them, and reveal unto them
The abundance of peace and truth. And I
Will cause the captivity of Israel to return,
And will build as the first.
And I will cleanse them from all their iniquity,
Whereby they have sinned against me;
And I will pardon all their iniquities,
Whereby they have sinned against me;
And whereby they have transgressed against me.
Amen."

The prayer was from God's promise to Jeremiah of 'The Restoration of Prosperity to Jerusalem" after it had been destroyed by the King of Babylon. Godfrey stood up and took the Cloth into both his hands and raised it into the sky, showing God his gratitude for what he had delivered to him. Then he kissed the Cloth gently, careful not to tamper with the fragile piece of Cloth. He took the True Cross and returned it to the vaults of the Holy Sepulchre Church.

Godfrey of Bouillon took the Cloth and folded it gracefully. His intention was to send it back to his Pope. But he felt this incredible urge to keep a piece of the Cloth for himself. He had after all, fought and killed many other men during the last two years in order to meet this objective. So with no one else in his chambers, he cut a piece of the Cloth for himself. This he would keep in his family and they'd guard it with their lives. Then he folded the rest of the Cloth and placed it into a leather sachet.

"General Peter…You may join me now!" he shouted.

"Yes my Lord…What is it that you wish I do?" Peter asked.

"Take this Cloth with you to the Pope in France. Guard it with your life. Take the best hundred men with you to Clermont" ordered Godfrey.

"Yes my Lord" Peter responded.

"And you can tell the Pope that the true cross is safe and back where it belongs!" added Godfrey of Bouillon.

January 1999.Cape Town, South Africa.

Father Khumalo enjoyed studying European history. It was not just because it was part of his course work for the Master of Arts degree that he was studying at the University of Stellenbosch, South Africa. He was also intrigued by the way the Church those days was essentially the government of the day. The Crusading armies that he'd just been reading about, were in reality the Pope's armies. Their sole purpose then was to entrench the political, commercial and religious control of the Christians in Europe.

He was also amazed that this "battle for Palestine and Jerusalem" was something that had been going on for many, many years. "It's no wonder that we are no closer to resolving the human and political crises that manifests itself every day today in the middle East!" he thought to himself.

"Father Khumalo. What are you reading today?" It was Patricia, his friend.

"Oh, nothing that would interest you my dear child. This is about something that happened several centuries ago!" he replied.

"Well exactly what father…try me?" she was smiling at him, daring him to pick on her young brain.

"Oh it's about the Crusaders!" Father Khumalo responded. He wasn't expecting Patricia to understand all this.

"Oh you aren't talking about the Crusaders of the 11th to the 13th Century, are you Father?" she asked with a victorious grin.

"Yes I am and you're such a bright child of God. One day you will be a great person…You have all that you need to make it in life my dear"

"Thanks Father, but I have to take what ever you say with a pinch of salt, because you always think I'm great!" she laughed.

"Ok Patricia it's time for your scripture lesson. Let's read" Father Khumalo suggested.

"Can't we talk more about the Crusader's and the part religion has played in the many wars over the centuries Father Khumalo?" she asked sincerely and with the curiosity given only to those with the fire of youth coursing through their veins.

"Now that is a very controversial subject my child. One that requires much thought!" Father Khumalo was trying to avoid that topic.

"I mean...Look at the 'Ethnic cleansing' in Kosovo, in Yugoslavia and Serbia, father. Isn't this all part of the remnants of the Crusader wars? I mean it's the Serb Christians trying to wipe out the Muslim Albanians over pieces of land in Kosovo the Serbs claim has special religious and historical importance to them. Doesn't it all point back to the days of the Crusaders again or at a minimum the issues they are fighting about are exactly the same as those of the Crusaders in the last century?" Patricia wasn't about to let this topic disappear, like the thousands of Muslim Albanian and Kosovo refugees that seemed to have disappeared into Kosovo and God knows where else.

"You're correct my child, over the years different people have mis-used the name of God for their own selfish reasons. They have plun-dered, raped, and murdered, all in the name of God. But that doesn't make God or any other religion wrong! It's the people that misinterpret the word of God, that are evil" Father Khumalo realised that Patricia was disturbed by all the madness that was erupting around the world, all because of religious and ethnic differences. So he decided to help her understand the complexity of mans' relationship with God.

"Remember my child what is written in Genesis and the creation of man?" Patricia nodded her head and went on to recite the relevant paragraph.

"And God said, Let us make man in our image,
after our likeness...
So God created man in his own image,
in the image of God created he him;
male and female created he them.
And God blessed them. And God said unto them,
Be fruitful, and multiply and replenish the earth,
and subdue it."

"Wonderful Patricia! You see, God created us all in his image…his own image!

So the differences that men see in each other are not of God's creation, but that of man and man alone!" added Father Khumalo.

"Just like the racial segregation that was law here in South Africa, before Nelson Mandela?" Patricia wasn't asking a question, she was, in fact, lamenting the futility and evilness of apartheid. She felt ashamed that her own had subjected people created by God in his image to such humiliation, torture and murder. This topic was close to the bone and it hurt. Father Khumalo noticed the pain, the guilt and the anger in her eyes, so he decided to take this as an opportunity to change the topic.

"Tomorrow Father James will be taking the juniors for Bible lessons…I know he would really love your help!" he asked, smiling at her.

"Oh, sure!" Patricia's mind was still roaming the centuries and corners of the globe, trying to understand why man was so evil. Why when God had given man every thing, he still wanted more and was prepared to kill others for it. And to make matters worse, to even use God's name to justify their murders.

Just like the Serbs in Croatia and Kosovo annihilating the Muslims in Kosovo and just like the Hutu's hunting the Tutsi's like animals. Just like her own people in South Africa had used the Bible to justify 'separate development'; apartheid, repression and murder. None of it made any sense in her young and innocent mind.

None of it made any sense too in reality to Father Khumalo. The seemingly random and endless murders in his province of KwaZulu Natal and Rwanda…Oh Rwanda! He shook his head in resignation as his mind drifted to that dreadful time he spent in Rwanda's 'killing fields.'

Seven

January, 1999. Honolulu, Hawaii. MIRC Laboratory

Manuel was in the cell culture laboratory. It was 10hr30 and he was back from the cafeteria. His mind was on the cells that Hans had said he was going to bring on the 12th of this month. He was alone in the lab, so it gave him time to reflect on the wonderful work they'd been doing on the chimpanzees. They had over the past eighteen months succeeded in cloning five chimps successfully.

They'd adapted their technique from their colleagues in Honolulu, at the University of Hawaii, led by Wakayama's team. Wakayama's team had managed to successfully clone more than 20 healthy female mice by the end of 1998. They published their groundbreaking research in the scientific journal, "Nature" in 1998.

But it all really started when Wilmut's team in Scotland, at the Roslin Institute, caught everyone unaware and announced that they had cloned Dolly the sheep, the first mammalian clone, late in 1997. Manuel recalled how excited he was when he heard that announcement by Wilmut. This was a significant breakthrough because the technique they used was new and full of uncertainties. He never for a moment thought that he would today, be the leading researcher in what was called Somatic Cell Nuclear Transfer or SCNT for short.

He recalled the history, debate and development of cloning in animals. You see each human cell has a nucleus at the centre. In the nucleus lies the genetic material clumped together as chromosomes. The human cell has a total of forty-six chromosomes, grouped together as twenty-three pairs. Twenty-three come from the egg of the mother and the other twenty-three from the sperm of the father. Together they made up the full complement of forty-six chromosomes that results in a unique individual. It was nature's way of ensuring that the best from one generation was passed on to the next. By the mixing of the chromosomes when the egg and sperm fused, this resulted in a better and more diverse individual. Eventually it leads to the very survival of mankind. Because if any of the chromosomes were defective, this process would not go on successfully, and a human foetus with major defects usually aborts spontaneously.

Now what made Dolly the sheep and the work done by Wakayama on mice so exciting is that they managed to extract the full complement of chromosomes from adult cells. Having done that, they then took the egg or ovum from the female and removed its chromosomes, which are only half the number of the adult cell. After that the full adult cells chromosomes, called a somatic cell in science, were placed into the empty egg from the female. This egg, now with the full compliment of the adult chromosomes, was then returned into the womb of the female. Miraculously, these went on to divide into the different tissues that make up the sheep or mice, and resulted in the birth of Dolly and the mice in Hawaii. Each an exact replica of the adult that had contributed the chromosomes.

Manuel and the rest of the world considered this miraculous because, adult somatic cells don't divide as quickly and regularly, as the young cells formed after the fusion of a sperm and an egg. Further, how these adult cells then still 'remember' to make the heart, the bones, liver, brain and so on, is still a mystery.

"Manuel my mate, a penny for your thoughts!" John interrupted him. He had a coin in his hands and a mischievous smile.

"Oh…I was wondering how on earth the adult somatic cell chromosomes still manage to divide from scratch into all the different organs and tissues; after being dormant for so long. I mean who would have thought that if I took a cell from your blood, and then placed it into an egg that's empty, that the blood cell would then develop into a full animal, heart, brain and all, when placed in the womb?" Manuel asked with a frown on his face. John's face lit up; this was the kind of discussion that fired him up. Science, genetics to be exact, was his passion. So he went on to add.

"Elementary my dear fellow, elementary! Let's journey back to Cambridge University. Remember Watson and Crick's discovery that all the chromosomes were made of DNA."

"Come on John, let's not get too basic" protested Manuel.

"No wait, I really think that if you start at that level, then this Somatic Cell Nuclear Transfer (SCNT) is really quite logical," added John.

"Ok." Manuel said with a sigh. "I'll pretend that I'm one of your undergraduate students, so go on!"

"Well the DNA in the chromosomes is made up of building blocks called bases. We know that the sequencing of the bases is highly specific for each section of the different chromosomes. These specific sequences of base pairs in the DNA, are called genes right?" Manuel continued to clear his desk but intimated to John that he was still all ears. John went on.

"So each chromosome has a specific number and type of genes. These genes control the manufacture of the different tissues, organs, enzymes and so on. That's why even an adult somatic cell taken from any tissue will still develop into the different organs that make a full animal" concluded John. Manuel turned around and feigned surprise.

"Is that all you have in your data bank up there?" pointing at John's brain. "Is that all you have to say. I mean how do you explain the fact those adult cells, let's say a blood cell, which is not actively dividing and has already matured to be a blood cell, then starts for some reason to divide again. What then triggers them to start dividing again and further, what says to them, forget about your life and duty as a blood cell; now it's time to make another baby with a heart and all?" Manuel was now intellectually sparring with John and enjoying it.

"Well if you were listening I said that all the cells have the genes in the chromosomes that are responsible for every part of the full adult species" responded John.

"I heard you John, but answer the question, what tells the cell to start those resting genes it has to start working all over again. I mean, imagine you are a muscle cell, and all you know is contracting and relaxing. Then all of a sudden you are required to stop all that exercise and start manufacturing a heart that beats, a brain that thinks, a stomach that digests food and even a liver that can handle as much beer as yours. How does that cell change its 'mind' and function differently?" asked Manuel.

John hesitated for a while, then smiled and said.

"Why don't you ask Suzie?" he asked.

"Suzie?" repeated Manuel.

"Yeah, Suzie your favourite chimp over there. After all you managed to clone her last week. Yeah, why don't you ask her?" John was laughing away now.

"Well perhaps I should have asked her first instead of wasting my time with you!" Manuel snapped back and winked at John as he joined in the laughter.

The phone ringing interrupted their hysterics.

"Hi John here, can I help you? Oh Hans how's Baltimore?" The atmosphere changed to a serious one now.

"I'm fine. Is Manuel there?" asked Hans.

"He's right next to me, hold on for him Hans," John gave the phone to Manuel.

"Manuel, is the other lab ready?" he asked.

"Everything is fine Hans. Don't worry about a thing," he responded and went on to ask. "Can we still expect you on the twelfth then Hans?"

"Yeah…in fact I will be coming with the Colombians. They want to make sure that the tissues are safe and get here in one piece. In fact Mr Paulo Galvez himself will be coming. So please make sure that they are no hitches!" Hans sounded as if he was pleading with Manuel.

"Don't worry Hans, we can handle any thing at this stage," Manuel said trying to re-assure Hans.

"Ok, then I'll see you all on the twelfth. We will be getting to the lab at 11hr00."

Hans then said good bye and put the phone down.

There was a minute or two of silence before John asked Manuel to confirm what Hans had said.

"Did he say that Galvez was coming along?" asked John with a look of surprise on his face.

"Yes" replied Manuel, looking blankly straight ahead of him.

"It's that important?" John asked. It was more of a statement, an acknowledgement of the fact.

Paulo Galvez was the chief sponsor of the Millennium Research Centre (MRC). In fact, he owned the centre and bankrolled everything. That was not the problem. The problem that Manuel had with that was, it was never clear in his mind how Paulo had accumulated his immense wealth. And he had an incredible amount of money. He had villas in Bogota, Columbia, an apartment in Manhattan New York, and in Baltimore at Fells Point. That was besides the luxury villas in Spain,

Monaco and Cape Town. He was a very wealthy and powerful man by all accounts.

The people that surrounded Paulo also concerned Manuel. Frankly they looked like gangsters and dressed and behaved the part. He wondered whether the fact that he resided mostly in Armenia, Colombia, had anything to do with the way he had acquired his wealth.

"Manuel, have you ever wondered why a man like Paulo Galvez would have any interest in gene manipulation and cloning?" asked John.

"You must have been reading my mind John!" answered Manuel." I really haven't a clue. I mean here we are, having managed to clone five chimps successfully and being the first in the world to do so, but we can't even publish this. Strange don't you think?" He asked. It wasn't as if he was expecting an answer.

"You don't by any chance think that he wants to clone himself…do you?" John asked. There was a moment's silence-an airy, deafening silence.

"That would be ridiculous!" responded Manuel.

"Why would it be?" asked John, looking rather surprised.

"Well for starters it's illegal. I mean both the United States Senate and the House have banned all cloning in human-embryo research. Remember that the Bond-Frist bill in the Senate and the Ehlers bill in the House, were both successfully passed last year."

"I know that, President Clinton has passed a moratorium on all human cloning research for the next five years and so have most of the European countries!" added John.

"As far back as the 12th of January 1998, in Paris, France, the Council of Europe's Bioethics Convention Protocol opened the discussion for the banning of cloning human beings. None of the world's major religions, be they Christian, Muslim or Jewish have supported human cloning. But what if Paulo really wanted to clone himself?" This was a question that although seemed frivolous now, may well end up as something they had to address later.

"That would be foolish. I mean just because it works in the chimpanzees, it doesn't follow that it would work in the human species. And even if it did, what would be the point?" asked Manuel.

"Well to make a copy of himself!" replied John.

"Now…John, you know that there are so many variables that make the full human being. There is the problem that the foetus would grow in an environment different from Paulo's mother's womb and…" Manuel was interrupted by John.

"Not unless he want's to use his mother to carry the baby around in her womb!" John interjected, sporting a mischievous smile.

"His mother is dead" replied Manuel in a matter of fact manner. He went on. "There are other problems and issues to be addressed if Paulo or anyone else for that matter thinks they can make exact replicas of themselves. Granted the clone would look identical to the cell donor, just like identical twins. I suppose you could call a clone a 'delayed' twin. But even amongst identical twins their characters are different." Manuel was now serious. These were issues that he had delved into, at length, besides the moral and ethical aspects, whenever he had the opportunity to do so.

"Further we now know for sure that the different parts of the baby's brain and personality, develop according to the environment they grow up in. That would mean that Paulo would have to not only recreate the exact conditions of his mother's womb, were he started as a foetus, but also the house and streets he grew up in, uncles and aunts that moulded his character and life, childhood friends, girlfriends and so on. The list of environmental features that mould the final person are endless." Manuel added sounding almost exasperated.

"Tell me about it," added John, looking resigned. "There is also the fact that our character is not static, but continues to change as we grow, until we die, depending on the events that we encounter in life. How can you stage-manage all that? Impossible if you ask me."

"The most important fact though John, is that if we are to use a cell from Manuel for the cloning, those cell's chromosomes and genes are already old. Every cell in the human body has a certain life span. It's possible therefore that we could clone him, but that his clone, or delayed twin, would only live for a few years because Paulo is over fifty. Maybe the clone would die at twelve years of age, thinking it's now sixty two years old!" Manuel went on.

"Yes we haven't really answered that question with the chimps have we. I mean since we are using granulosa cells from the female ovary, these are fairly young cells because they are made every month. I agree with you that it would be a totally different proposition if we used mature adult cells." Added John. Granulosa cells are the cells that surround the developing ovum or egg in the ovary. Since the female makes an egg once a month, there is a recycling of these cells every month. This makes them a good source of fresh and young cells. That explained why all the mammalian clones so far had been female; Dolly the sheep and the mice at the University of Hawaii, were all female.

"Well let's not speculate. Maybe we are jumping the gun a little and Paulo has no intention of cloning himself!" concluded Manuel.

"I must say though Manuel, it does make one wonder…This is frightening for mankind isn't it?" John was serious now.

"It's only frightening if we do research with the aim to clone humans. But I see no problem if we only clone certain tissues and organs. I mean that could revolutionalise organ transplantation and the treatment of diseases like diabetes. Imagine if we could produce buckets of pancreatic cells. If anyone was diabetic, we would simply supply the patient with pancreatic tissue!" added Manuel.

This was a debate that had been going on Internationally for years. However, the politicians, who respond to public opinion, had developed a knee jerk reaction to human embryo research and banned all forms of research dealing with human embryos. They failed to distinguish between cloning of human embryos and placing them in the womb of a woman with a view to creating another replica human, and that of culturing human tissue only in the lab, for the benefit of medical research and disease treatment.

"I guess we'll have to wait until the twelfth of January to find out!" Manuel said, resigning to the fact that all they were discussing at the moment was pure speculation.

Needless to say the lengthy discussion that John and Manuel had, got them thinking.

Besides the ethical and moral aspects of cloning in whatever forms it occurred. There are those that felt that even the cloning of crops and plants for agriculture was going to backfire on us one day. That as a result of the cloning of these plants had limited the genetic diversity of certain crops. In time, all that was needed was a fungus or bacteria, that developed an affinity for these cloned crops and that would wipe out the entire year's crops. Those concerned about this occurring, had even suggested that perhaps we should keep a nursery of all the original wild plants and crops. Kind of a "Jurassic Park" for plants and crops. That way if such a disaster occurred, it would be easy to repopulate the world with the original plants that had adapted by evolution, naturally to the earth's environment.

Philosophically for John and Manuel, therein also lay the problem of trying to clone mammals and humans. In the end, we would populate the world with people we have no guarantee can adapt to the changing requirements for the next generations. The mere fact that Rembrandt was an artistic genius in 17th and 18th century Holland and Europe, does not mean that if we cloned him today, he would still produce those fine works of art. He would also need the same parents, teachers, friends and lovers that inspired him then. Perhaps without them, a Rembrandt clone born today, in this modern world where art had been replaced by digital cameras and videos, would end up being a gifted social misfit. A nuisance to society. Perhaps he'd even be classed as schizophrenic.

After this reflective mood and a minute had elapsed, Manuel concluded by adding.

"If people really wanted to develop the best individuals for the world, what is needed is for us to ensure that every child is brought up in a loving and stimulating environment. We know that in the third world, millions of children are malnourished and as a result their intellectual growth and capacity is stunted. That more than anything else, denies the world of dozens of Rembrandts, Picassos, Muhammad Alis, JFKs and Mandelas!"

"You're so right mate," concurred John. Manuel was now very serious and deep in thought. After a while he added, slowly.

"If man ever clones another man…the Lord will surely curse us all!" This was his Catholic part talking now. He was now speaking from his heart. Cloning suddenly for him was no longer simply a scientific issue. And in that sombre mood he went on to recite the Bible, on the "Consequences of Disobedience" of the Lord.

> *"Cursed shall be the fruit of thy body,*
> *and the fruit of thy land,*
> *the increase of thy kine,*
> *and the flocks of thy sheep.*

> *Cursed shalt thou be when thou comest in,*
> *and cursed shalt thou be when thou goest out.*

The Lord shall send upon these cursing, vexation, and rebuke,
In all that thou settest thine hand unto for to do,
Until thou be destroyed, and thou perish quickly,
Because of the wickedness of thy doings,
Whereby thou hast forsaken me."

Leviticus. 26:14-46.

Eight

Galvez was at his penthouse in Fells Point, Baltimore when he got the call from Senator Bell. He'd just returned from a very successful European trip. The welcome was unpleasant, not what he expected at all. The hair on the back of his neck rose when he heard the news.

"My bodyguard has been murdered!" said Bell

"How?" asked Galvez.

"Some bastard put a bullet behind his ear…damn!"

Galvez mind raced back to the previous week. Nicky had been murdered after they had parted ways from Wilts place and he had set off for Europe to complete his mission. Again it was Bell who had called to inform him of Nicky's murder. He remembered asking Bell how it had happened.

"Really crazy thing Galvez…Someone laced his champagne with nitrates". Bell was still in a state of bewilderment then. Nicky's death had visibly shook him. Within the M.C he had been the closest to Nicky. Now in a space of seven days two people that he knew well were murdered, he was really concerned. He knew that he couldn't exactly go the police or the FBI and share his thoughts with them.

"What the fuck are nitrates?" Galvez remembered asking. He hadn't a clue then what sort of drug or poison it was. Although 'hits' were part of his trade, this was a first. He was irritated more by the fact that someone had used a kill method he hadn't heard of. In his line of business, premature violent death was part of the package; in fact it was inevitable.

"They're anti-angina tablets or some sort of anti-hypertensive tablets" explained Bell.

"So, if it's a prescription drug, how did that kill him?" Galvez still wasn't clear how this all worked.

"No Galvez, the tablets are safe but the problem is that Nicky was taking Viagra as well. The combination of the two causes your blood pressure to drop so fucking low that not enough blood goes to your heart!"

"So Nicky had a heart attack…fucking some broad?" Galvez was pissed off but he could see the humour in it all, although he didn't elaborate because he knew how close Bell and Nicky had been. "Did they catch the broad who did it?" asked Galvez.

"No, the Broad isn't the problem. In fact Ms Genevieve, yeah you know her, called me early in the morning to inform me of what happened and then I called the police!" Galvez knew Genevieve well as he always used her escort services whenever he needed company in Washington. There was no way she would have been into this. Their relationship went back along way and she had a business to protect. The fact that she'd called Bell before the cops found out further proved her innocence. She could easily have kept quite and they would have not been the wiser.

"It gave me time to go and clear Nicky's penthouse of all evidence linking him with the Millennium Club. Thanks to her, or else we'd have half of DC's police force onto us by now!" added the Senator.

And now the Senator had just had his shadow whacked right in front of him and Galvez. Galvez sixth sense told him to watch his back. "Bell someone is on to us…I knew it the moment they killed Nicky. That was the first message! Bastards!" Galvez was really upset. He hated not knowing who his enemy was and right now he didn't have the foggiest clue as to whom and when next. He knew the why though; it had to be because of The Cloth. But he had been through similar difficulties before and had always lived to tell the story.

"I'll personally castrate the bastards…That's a promise!" Galvez added.

"But who can it be?" the Senator was almost pleading and Galvez sensed the panic in Bell's voice. This was no longer in Bell's terrain. Bell was comfortable in the wheeling and dealing in the Washington political circuit. He had, until recently, been confident about taking on Bill, using sleaze journalism, rightwing funds and the office of the Independent Prosecutor. Digging up personal dirt was in his line of work, but these…silent assassins were way above him. For the first time since Vietnam he actually felt frightened for his own personal safety. The assassins obviously knew his every move; hence they killed David his bodyguard as a message to him. Now they followed this up with Nicky's murder, a very close friend. Soon they would decide to get close enough and take him out and he wouldn't even know when and where to look out from.

"Listen Bell, the plan proceeds as we originally agreed. I'm going to delay my departure to Hawaii for a while. Lets allow things settle and I'll find out who the fuck is trying to fuck with us. In the meantime no landline calls to each other. Increase your personal security and try to get any leads from the FBI and the local cops" Galvez was in control now. Nothing was going to stop him now. He was too close to so much power, absolute power and wealth that he was not going to let this project die. In fact he was prepared to die for this. If ten people were behind this then he would kill all ten. If a hundred were behind this, then a hundred people would surely die!

"Ok Galvez, I'll inform Wilt and Oneal!" answered a some what more confident Bell. It occurred to Bell that they were now down to four men in the MC." And let's meet at Wilts place tomorrow so that we can put some sanity into all this shit!" he added. He was still upset about the death of his close friend.

As soon as Bell had put his phone down, Galvez decided to leave his penthouse. He was escorted by three of his bodyguards and he instructed one of them to get the car and meet them at the entrance of the apartment building.

Once he settled at the back of the Mercedes 600 SEL, he told the driver to head for the Aquarium in down town Baltimore. Then he used his cell-phone to call Professor Hans Schmidt. Hans was in Baltimore, waiting for the samples from Galvez.

"Hans, it's me, no names on the phone ok! Meet me at the aquarium, near Planet Hollywood in thirty minutes. You do know where it is?" it was more an order that a question.

"I'll be there!" Han's knew that something was up. He assumed that Galvez was bringing him the tissue specimen and it was time to head back to Hawaii. He'd prepared the laboratory and the team in Hawaii, so he wasn't unduly anxious. He'd performed his duties efficiently as usual. Perhaps it had something to do with his German upbringing, but he loathed inefficiency. He detested laziness and time wasting. So he called for a cab and directed the driver to head for the aquarium.

When Galvez arrived at the aquarium, Hans was already waiting outside. He summoned Hans to get into the Mercedes and they drove off to find parking near Planet Hollywood. They managed to find parking off street and Galvez ordered the driver and one of the other bodyguards to stay with the car. The idea of coming to a car booby trapped with a bomb was on his mind. He wasn't taking any chances. He and Hans with the other bodyguard then went into Planet Hollywood. They chose a corner table, so that they had full view of the restaurants entrance and the diners. Tina Turner was blasting off in the background singing that she was 'Simply the best!'. Galvez hummed to the tune. He liked Tina Turner.

"We have to postpone our visit to Hawaii. Maybe in about two weeks we can go. Something has come up that has to be settled before we proceed!" said Galvez. Before Hans could respond, Galvez summoned the waiter. "Some real Colombian coffee for all of us…and bring some bacon and egg toasted sandwiches!"

"Yes Sir! Coffee and sandwiches will be ready in five minutes!" she responded. Hans still hadn't said a thing. He knew never to pry into Galvez's business. He'd known him now for five years and knew that he was a violent but extremely intelligent man.

"Is everything fine at the laboratory?" Galvez went on.

"All is fine and waiting for the new tissue. We are on schedule." Hans was always to the point with his answers.

"Thanks!" Galvez said to the waitress after she had brought the coffee and toasted sandwiches. After tasting the coffee he nodded in satisfaction, it was real coffee all right. He was nodding also in appreciation of the waitress' butt. She had one of those ramp model figures. Galvez figured that she must have tried her luck as an actress in Hollywood and when she failed, she reckoned that working in one of the Planet restaurants was the next best thing. "Damn…I bet she even dreams Bruce Willis will one day walk into this joint of his and spot her for the talent she really is!" Galvez mumbled to himself. He felt sorry for her in a way. He knew that in life no one ever gave you anything for free. There was no such thing as luck in his book. All he had today he had to kill for. He shook his head this time, in sympathy for a waitress that didn't even know him!

"Now Hans I want you to go back to Hawaii tomorrow…keep an eye on things and keep me informed. If anything strange happens, I want to know every detail".

"Consider it done Mr Galvez!" Hans responded after swallowing some of the coffee in his mouth.

"How do I get in touch with you Mr Galvez, if the need arises?" asked Hans.

"I'll contact you in two days time. Then I'll inform you which mobile number I'll be using". Galvez never let anyone know his exact whereabouts. That's the way he operated and that's why he was still alive today. Even with his bodyguards, he only told them the day they were leaving where they were going. He had a famous saying about trust; 'There is only one person I trust and that's my mother!' Those who knew him well also knew that his mother had long passed away. What Galvez was saying in reality was that he trusted no one.

The following day Hans left for Hawaii. He decided not to call Manuel at the laboratory because he saw no point since he was not coming with the tissue or
Mr Galvez. Hans was disappointed to say the least, because he was keen to get the project off the ground. Galvez had been secretive about the project for some time. But in the last few weeks, he had hinted to Hans the enormity of the task. Hans was taken aback at the audacity of it all at first. But he never showed his emotions to Galvez or anyone else for that matter.

After a while, the idea became quite appealing to Hans. He could see the true potential of it. He was exited that he was part of such a noble cause. It reminded him of his motherland, the two world wars that were fought to make this world a better place. Now he was sure that this world would once again become pure, clean and holy. He grinned and then put his seatbelt on as the Captain announced that they were about to land at Honolulu Airport.

Meanwhile the same day, Bell was sitting in the conference room at Wilt's house with the rest of the Millennium Club, licking their wounds. They were now down to four men. Nicky had been the fifth. A select group of individuals, wealthy, ultra conservative and all with the same blinding ambition. But as powerful as they all were, they were being stalked and eliminated by an invisible enemy. An enemy that was obviously just as powerful and ruthless. That disturbed them all.

It was 10h30 and Galvez was there as he'd promised. Although he had good news for them, he wasn't the centre of attraction at that moment. That belonged to Bell as he recounted the previous events. Namely the murders of his bodyguard and that of Nicky. "Damn scares the living day lights out of me," Bell concluded when he had recounted in detail what had happened.

"No FBI?" asked a serious and concerned Galvez.

"Don't worry, that's been taken care of. And they don't know that I had a meeting with you either" added Bell.

"Who the fuck has the balls to be messing around with you Bell?" it was William O'Neal. He was known for his short temper. I suppose it was in keeping with his height, you know the 'Little Napoleon Syndrome'.

"I'm not sure. I don't know what this all means yet" Bell was telling the truth.

"Maybe this David of yours was robbed plain and simple!" interjected William O'Niel. He stood up from his chair and started to pace the room. He was obviously worried. He felt as if they were beginning to lose control just when it seemed that their plan was about to take off.

"No it wasn't a robbery. They took nothing from him or the car. Damn!" Bell hissed and cursed.

"You don't believe that someone is on to us do you, Bell" asked Wilt.

"I don't think so. Anyway who could it be and what would be gained by killing my shadow?" Bell protested.

"If you ask me I think this shadow of yours had a personal problem and someone took care of things. Gentleman I wouldn't lose sleep over this. Let's get on to the business of the day, the reason we're all here!" Oneal had made up his mind that this issue was pure coincidence, bad luck and nothing to waste time on. He was used to making quick decisions. As the senior partner in the largest law firm in Washington, making decisions was what he was paid to do.

"But if it turns out that someone is trying to fuck with us, they're not going to know what hit them!" He moved his short, pot-bellied frame, fidgeting about in the leather chair that was almost submerging him.

Galvez kept rather quiet all along. He sensed something more sinister. This was more in his line of work, his speciality. In this business he had learned to develop a sixth sense. That's why he was alive and a billionaire. That's why in Columbia all the Cartels treated him with respect. He had earned that respect by the only means possible in the narcotics industry. He liked to call it the recreational, over-the-counter drug market.

He'd murdered his way to the top, systematically getting rid of any rivals. Rumour had it in his hometown of Armenia, that he'd personally killed thirty-six men with his bare hands. To him, killing was always a means to an end. He sensed more to this story than the rest of the MC gang did. It was that simple. He learnt in the trade that there are never any coincidences or accidents. Accidents? Well yes, he had learnt to create them against his enemies. Surprise was always the best means of attack.

The killing of David had all the signs of a professional hit. The fact that a highly trained shadow didn't even have time to reach for his gun, the neat bullet placed behind the head and most importantly, done right in front of him and Bell. And Nicky's death…that was the most bizarre murder case he had ever heard of. Someone was trying to send a message to them. He was going to find out on his own. He learnt a long time ago that you could only defeat an enemy that you could see or knew. That if you didn't create your own future someone would create it for you.

"Common Galvez, the fucking suspense is killing me, tell us what's going on?" O'Neal said impatiently.

"Oh!" Galvez's mind was brought back to the room and the attention of the rest of the MC. He stood up and positioned himself so that he was facing all of them.

"Amigos…I have The Piece of the Cloth with me!" he said with pride. He had this air of accomplishment about him, of having done the impossible, of success and victory. There was a moment's silence.

"How did you convince them to release it to you?" asked a shocked O'Neal.

"Two hundred million US dollars and 5% of our stock in Microsoft and Amazon.com. And of course, I told them that the alternative was too ghastly to contemplate" Galvez added with a deep throaty laugh.

"You son of a gun! The real thing hey?" O'Neal was trembling with excitement.

"You bet it's the real thing!" Galvez sounded almost irritated. The notion that anyone could even consider that he would be conned was insulting. "I had the blood samples from the Cloth tested in Europe. The analysis showed that it was a male and that his blood group was AB-positive. It's the real thing all right. The carbon dating also fits with what we know!"

"Galvez you're bad!" O'Neal was up from his chair. He couldn't sit still with all this excitement. "You mean you actually stole the 'Cloth of Turin' from the Europeans?" O'Neal wasn't the brightest of them when it came to European history.

"O'Neal you're crazy! Even I couldn't touch The Cloth of Turin, even if I spent all my money and time on it." Galvez was revelling in this. He knew he had their undivided attention now. If this wasn't The Cloth of Turin, then why did he pay so much money for this one?

"I know some of you are confused. Let me put you guys into the picture!" Galvez sat on the desk, giving him self a height advantage, a stage on which to deliver his coup de grace. "Some time during the 11th to 14th Century, the Shroud was seen in Constantinople by a "Robert of Clari" of the Fourth Crusade. He's said to have seen the shroud himself, publicly exposed in the church of "Our Lady of Blancherness' in the year 1203. The year after that Constantinople was invaded and looted by the Crusaders and that's when the Cloth went missing. Apparently the Crusaders cut pieces of the Cloth and distributed some of the fragments amongst themselves. Some people even think that they did this as early as the 11th Century. This explains why today, it is acknowledged publicly that a piece of the Shroud is missing, the part below the frontal image. It's believed that the Cloth or fragments of it were sent to Lirey in France for safekeeping.

Our client says that the missing piece of the Cloth of Turin was taken and kept by one of the French Noble families. They kept it within the family vaults from one generation to the next. It was sold to our clients during the Second World War. The French family was afraid that it would fall into the hands of the Nazis. Hitler, it is said, actually had the family killed when he discovered that they had disposed of the Cloth. He wanted The Cloth desperately, because he was convinced that if he had it, he would win the war. The French family knew that it would be safer in England, that Hitler would find it difficult to conquer England". Galvez was speaking slowly and with a sense of the occasion at hand. The room was quiet except for the occasional crackling of the burning wood on the fireplace. Galvez paused to allow the moment to soak in.

"Galvez if you don't go on I'm going to piss on my self with anticipation" O'Neal interrupted like an impatient child being told a never-ending story by a grandparent.

"My contacts in Europe have been tracing this missing piece for the last ten years. They actually stumbled on the evidence when they were in Paris. They met an old monk who told them about the French family that was killed by Hitler's SS troopers. The family had one surviving relative. She was a little girl during the war and was hiding with the French resistance movement. My contacts traced her to an old age home in Paris and interviewed her. Low and behold, she actually had a copy of the letter and document of sale of "The Cloth", to our clients. It was dated 13 October 1943. She had no clue what this cloth was all about!" Galvez lit a Havana, asked for some Remy Martin cognac and filled his glass. The others did likewise. There was an air of celebration, mixed with the thick rich aroma of the Havanas.

"Once we had the name of our client in London, the rest was easy. Fortunately for us our client was a victim of the Long Market Investment Hedge Fund. The family lost almost their entire wealth because of the Russian and Asian financial crises. I simply gave them…well, 'an offer they couldn't refuse' and now we have The Cloth with us, here in Washington!" There was a moment's silence then Wilt started clapping slowly. Soon the others followed, in synchrony. If one didn't know better, it sounded like a communist party gathering with that synchronised clapping. This went on for at least a minute. Galvez was serious, nodding his head in approval and accepting the sincere acknowledgement and gratitude from the rest of the Millennium Club.

"Gentleman fill your glasses, I propose that we toast to Galvez for the brilliant work done!" Wilt suggested, so they all rose to their feet.

"To Galvez, to Galvez, to Galvez!" they all toasted. Then it was O'Neal's turn.

"This is to the Millennium Club!" and again the chorus, the Millennium Club echoed in the room.

"To the year 2000 elections!" It was Bell. He was back to the Bill bashing theme. Again they all echoed his toast. Finally it was Galvez's turn. He asked that they all kneel instead and they did.

"This is to Coming of the Son of Man!"

"To the Coming!"

"To the Coming!"

"To our friend Nicky!"

"To Nicky!"

"Gentleman let's sit and have something to eat. The table has been set in the dining room. We have much to discuss and celebrate!" said Wilt as he ushered his guests to the adjoining dinning room.

"I'll drink to that," added Galvez. He was famished and all this tension and discussion had whipped up his appetite.

"Now this is a feast befitting the rulers of the Earth!" said Bell looking at the spread on the table. There was crayfish, lobster, prawns and roast duck, amongst other things.

Once they had settled down and indulged themselves with the food and drink, it was back to serious business. Time and planning was of the essence if their plan was to work.

"We will need the virgin girl next month Bell!" It was Galvez this time. He handled all the details about the Millennium International Research Centre (MIRC). That was his baby." Can you arrange that in time?" he went on to ask.

"Not a problem. I'll set the ball in motion. I'll notify our contact in Cape Town South Africa, today. I don't foresee a problem!" Bell had done his part and he was sure that things would run smoothly.

"When do you leave for the MIRC in Hawaii Galvez?" asked Wilt.

"Well Hans has already left for Hawaii! By Friday I should be in Hawaii with the Cloth!" Hans had briefed him about the progress of the experiments and that it was all systems go. The laboratory had been prepared and they were waiting for the tissue samples to arrive.

"The obstetrician?" asked Wilt looking at Bell for an answer.

"No problem there again. I have convinced Dr Brock from London to perform the procedure and to look after her" replied Bell confidently.

"Can he be trusted?" Galvez asked. He wasn't about to put his $US200 million and more investment, without having all the guarantees and angles checked out.

"He can be trusted…and he doesn't have much of a choice anyway. I haven't given him all the details though. As far as he's concerned he will be doing a simple in vitro-fertilisation for a high-profile family. I've had him under surveillance for the last eight months. He can't as much as breathe in London and I'll know when he does! Don't worry about him! He's my responsibility!" Bell was sure that all the necessary groundwork had been done.

Nine

January 1999, Cape Town, South Africa.

Patricia had been seeing Jos Leon for almost two months. She recalled the first time they met. It was at the Victoria and Alfred Waterfront, in Cape Town, South Africa. It was a Saturday morning and she was with her cousin Ruth, who was visiting from New York. She and Ruth were the best of friends and were born in the same year, separated by a few months and a few thousand miles.

That day Patricia had decided to take Ruth on the ferry that leaves from the V & A Waterfront to Robben Island. Ruth was keen to see the infamous Island and the matchbox cell that was Nelson Mandela's home for twenty-seven years and some months.

She recalled how they had arrived at the Waterfront early that morning and parked quite near to where the car bomb had exploded the week before. She did this with intent and thinking that there was no way that they would plant the next bomb in exactly the same place. Now almost ten years after the release of Nelson Mandela a State of Emergency of another kind was called for to stop the new urban terrorism that was threatening to paralyse the tourist industry that was the lifeline of the city. This urban madness was motivated by both by political and religious factors, with the control of the illicit drug industry as the key factor. Ruth was excited about visiting South Africa's Alcatraz, 11.5 km out to sea and clearly visible from the city bowl. This maximum-security prison only opened itself to the public after 1990.

Patricia and Ruth went to get their pre-booked tickets from the booth alongside the quay. They boarded the Makana catamaran, which left promptly at 7:30. The water was a bit rough as the trade winds came up over the ocean.

"It looks as if it's going to be quite choppy this morning'" said the pilot as he steered the boat out of the harbour and through the wake of the Safmarine cargo ships being escorted by tugs out of the harbour and up towards the Indian ocean. Ruth leaned over the side to get sick. Her stomach was in a cramp and she managed to bring out the morning's breakfast. She still hadn't completed the digestive process because you could still see the streaks of bacon and egg yolk.

"Should we turn back?" asked Patricia. "Perhaps we should have flown there. Court helicopters offer a flip from the Waterfront."

"Oh God no" replied Ruth, "that would be far worse." The forty-minute boat trip was not a pleasant experience although quickly forgotten when they docked at the Island. On the way over Patricia imagined what it must have been like to have been cut off from the mainland by the icy Atlantic sea as they moved further and further away from the mountain, Table mountain.

They were taken on a tour of the prison and led to the tiny cell that used to be President Nelson Mandela's home. It was unimaginable that such a revered man had for so long been confined to this matchbox of space. The reality of apartheid and the former regime became quite evident to the two girls. Tears filled Patricia's eyes. Ruth was silent, her heart filled with anger.

Patricia remembered how little she'd known of this man, how she'd grown up on a wine farm in Stellenbosch so close to Robben Island yet so far from her thoughts. At school no one had told her about Mandela. What made her angry was that her so-called Christian-liberal upbringing didn't encourage much interaction with black people and discussion was limited to interaction with farm labourers and their dependants who her family 'looked after'. As a child she was raised by Mercy, an elderly Xhosa lady who had six children of her own. She was their maid and it took Patricia some time to realise that. She had fallen in love with Mercy and, in fact, had spent more time with her as a baby than with her mother. She brought her up and before her mind was fed all that stuff about apartheid and racial superiority, she was her best friend. She loved Mercy.

The other black farm labourers were paid a monthly wage and given a bag of maize meal, sometimes flour and meat too, depending on whether it was a good month. And, of course, they were all given the fruits of their labour, wine, gallons of the cheap stuff as part payment for they labour. At first it seemed logical that they should be given the wine. But with time she realised the evilness of the scheme. The labourers become alcoholics; they became dependent on the farm not only for their accommodation but also for their monthly fix. As a result, today the Western Cape of South Africa has the highest incidence of the fetal-alcohol-syndrome (FAS) in the world.

The female labourers continued to drown themselves with the wine even when they were with child. Patricia visualised the hoards of children, born with small heads and ears, and a tiny body to match. In her naivety as a child she actually thought that, these were the normal features of the Xhosa and the so-called coloureds that worked on the farms. When she went to high school and learnt the truth about this FAS, her heart despaired and the thought that her parents had actually perpetuated this 'congenital' affliction hurt her like hell. She felt guilty and ashamed, but there was nothing she could do about it. The labourers were now addicts and actually demanded the free, cheap wine. Their houses were situated at the bottom of the farm near the river and every evening before Mercy put her to bed, she would hear the drunken brawls; of husband against wife, brother against brother. And sometimes this drunken domestic mayhem would result in a fatal stabbing. Mercy, her friend didn't come back one morning to wash her, her drunken husband had killed her. To this day she still looks down to the houses and the end of the farm in the morning, hoping that Mercy would reappear and walk up the path to their farm house.

Patricia asked her parents why Mercy couldn't have slept with her in her bed. Surely she would have been safe with her. Her parents tried to explain to her, but it all didn't make sense to her young mind. All she knew was that she had lost her best friend when she was only seven years old.

Now as she roamed around Robben Island with Ruth, she wondered what her parents had known of Nelson Mandela then and why they'd never mentioned him. That they now saw him as a darling, a godsend and even saintly, she felt was hypocritical. In retrospect she saw her past as feudal and meaningless. A life of squires and serfs, of masters and servants.

The first time she'd become aware of the struggle was at the University of Cape Town, where out of curiosity she'd attended mass meetings and political rallies on campus. Although she attended the demonstrations, mass marches and protests and supported the ECC (End Conscription Campaign). Scores of boys who she knew as they grew up on the farms had been forcibly conscripted in to the South African army to fight wars in other parts of Africa. Ostensibly to fight for Christianity.

Some of them never came back. Michael was one of them. She vaguely remembered Michael now. She was too young then, since he was twelve years older than she was. She remembers that fateful day though, with clarity even today. She'd just returned from high school at midday and when she arrived home, she could hear her mother crying. She had never heard her mother wail before. It sounded as if her heart had been torn apart, her soul emptied of all hope and her life, not worth living.

When she entered the living room, it was packed with her aunts, uncles and neighbours. Her Aunt Margaret was comforting her mother. Michael, her brother had been killed by terrorists in Angola. His coffin, draped with the 'old' South African flag, lay alone in the middle of the living room. He was the first-born and Patricia loved him dearly, just as much as she loved Mercy. He doted on her and was like a guardian angel to her. God had taken him they told her. They said that he was too good for this earth and that God decided that he wanted Michael next to him in heaven. She recalls being upset with God. First it was Mercy, now it was Michael. She even felt that perhaps she too should die, so that she could be with Mercy and Michael and, of course God. As she became older, her anger turned to her parents for having allowed Michael to join the racist South African army. They were Christians and should have known better. That's when she decided to support the End Conscription Campaign, even though she was still at high school.

Today, ten years after the release of Mandela she was visiting Robben Island for the first time. It had now become a pilgrimage for many non-white South Africans. Patricia thought to herself that perhaps someday, white South Africans would see that their heritage lay here too below the limestone.

The ferry headed for the island was packed with Japanese, German and French tourists. Patricia had studied languages, spoke German and

French fluently and assumed the people with the slightly oriental look and expensive cameras were Japanese. It was this naivety that had brought South Africa so much trouble in the past. These blatant assumptions based on definitions of identity and stereotype classifications that confined people to boxes they could not escape.

The guide from the ferry led them into the prison and straight to Madiba's tiny cell. The man at the prison, an ex-prisoner himself took over and told them how when he lay down, Mandela's head touched one side of the cell and his feet the other. He was too tall; or rather the cell they gave him was too small. It occurred to Patricia that the vindictiveness was so petty, so mean. Mandela was 46 years old then, a political prisoner and he was supposed to spend the rest of his life there. Far from the loving arms of Winnie his wife, the tender embraces of his daughters and denied the privilege of raising his son to be the man every father wants their son to be. Looking around she could just imagine the night warden waking him up at 5:30 every morning. And Mandela being the man that she now knew would probably have thanked the warder for doing so.

"I would have told him to piss off!" Ruth whispered.

The guide went on to explain that Mandela was only allowed to receive one letter every six months. He told them so many stories of the working conditions at the quarry, of the hardships, the lousy food and cruel racist wardens. The most touching of all was the time when Madiba's mother died and he was refused permission to go and bury her, then the time he received a telegram that his eldest son, 25 years old at the time, had been killed in a motor accident. Another was the helplessness and worry he said he felt when he heard that his wife Winnie had been arrested and detained without trial and banished to a remote village.

Walking through the courtyard seeing the shadows of the late morning sun across the barred windows brought back a time that Patricia really was so much a part of yet had nothing to do with. She kept wondering what her parents knew and what they'd chosen not to tell them as they children.

"Were we not locked in our own prison of propaganda?" Patricia asked herself. She noticed that her cousin Ruth was also silent. She was going through her own torment and enlightenment. In her mind she raced through the similarities between what blacks in southern Africa had gone through and her fellow citizens in the States, the Afro-Americans. She couldn't help but draw the similarities between Nelson Mandela and Martin Luther King. It suddenly dawned on her that nowhere else in history had she encountered a people that were so willing to forgive, after such grave injustices had been done to them. There were no calls for Nuremberg like trials to address the crimes of slavery in America or the brutal apartheid in South Africa, Zimbabwe, Namibia, Angola and Mozambique.

Patricia noticed a tall, well-built man standing in the prison courtyard, taking pictures. Ruth actually nudged her on the ferry earlier that morning and said that he was looking across at Patricia.

"I think he likes you!" Ruth added with a mischievous giggle.

"Oh don't be silly, he's looking at you" Patricia fobbed off the idea. No one ever just stared across at her. She wasn't the type that made an on first sighting or flirted in a nightclub with a stranger. Usually people got to know her first and then through conversation they'd usually get interested in getting to know her better. So Patricia didn't believe a word she was saying.

Patricia admitted though that he was quite striking. There was an almost arrogant independence about him. She liked that. He appeared confident, intelligent but at the same time relaxed and at peace with himself. He definitely looked foreign, perhaps from the States. He had the usual 'tourist' gear with him, a video camera, a map of Cape Town city that he had folded and which was peeping from one of the pockets of a safari 'out of Africa' jacket. His levy jeans held his firm butt tightly and she felt a rush when she found myself looking at the bulge between his legs. Ruth noticed it too and nudged Patricia…That made it even worse as all these girlish gestures they were making attracted his attention. He looked at Patricia and smiled, then he walked towards them.

"Hi I'm Jos!" he said with an American accent.

"Oh…I'm Patricia and this is Ruth" she blurted out, trying to remain calm and hide the excitement that was welling within her.

"You guys from Cape Town?" he asked. It was obvious that he wanted to know more about Patricia.

"Well, she's Capetonian and I'm from Washington, DC" Ruth buttered in.

"Gee what a co-incidence, I'm from Baltimore actually!" he responded.

"Patricia thinks you're great!" Ruth blurted out. Trust her to have done that. She was more straightforward, wasn't shy at all or was it that she was American and courting was different there than here in South Africa?

"Ruth!" Patricia said, dragging her name along in the mud, trying in vain to stop herself from blushing.

"I was just about to say the same thing to you". Jos came to her rescue and added." If you don't mind I would really appreciate it if I could take you out for lunch or dinner, of course you would have to choose the resturaunt because I have no clue of what's in here".

"Well, I'm sure that wouldn't be a problem, it all depends how long you're going to be around in Cape Town" Patricia responded.

"Oh, I'm here for another three months or so. I'm doing some research at the University of Cape Town, so I'm sure there will be plenty of time Patricia!"

That's how Jos and Patricia met and he was her first true love. She'd had one or two other boy friends but it was never serious. She truly believed in sex after marriage, in stark contrast to her dear good old cousin Ruth, so most of the guys would quit after a few weeks when they realised that she was serious about the no sex issue. Patricia hung on to her virginity.

By the time they left Robben Island, Jos and Patricia were chatting as if they had known each other for years. He was also into theology and philosophy, and was studying for his Masters. She found it so comforting that at last she'd met a man she was sure she could love, but who appeared to have the same religious convictions she had. Patricia felt that day that Jos was the man she would be spending the rest of her life with. She thought to her self that all he had to do was to ask her. She knew that he was the right man, she just knew it!

"Thank you for having sailed with us!" the skipper of the catamaran shouted as they docked at the Victoria and Albert waterfront. The return journey was just as rough and Ruth had that look on her face that said, "I'm about to spew my guts out". That kept her quiet for a while and allowed Patricia to get to chat with Jos, without her cousin interrupting and barging in.

"Is next week Friday at seven in the evening fine?" Jos asked.

"That's perfect with me" Patricia replied.

"We meet here at the Hard Rock café then?" he continued.

"Ok!" With that they parted ways and before Ruth had recovered from the trip, Jos was gone.

"You're looking horny" Ruth managed to fight back. She wasn't going to let the seasickness stop her from at getting at Patricia.

"Oh Ruth, he's a nice guy that's all"

"Yeah…I'm sure even nicer in bed, butt naked!" she went on.

"Ruth you really are the limit you know" Patricia said laughing and shaking her head. Patricia decided to hit back at her, just to keep her quiet and change the topic, so she went on to suggest. "How about some Tequila, Ruth?" To her horror she agreed.

"Yeah…why not, that should do the trick for my stomach. And by the way I still think you should screw him next week!" Ruth was back!

Ten

February 1999. Cape Town, South Africa.

Patricia had just spent the afternoon in Cape Town with Jos. They had lunch together and she was surprised and excited about the events of the day. In fact she was ecstatic.

As she was having a shower at home, she recalled the events of the day. Jos had called her last night and asked that they meet at Marko's for lunch. They'd been there before for dinner and they'd enjoyed the food, because it was the only restaurant in Cape Town that served genuine African cuisine.

Jos was waiting for her in the restaurant when she arrived at 13h10. He was sitting upstairs at a corner table. Marko the owner greeted her. He was a hands-on manager, always friendly and bubbly. She walked up the stairs and when Jos saw her he smiled and stood up to meet her. She actually quickened her pace as she rushed to hug him and snuggled into his chest. They kissed each other. Patricia felt for a moment that Jos kissed her with more passion than usual. She looked into his eyes; he simply smiled and kissed her again, this time lightly on her forehead. Their relationship had been blossoming and she was grateful that Jos hadn't insisted on sex. They'd cuddle into each other, discovering each other's body and at times the petting would be heavy. But not once did Jos insist on sex. At one time, she was willing to give in to the physical craving and lust that had built up within her. She was ready to give Jos all of her, everything. But it was Jos who cooled things down. After that her love for him became intense and she even introduced him to her family, Father James and she even arranged that he meet her best friend, father Khumalo. That's how much she loved him.

"You're looking lovely as always Maria!" said Jos as they sat down. Jos preferred to call Patricia by her second name, Maria. He said that he preferred that name and so he always called her Maria when they were alone. He'd use Patricia when they were in the company of other people. Maria was wearing a stunning red dress that wrapped itself around her body. It brought a beauty and sexuality that was hidden within her.

"Are you guys ready to order?" It was Marko, the owner of the restaurant.

"Can you give us another five minutes please" Jos replied.

"Fine, and anything to drink in the meantime?" asked Marko.

"I'll have a Grapetizer", Patricia chipped in. She had worked up a thirst. After Jos and Maria had placed their drink orders, Jos stood up and went down stairs to chat with Marko, the resturuant owner. It couldn't have been for more than five minutes, but Maria was already missing him.

"Jos...where have you been?" she asked, stretching out to clasp his hands into hers.

"Oh, I had to use the gents."

"Oh! Sorry I asked. It's just that I was missing you." Maria was apologetic.

"Why don't we order some food now...I'm starving," she added.

"I think I'll have the putu and oxtail," she said, lifting her head to see if Jos thought that was a good idea. She had made up her mind. "What are you going to order?" she asked.

"I only want one thing Maria" Jos replied. That's when Patricia noticed that Jos was a little nervous and he become quiet serious.

"What's wrong Jos? Is everything all right?" Patricia was a little concerned with the change in tone.

Jos looked straight ahead over Patricia's shoulder and nodded to Marko. Marko signalled to the receptionist. The music changed and "Lady in Red" by Chris De Burg started.

"Oh I love this song" Patricia commented, oblivious to what was going on.

"You do?" asked a nervous Jos.

"Yes. What about you…" Patricia stopped herself half way as she looked at Jos. He had moved away from his chair.

"Maria, will you marry me please?" Jos was on his knees. He had opened the velvet box and inside was the most gorgeous diamond engagement ring.

"What?" Patricia responded, covering her mouth in shock and was embarrassed at the sight of Jos on his knees. She giggled and looked around the room to see if any one was looking. She felt shy and was completely taken by surprise. She giggled again not knowing what to say. Before she could string an answer together, there was a chorus behind her back chanting.

"Say yes Patricia! Say yes! Say yes!" Marko and all the staff had formed a group around their table. She turned back to look at Jos, her hands still covering her mouth and before he could ask her hand in marriage again, she blurted out.

"Yes! Yes Jos I'll marry you!" With that the crowd that had surrounded them burst into applause and song. The volume was put up and everybody, including some of the lunch time guests were singing the chorus to 'Lady in Red'. Jos put the ring onto Patricia's finger then asked.

"May we dance?" Patricia was shaking with excitement now.

"Yes Jos…Yes Jos!" she kept repeating. They waltzed and snuggled into each others arms as the song played, helped during the chorus by the waiting staff and the other lunch time guests.

"Father Khumalo! Father Khumalo!" Patricia was back at the Parish. It was 17h00 and she had managed to catch her spiritual friend as he was walking to the church. She was besides herself with excitement and found it difficult to hold her breath.

"Father Khumalo…look at this!" she said as she stretched her hand to show her friend the diamond ring Jos had given her.

"What?" Father Khumalo exclaimed as he took her out stretched right hand to look at the ring.

"He proposed, Jos proposed this afternoon Father…and I accepted!"

"Congratulations my dear child…siyakubongela!". Father Khumalo was genuinely happy for Patricia. He was happy to see he so overjoyed and this brought a smile on to his face, exposing his clean white set of teeth. Patricia was hugging him and they embraced each other, laughing with joy as they did so. Such was the intensity of their friendship that Patricia had decided that Father Khumalo should be the first to share her joy. She was going to inform her parents later on tonight and then Father James in morning.

"Patricia, you caught me on my way to the church. I think this calls for a little prayer, so that we can thank the Lord for what he has done for you and also to ask him that he guide you in your new found love!" suggested Father Khumalo.

"Well let's go Father Khumalo!" Patricia was still beaming and she was pleased that Father Khumalo was happy and approved of her engagement.

As they entered the church, they both dipped their right hands into the water plate at the entrance and made the sign of the cross. They walked hand in hand till they were at the front row and then they both knelt down in prayer. Father Khumalo started the prayer.

"God I thank you for the kind love that you have bestowed on my dear friend Patricia. I know it is because of your love and guidance that Patricia and Jos have met, grown to love each other and now, because of you, their relationship has blossomed. I know that you will continue to look after my little Patricia and guide her to happiness. Thank you Father!" Father Khumalo then looked at Patricia and motioned that they stand up and leave. She held his right-hand back and pulled him down to his knees again. She wasn't quite finished with the prayers yet.

"I want to ask God for guidance and give him thanks" she said, looking at Father Khumalo.

"Go ahead my child" Father Khumalo responded as he settled down on his knees again. Patricia took out the bible and opened to the Psalms 22-25 section. She zoned in on "A prayer for Guidance, Pardon and Protection. A Psalm of David".

"Unto thee, O LORD, do I lift up my soul.
O my God, I trust in thee:
Let me not be ashamed,
Let not mine enemies triumph over me.
Yea, let none that wait on thee be ashamed:
Let them be ashamed which transgress without cause.

Show me thy ways, O LORD; teach me thy paths.
Lead me in thy truth, and teach me:
For thou art the God of my salvation;
On thee do I wait all the day.

Remember, O LORD, thy tender mercies
And thy loving kindness;
For they have been ever of old.

Remember not the sins of my youth
Nor my transgressions:
According to thy mercy remember thou me
For thy goodness sake, O LORD

Amen!"

Father Khumalo was impressed and proud. He had watched as his little Patricia had grown from a shy teenager to a mature woman. She had mastered the bible and was a fine example to all the other youth in the town. She was intelligent but modest, beautiful yet never flaunted her beauty, well off but never forgot those that were less privileged than she was. Now that she had become of age, she still saw and believed in the wisdom of thanking her Father in heaven and asking him for guidance.

"Patricia…Remember that I'll always be here for you when you need someone to talk to!" Patricia sensed that Father Khumalo's mind was racing ahead in time. It was obvious to her that he was worried that since Jos was from the States that she would have to leave them in Cape Town when they finally tied the knot. She could sense that he was already hurting at the thought of her being so far away from him, of her being alone with no close friends in a new and strange country. His concern touched her.

"Don't worry Father Khumalo…I'll never ever forget you and I'll come home every year to make sure you're all right!"

Patricia took Father Khumalo's right hand into her left hand and gave it a gentle-reassuring squeeze. He turned round to look at his angel. He felt in his heart, that he was prepared to protect her with his life. Patricia wiped a drop of tear that had found its way down Father Khumalo's left cheek. She felt very protective towards him. She was acutely aware of the trauma that he had been through in Rwanda and in Richmond, KwaZulu Natal. He had confided in her and she had felt his anguish, pain and despair. She sometimes accompanied him when he went to visit the psychologist and psychiatrists in the city. He appreciated the moral support and she felt honoured that he had opened his heart to her. After all he had literally brought her up at the Parish.

Meanwhile in Baltimore, Galvez had just been woken up at 03h30 by the phone ringing. It rang at least five times, before he concluded that he wasn't just dreaming of the phone ringing.

"Who the fuck could this be?" he muttered to himself as he stretched across Yvonne's head to answer the phone. Yvonne was one of his favourite girls. She was a kept girl. She was twenty three, lived in a swanky apartment in Fells Point, Baltimore and she drove a BMW M3. A red one. She had platinum American Express credit card to make her happy. She was Galvez's girl. She knew that, everyone knew that and that's the way things were.

"This better be fucking important!" Galvez was clearly upset at being woken up at such an unholy hour. It had been a busy week. He'd come back from Honolulu where he'd gone to inspect his research laboratory at the MRC. The operation required a lot of preparation and tight security. Although he didn't leave the Cloth there on that occasion, carrying a piece of Cloth that was worth well over $US 300 million in cost in a brief case and having to make sure that it was well protected, was easier said than done. Ordinarily the logical thing would have been to ask Lloyds of London to insure it. But then again this was not something that you went about showing to the rest of the world. It had to be done privately and secretly. He'd succeeded in doing so and he had come back to Baltimore to chill and wind down before he delivered the Cloth to the scientists. He enjoyed being with Yvonne. She doted on him and she did things to him no other women could. She managed to bring out the sexual animal in him. And when he was with her, he felt respected. Not because of the money he had or the power that lay within his reach. But respect, a genuine respect for the man that he was. She made him feel like a man.

"Galvez...Who the fuck is this calling me at this hour?" he asked angrily.

"Senor Galvez...I'm sorry to be the one to tell you this. There has been an earthquake in Colombia!" The voice at the other end of the line was frightened. To have the duty to tell Galvez that his wife and his two kids were wiped out in the earthquake was almost akin to committing suicide. Galvez was an unpredictable man, a very violent man. Munoz at the other end of the line knew this, but in the same light, if Galvez wasn't told of the disaster that had befallen his hometown of Armenia, Munoz and those who worked for him could consider themselves dead.

"What did you say?" asked a shocked Galvez as he sat upright in bed and put the lamp on.

"What's wrong honey...?" asked Yvonne. Galvez motioned her to shut up. She did as she was told. She knew Galvez well and she could sense that something serious was wrong. She had learnt very early on in their relationship that the less she knew about his business the better. She had also learnt not to ask too many questions.

Galvez put the phone down. He was quiet. He moved his naked body out of the bed and set on the edge, his face buried in his hands. He kept shaking his head, muttering "Oh God no...Oh God no!"

"Darling..." Yvonne tried to rub his shoulders, to give him some kind of support. She sensed that something serious had happened that hurt Galvez deeply. She moved across the bed to him and cautiously at first put her arms around his broad shoulders. To her relieve and surprise, he didn't brush her aside. Instead he leaned towards her, looking for some comfort from all this pain.

"My family...I mean my wife and two sons..."Galvez didn't want to say it. It was as if saying it meant that it really happened and he didn't want to believe that it was true. Yvonne knew instinctively that they must have been killed. To ease his torment, she led him on.

"How did it happen?" she asked.

An earthquake!" Galvez replied. Then he turned to Yvonne and buried his head between her firm breasts and started crying out aloud. Yvonne was taken aback by Galvez's outpouring of emotion, exposing his vulnerability. This was a side of him she had never seen before in the five years that she'd known him. She stroked and kissed his balding head and repeatedly told him that she was sorry.

"Shoo…don't hurt yourself my darling," she added as she continued to cuddle and stroke him. He in turn regressed further. He was almost like a baby now. Nestling in its mother's breast, searching for nourishment and support from her breast. January 25 1999 is a day that Galvez and all of Colombia will never forget.

Galvez took his private jet to Colombia the next day on the 26th of January. When he arrived in the capital, Bogota, the heads of the other cartels were out there to meet him to pass on their condolences and to show respect. Galvez was a native of Armenia. His family lived there whenever they were in Colombia. He had built a villa there and his extended family of uncles and aunts all worked for him. Being a billionaire he was able to employ all of them who wanted work. Family meant everything to him. His wife and two sons had decided to spend the New Year and the rest of January in Armenia at the villa while Galvez ran around Europe and America sorting out his business. They loved being in Armenia because it was their hometown and they were surrounded by family and friends. Everyone knew them well and they were safe there. In Galvez's line of business, there was always a threat to the security and safety of his family. In Armenia they couldn't have been safer. Only a lunatic would've had the guts to venture into Galvez hometown and threaten his family. The community there would have eaten that lunatic alive. But not even Galvez could have dreamt that an earthquake would have struck his hometown. It was the worst earthquake to hit Colombia in more than a century, measuring 6.0 on the Richter scale. The last deadly earthquake in Colombia had been in 1875, which killed about 1000 people in the city of Cucuta, which borders Venezuela.

When Galvez arrived at the airport in Armenia, it was total chaos. There were ambulances arriving every hour or so, carrying the wounded so that they could be flown to hospitals in Bogota and other cities. The earthquake had been so violent that it even shook buildings in Bogota, 140 miles from the epicentre. Galvez headed for the northern section of the city, the wealthier part of the city. His villa was there. This part of the city had been largely left intact because the houses there were well built as opposed to the flimsy shacks and residence of the poorer sections of the city.

When he arrived at his villa, he was met by the wailing of throngs of relatives and staff. His older brother hugged him and the two of them started crying in the doorway. After a few minutes his brother led him to the main reception area. The three coffins had been placed together in the centre of the vast room. The larger coffin, which his wife was in, was in the centre and at her sides were the smaller coffins of his sons. As Galvez approached the coffins, he felt his knees give in. His brother and Uncle came to his support and as they helped him walk towards the coffins. Galvez was sobbing loudly, crying. He was a man torn and deprived of everything he treasured. He loved and lived for his family. Especially his two sons, he really loved them.

Galvez was helped along until he managed to get to the coffins. Then he reached out to touch his wife's beautiful face. It was cold and expressionless.

"I'm sorry I wasn't there for you!" he whispered to her.

"Don't torture yourself" Galvez's uncle tried to ease his pain.

"There was nothing you could have done. It was the devil, Galvez. It was the devil himself that had descended on us. It was so violent and explosive. There was nothing any one of us could do!"

Galvez then turned to his youngest son. The left side of his face was depressed and there was an ugly gash. His left eye was missing. Someone had been kind enough to stitch his left eyelids together. So that he still looked as handsome as Galvez remembered him. This sight was too much for him. His knees caved in again and this time he fell to the ground and broke down. He wept and wept. He asked God why he had to take his family.

He buried his family in the family graveyard the same day. As the three coffins were lowered into the earth, Galvez broke down again. He was an emotional wreck. It was obvious to him that they would not come back. Reality sunk in as their bodies sunk six feet below the surface. There was a shortage of mortuary space in the hospitals, so burials had to be done quickly before the bodies started to decompose.

The next day he walked around the city to examine for himself the extent of the tragedy and damage that had befallen his hometown of Armenia. He also wanted to see the central business district downtown, which was hit the hardest. He owned a lot of the property there. There were the shopping malls and other buildings that housed most of the business corporations and banks. All that was left of them was a pile of rubble. His family had been shopping at one of the shopping malls when the earthquake struck.

"If only they had been at home in the northern suburbs of the city, they would have been alive today. If only!" Galvez thought to himself.

He was still trying to bargain with God, trying to turn back the hands of time and alter the events of January the 25th.

As he walked the streets, bodies were strewn all over the roads. People were crying and praying. Some were using their bare hands to dig and displace the tons of rubble that had created makeshift graves for loved ones.

Even coffins had run out and had become a precious commodity. The situation was so bad that some of the victims were laid into the graves naked, covered only by a blanket or wrapped in a plastic.

As Galvez approached Calarca, south of Armenia, he went to his favourite church, the San Jose. It was a mess and even the silver bell tower was leaning dangerously at an angle. Galvez knelt down in front of the San Jose church and decided to pray.

"O LORD God of my salvation,
I have cried day and night before thee:
Let my prayer come before thee:
Incline thine ear unto my cry;
For my soul is full of troubles:
And my life draweth nigh unto the grave.

I am counted with them that go down into the pit:
I am as a man that hath no strength:
Free among the dead,
Like the slain that lie in the grave,
Whom thy rememberest no more;
and they are cut off from thy hand.
Thou hast laid me in the lowest pit,
In darkness, in the deeps.
Thy wrath lieth hard upon me,
And thou hast afflicted me with all thy waves.

Thou hast put away mine acquaintance far from me;
Thou hast made me an abomination unto them...

Galvez was at the lowest point in his life. He was beaten. Earthly things he could handle. But against the hand of God he was powerless. And ironically, for someone who was used to playing God on earth, he was always the first to turn to God for forgiveness and mercy. He learnt that early in his career as a gangster. If the enemy was more powerful than you, it was wiser to make peace with him. There was no point going to war when the outcome was obvious. So he begged God for deliverance and mercy. The only other choice his mind flirted with was taking his own life. But the only reason he decided not to take his live in that week of January 25, when the devil had struck across the earth and soil of Armenia, was the research project he was overseeing in Honolulu. For that reason alone, he would soldier on and rebuild his life.

"For sure the Lord giveth and the Lord taketh!" Galvez thought to himself.

"Senor Galvez we better leave soon, there are riots in the city. People are looting the shops. They are hungry and desperate. It's not safe Senor Galvez!" It was one of his bodyguards. The violence had started in the city. So Galvez decided to leave Armenia and head back to Baltimore. He needed to regroup his thoughts and make sure that his plan and the work in Honolulu would run smoothly. Now more than ever he wanted to have this child, this boy as his. Now that his two sons had been snatched from him by the devil, he wanted to have another boy. But this was not going to be just any other boy! This boy would be immortal.

Eleven

March 18th 1999. Cape Town, South Africa.

Jos and Patricia's wedding was a simple one. Only family and close friends were invited. Ruth was back from the States and she was the Maid of honour. Jos had asked Father Khumalo to be the best man. He knew that this would please Patricia. Father Khumalo agreed. He was however, concerned that Jos had not invited any of his family to the wedding. He asked Patricia about this, but she was too excited to worry about that.

"Patricia…doesn't Jos have any family? I mean you do know that in our custom, marriage is not the union of two people only, but that of the two families?" Father Khumalo was talking about the African culture. Such was their relationship that he considered his Patricia to be African in all respects. He had taught her everything he knew about the Zulu customs. She was fluent in Zulu.

"I know Father, but Jos was adopted and has no living relatives. It's so sad what happened to him. I mean having to grow up with no parents, brothers and sisters. I really want to make him happy Father. I want to give him that family and love he never had!" Maria was so genuine in he response, that Father Khumalo decided not to pursue the matter further.

126

What counted most was that she was happy. That to him was all that mattered now.

The reception was held at the Old Castle in Cape Town. There, sheltered by the walls of the castle in the central courtyard, with the Soweto String Quartet belting out their melodies, they took photos and danced. Patricia's parents had arranged everything. From the Soweto String Quartet to the lamb spit barbecue, South African style of course. Patricia was dressed in the most beautiful white silk dress.

"You sure your dress shouldn't be cream instead?" teased Ruth her best friend.

"Ruth, I'll have you know that Jos and I still haven't done it yet!" Patricia replied, sticking her tongue out to her friend. She was obviously proud of the fact that she had remained a virgin right until her wedding day.

"What? Then what have you guys been doing the last three months? Damn you guys must hate each other!" Ruth was still teasing. She had lost her virginity when she was sixteen. That was almost ten years ago. "Have you even seen him naked...I mean what if he can't do it?" she asked. They were in the ladies and were catching up with gossip.

"Do what?" asked Maria rather naively.

"I mean what if he can't get it up?" Ruth added. Realising that Patricia still hadn't caught on to what she was talking about, she decided to be her true self.

"What if Jos can't fuck?" That was the real Ruth now.

"Ruth how can you be so crude? We'll learn together. I'm sure he can do it and who says sex is everything anyway?" answered Patricia.

"Girl! There is no way I would sign a contract to live with a man for the rest of my life without first seeing what he can really do to me. No way girl!" Ruth was shaking her head. She made a bubble with her chewing gum and burst it. It made a loud pop. It was as if she wanted to emphasise her point.

"Ruth all you think about is sex! Jos and I have a perfectly wonderful relationship…" "Yeah…yeah. I've heard that one before!" Ruth was sounding rather sarcastic. She had a point though. Most of her friends who had tried marriage in New York had either divorced or were living miserable lives. She was clear that she wasn't putting her signature on any marriage contract.

"Maria are you still in there?" It was Jos shouting from outside the ladies. That hushed the girls for a second.

"What's with this Maria issue?" asked a surprised Ruth. She knew that Maria was Patricia's second name, but no one ever called her by that name.

"He prefers to call me Maria" Patricia whispered then she giggled.

"I'll be out there soon my darling!" Patricia shouted back at Jos.

"Don't take too long Maria, I'm already beginning to miss you!" added Jos.

"You're sure going to get fucked to night!" Ruth commented with a smile on her face.

"Ruth girl" Patricia whispered, putting her right index finger on her lips, indicating to Ruth to talk softly. "Anyway that's not going to happen this week because I just started my period today!" Patricia added and pulled out a box of Tampax to show Ruth.

"His fucking luck!" Ruth added shaking her head. "But the way he's been looking at you today, I wouldn't be surprised if he changes into Count Dracula tonight just for you!"

"Oh Ruth you are so gross. Sis!" Patricia was truly disgusted. There was no way she could imagine having sex when she was having her period. Jos would just have to wait for another four to five days she told herself." I'm sure he'll understand," she thought to herself.

Then they left the ladies. Patricia in front and her best friend Ruth behind supporting her wedding dress and sporting a fake smile of innocence. Jos rushed to Patricia's side as soon as they had reached the rest of the crowd. He took her left hand into his right and asked for a dance.

"Sure Jos" Patricia was beaming with love as she looked into his eyes. She had a smile on her face that clearly said how happy she was. The Soweto String Quartet started playing an instrumental version of 'Lady in Red'.

"Oh Jos…You're so special!" Patricia realised that Jos had asked for this song. It reminded them of the day he proposed at Marko's restaurant two months ago. The rest of the guests created a ring around them and they danced alone in the centre. Patricia's mother and aunts were so touched at the site of their little angel dancing in the middle. It brought tears of joy to some of them. For some they were tears of anxiety and fear. Fear that their little Patricia would be leaving them and going to settle in the States.

Father James was having a whale of a time. He had looked after Patricia from when she was in kindergarten Sunday school. Now here she was a beautiful woman. Getting married to a man he personally approved of. His plan had worked out well and he was sure that his dreams would now become reality. Father Khumalo though was a bit moody. He would only smile when he saw Patricia. People generally left him alone. They all understood that he was seeing a psychiatrist and was on medication for his 'post traumatic depression' that he was suffering because of the horrors he had witnessed in Rwanda and Richmond; KwaZulu Natal's own killing fields. He preferred it that way because it meant that people didn't bother him too much.

It was as if they were afraid to talk to him. He figured that they were worried that he might break down emotionally on them and they wouldn't know what to do to comfort him. Patricia knew better though. Although he had been depressed by his experiences, she knew that he was not psychotic or on the verge of a nervous breakdown. She appreciated his wit and intelligence and guessed that he pretended to be on the edge of insanity to the others simply because he preferred to be on his own so that he could read. Father Khumalo was an avid reader. History was his favourite subject, but he went through everything from philosophy, medicine, music and art. He, more than anyone else had taught her so much. She loved him dearly.

The evening reception was held at Patricia's parent's farmhouse in Stellenbosch just outside Cape Town. The evening was warm and it being summer still, the sun was still basking in its glory at 19h30.

"Jos…There's a call for you in the office!" shouted Father James.

"Thank you" Jos shouted back. "I'll be back soon so don't disappear with Ruth again," he said to his Maria. He squeezed he left hand warmly and kissed her lips before he left.

When he got to the door where Father James was standing, waiting for him, he noticed that Father James had a serious expression on his face. Father James didn't say a word. He simply nodded and showed Jos were the office was. Jos nodded back.

Father Khumalo saw this and for no apparent reason this disturbed him. It was nothing specific, except that the expression that Father James shared with Jos was rather strange. It was as if they knew each other. Of course, they'd known each other for the last two months ever since Patricia had introduced Jos to Father James. But no, this was a deeper expression, as if their relationship spanned years rather than months. It was almost the kind of look a father would give a son. "Fair enough" thought Father Khumalo, "he is after all a priest and he had every right to treat Jos as a son now". But still Father Khumalo sensed something more.

"Please can we dance?" It was Patricia. She managed to startle Father Khumalo.

"Is everything all right Father?" asked a concerned Patricia.

"Oh Patricia, you know me, I was just thinking about how I'm going to miss you!" Father Khumalo had regained his composure and managed to lie well enough even to convince Patricia. They hit the dance floor for the next two or so songs.

"Yes Senator Bell, everything is going on as planned" answered Jos. Senator Bell was on the other side in Washington D.C.

"Now remember Jos that she must remain a virgin! Don't spoil it all and fuck her tonight. You'll have to give some excuse, but she must remain a virgin. Do I make my self clear?" Senator Bell was serious. He had waited for this to happen for some time now. He wasn't about to allow his plans to go up in smoke just because Jos became horny and failed to control himself tonight.

"Let me speak to Father James!" Senator Bell ordered. Jos looked around and saw Father James. He had been standing at the doorway of the office all along. He offered him the phone.

"Senator Bell?"

"Yes it's me, Father James. Congratulations so far!" the Senator started.

"Now we need to make sure that she remains a virgin until next month. I've just reminded Jos about his duty to God. Make sure that he follows the plan accordingly. We are almost there now and we can't afford to make any mistakes now!"

"Don't worry about a thing Senator. Jos is a good boy and he understands the importance of sticking to the plan as arranged" replied Father James, starring Jos in the eye as he did so.

"Well that's comforting to hear. Give my regards to Mr and Mrs Oppenheimer and tell them I appreciate the honour they have bestowed on us. And hopefully we'll see them next month!" said Senator Bell.

"I will and God bless you Senator!" With that Father James put the phone down and turned to look at Jos, who had shut the door.

"You heard what the Senator said?" he asked

"Yes! Loud and clear. Don't worry Father James I'll play my part. You can rely on me" Jos answered.

"Jos where are you?" it was Patricia, she had opened the office door looking for Jos. She was a little surprised to find Father James with him.

"Oh sorry Father. I hope I'm not interrupting any thing serious…am I? "She asked giggling.

"Oh no my child, I was just reminding Jos that I'd personally advise the Lord and make sure that he goes to hell if he ever mistreated you!" he replied jokingly.

"Don't worry Father James. Jos would never do such a thing!" she hit back defending her husband. Then she grabbed Jos's right hand and pulled him towards the door.

"I've been waiting for this song for a long time now. So let's go and dance!" She was happiness and innocence blended into one glowing and joyous bundle.

Father Khumalo had taken note of the fact that Father James and Jos had spent so much time together in the study. It all started with the phone call for Jos, then that rather strange expression and nod his mentor had given Jos at the doorway and now the unusually long time they'd spent in the office together behind closed doors.

"If the call had been for Jos, a private call, then why did Father James have to be there too? Why the closed door?" All these questions kept nagging Father Khumalo. "Perhaps" he thought to himself "Father James wanted to give Jos some fatherly advice. Him not having any parents and all. Perhaps that's why!".

Father Khumalo decided to rejoin the party and this time managed to get a dance with Ruth. He knew that she thought that he was conservative and most likely couldn't dance. He had a surprise in store for her. After asking her for a dance and she politely agreeing, he took he across the dance floor towards the DJ.

"I'm sure you must have the Mary J Bilge and George Michael version of the Steve Wonder classic, 'Loving you' he asked the young DJ?" Ruth and the DJ almost shrieked. As soon as it was on, Father Khumalo got down to some serious dancing. Ruth was more than impressed.

Father James, on the other hand, was a little concerned. The thought occurred to him that perhaps Father Khumalo was not taking his medication as his psychiatrist had prescribed!

That evening when Jos and Patricia were finally alone, Patricia was nervous. She had heard about how on the first night she was supposed to become a woman. But besides being anxious about all that, she was bleeding heavily now and she had to use two pads to prevent the blood from soaking her underwear. Jos was in shower and he had hinted to Patricia that she join him.

"Look the water is really nice and warm. Come on and join me!" Jos shouted from the bathroom.

"I'll be there in a minute!" Patricia shouted back, stalling, trying to think of what to say. This was uncharted territory for her. She was nervous, really nervous. She took off her wedding dress and then her bra. Her tits were firm and tender. They always became engorged and sensitive during her periods. She went to the bathroom to join Jos, who by this time was singing in the shower. He'd had his fair share of champagne.

"Jos" Patricia called shyly as she walked into the bathroom with her hands crossed over her chest, trying to hide her tender breasts. Jos opened the shower door.

"Oh my Maria! You look wonderful" He took one foot out of the shower and stretched his right hand to her. She gave him her hand and then he pulled her towards him. Maria obliged but did so rather clumsily as she was now caught between holding on to Jos's hand and covering her breasts.

"It's ok Maria. Don't be nervous. Remember it's only me and we will take our time until we are comfortable about it" Jos was also stalling as he had been instructed by Father James and Senator Bell.

"I'm…eh I'm sorry Jos, but I…I started my periods today" Maria was looking down, to the floor. She spoke as if it was her fault, that she had spoilt everything on this their first night together as husband and wife.

"Oh…that's not a problem. Don't let that bother you!" Maria was taken aback by his response. It was as if he was almost as relieved as she was. She didn't know it, but she'd actually removed a huge load off Jos's mind. Jos decided to pull her into the shower.

"Jos I can't. I mean I still have my panties on!" Maria tried to protest.

"That doesn't matter". He pulled a now giggling Maria into the shower and then kissed her passionately. He was keen to show her that just because she was having a period didn't mean that her loved less, that they couldn't cuddle and love each other. It worked. Maria was touched by Jos sensitiveness, his patience and she was convinced more than ever that theirs was a true love. A match made in heaven and blessed by God.

"I usually only bleed for about four to five days" Maria added inbetween the kissing and cuddling. She felt obliged to let him know that she was his to take then. "So maybe next week you can guide me!"

"Shoo!" Jos responded and then continued to kiss her. He had been given a reprieve and he wasn't about to make any promises to her. Before her next period on the 18th of March he would have come up with some rational explanation. He had to buy time. He needed to make sure that she remained a virgin until then. He hadn't exactly figured out how he was going to convince her, but he had to succeed. The success and timing of their plan was now crucial. It would have to happen in March, the end of March to be exact.

That evening they cuddled each other and romanticised about their honeymoon. Maria's parents had bought them tickets to go to the States and London.

"I think we should start in London" Jos suggested.

"Why not. I don't care where we start as long as we are together!". Maria was in love and all she cared about was being with Jos and making him happy.

Twelve

March 15 1999. MIRC LAB-Honolulu, Hawaii.

Manuel and John had been invited to Hans's office. Well it was more like they were commandeered. Mr Galvez was around so no one could blame them for being a bit nervous. They had heard of the tragic earthquake, which wiped out Mr Galvez's family in Armenia, Colombia on the 25th of January. This further fuelled their speculation that Galvez wanted to have himself cloned. It all had begun to make sense now. Galvez would be all the more desperate to have him self cloned, now that he'd lost his only sons. They figured that he was desperate to have a heir to his vast fortune. The very thought of this sent a cold shiver down both Manuel and John's spines.

Although Manuel could understand Galvez's grieve and loss, the haunting pain of having lost close family, all your family, there was a line, which he was not prepared to cross. He knew that he could never bring his family back. He would rather God did that. Cloning the chimps was Ok, but God no, not cloning a human being. Manuel and John had discussed their strategy the previous night. They were going to spell it clearly to both Galvez and Hans about their reservations about cloning Mr Galvez.

136

Galvez's private army lined the corridor leading to Hans's office. It reminded John of his high school days. He went to one of the private boarding schools in England. The headmaster to the best of his memory, was a mean bastard. Every Friday evening between 19h00 and 20h00, was reserved for caning those pupils who had been caught during the week doing some sort of mischief. John was a regular at the Friday night sessions. The headmaster was a big man, bald and with a belly to match. They nicknamed him "Puttapoof".

When he swung the cane down, his eyes would pop out of their sockets. John suspected that he was kind of turned on by wrapping the cane around the naked boys' buttocks. They would form a long cure as they each waited their turn. Somehow today as he approached Hans's office, with all those goons lining the corridor all the way to the door, he felt as if he really was a schoolboy again going to be punished. He was scared shit. For once he was more than willing to follow behind Manuel.

"Oh please do come in and have a seat gentleman!" It was Hans and he was being uncharacteristically polite. They had never met Mr Galvez before, but John recognised that structure. The one that belonged to the headmaster who today still haunted his childhood memories.

Galvez was sitting at the corner of the office on one of the leather couches. He had one of the other school boy baddies to his right, wearing shades even though it was a little dark in the office. Galvez offered no smiles or recognition of their presence. He sat passively clutching a small silver box. It was at least a metre long and half a metre wide. John and Manuel sat down opposite Galvez as they'd been instructed.

"Gentleman…this is our benefactor, Mr Galvez!" Hans said. He introduced Galvez with some pomp and pride, with a lot of respect.

"Morning sir!" John's response was spontaneous. Perhaps it was because he was English or maybe he had actually regressed into his boyhood era at boarding school.

"Morning!" added Manuel. He was a little more composed.

Galvez nodded. That's all he did, he nodded as if to say, fine now that we have dispensed with the formalities let's go on to the real business he had called them for. Hans took the hint. Galvez was still in mourning. This wasn't exactly the time to crack a joke or start some idle chitchat.

"Manuel, Mr Galvez has some cells that he wants you to isolate. He wants you to clone these cells. They are very delicate cells…but I have assured Mr Galvez that we are capable of doing it, that his investment in all of us has been well spent!" Hans was being very polite and at the same time cautioning Manuel and John. He couldn't have them showing any disrespect to Mr Galvez. So he gave both Manuel and John a long stare after he had finished the introductory warning. He managed to pass this non-verbal message of caution on to Manuel. John didn't need any more verbal or non-verbal warnings. He was convinced all right that Galvez and his goons could if they wanted, thrash him with impunity like his headmaster.

"Thank you Sir! I'm sure that we can clone the cells." He hesitated for a while then went on to ask.

"If I may inquire Sir, how delicate are these cells?"

"Very delicate…very delicate" Galvez almost murmured the response in a flat tone. It was the first time that Manuel and John had heard him speak. His voice was deep and commanding.

"As you are aware Mr Galvez lost his family last month. He has the cells of one of his sons with him. He would be eternally grateful to the two of you if you could clone his son…bring him back. Mr Galvez has assured me that he will reward you all handsomely, above and beyond what he has already given you in the last two years!" John thought that Manuel was going to raise the issue about the law and their own ethics being against human cloning. Manuel thought that John would do the same.

None of them objected. They remained still and quiet. In fact, Manuel suddenly felt sorry for Galvez. Here was a man who like him, had lost everything and everyone he loved through no fault of his own. Manuel even conceded that maybe, if he'd had children and lost them the way Galvez did, perhaps he too would want them back. He had lost a father, a mother, uncles and aunts. But God had already blessed all of them with many fruitful years on earth. Surely the loss of them could not be compared with the loss of a young child. Manuel decided not to argue this point. Further he was at least pleased that it wasn't Galvez that wanted to be cloned. He felt sure that he would have objected to that. But an innocent little boy killed by a violent earthquake…surely even God would understand. The boy had left the world before his time. He was a healthy boy, who if it weren't for the earthquake, would have probably lived for a very long time. Manuel made up his mind. He would disregard the guidelines on human cloning and go ahead. He would bring back one of Galvez's sons!

"If I may ask Sir?" Manuel was treading cautiously. "We need to obtain the egg from the woman who will carry your son once we have managed to transfer his chromosomes into her egg cells. It might be wise, I mean correct if we knew the woman so that we could make sure that she would be ready for the egg once we are through."

"Don't worry about getting the eggs or fertilising the woman. Another person will do that. He's an in vitro fertilisation (IVF) special-ist. I do belief that in the case of humans, he would be the right person to do that! That's correct isn't it?" asked Galvez. This time there was a little more life in his voice. He had expected some grumbling from the team, but now that they had agreed, he was feeling a little upbeat. Not that he would have taken no for an answer anyway. He would rather have killed them both if it had to come to that.

"Oh yes Sir! An IVF specialist is the right infertility specialist. We will have to work closely together so that we can synchronise the preparation and culture of the cloned egg with the preparation of the surrogate mother's womb. She has to be made ready to accept the egg or else she will abort spontaneously!" Manuel was trying to be constructive. Galvez noted that. He nodded his head in appreciation of the advice and concern.

"You will get her eggs to work on soon. First you must isolate Mr Galvez's son's cell and chromosomes. Make sure they are healthy and then you can work on the eggs from the surrogate mother!" Hans chipped in. He was pleased with the way the events of the morning had transpired. He too had expected problems, particularly from Manuel. That would have resulted in an ugly situation, which he was more than keen to avoid.

"Fine" John pitched in. He had woken up from his high school nightmare. "When can we have Mr Galvez's son's cells? The sooner we start working on them the better. As the cells get older, they start to disintegrate and the chromosomal material becomes very fragile!"

There was an airy silence for what seemed like an hour to John. He was beginning to regret asking the question. Perhaps reminding Galvez about the death of his sons wasn't the right thing for him to have done. He was saved by Galvez.

"Yes…Yes you are correct" he said very slowly, keeping his gaze firmly on John as if to emphasise John's point about the fragility.

Galvez shifted nervously from side to side on the couch as he reached for the silver case on the table in front of him. Manuel noticed that Galvez had a slight tremor. His heart sank. He imagined the agony Galvez must have been going through, having to examine a specimen of his son. The only remaining tissue of a once lively boy. A boy that laughed, sang, loved and cried. Now reduced to only a few cells. But this is were Manuel felt the glory of science lay. In those tiny cells was all the genetic material, lying dormantly as chromosomes, that was needed to make another boy. Such was the progress of science. He mused to himself that because of science, what people had witnessed in the movie "Jurassic Park", was actually possible. In that instance it was to bring back a species, the dinosaurs, that had been wiped out millions of years ago again by some freak of nature. Nature than had changed the weather so much, heating the earth's environment to the extent that the dinosaurs could not continue to live and propagate as a species.

The irony that Galvez's son had also been destroyed by a freak of nature, just like the dinosaurs, hit him. However he felt mankind was now in a position to fight these aberrations that occurred not through man's fault, but nature getting its timing all wrong. Or perhaps it was the work of Lucifer. And if it was, as had happened to his family when Lucifer sent Hurricane Mitch to destroy his family in Honduras, this time he was going to spoil Lucifer's celebration. He was going to bring this boy back!

Galvez slowly and gently opened the silver case. It was as if he was handling the mortal remains of a cremated loved one. The inside of the case was covered with red velvet. John and Manuel couldn't hide their curiosity. They both stretched their necks, as if they were trying to get a sneak preview of something major to come at a later date. Galvez lifted his gaze from the box and moved it to John and Manuel. He did it instinctively, as if he was guarding something that was his and precious from them. Perhaps he did it just to scare them. Whatever the reason, it had the desired effect. Both of them recoiled quickly back into their seats. John even shifted his gaze to the floor as a sign of his submission in this non-verbal war of superiority.

Galvez's eyes moistened when he took the Cloth and cradled it in his hands. He lifted it slowly and gently for all in the room to see. He sniffed to stop the tears that wanted to escape via his nose and followed with a cough as the tears had again entered the wrong pathway, into his air pipe. Manuel was moved by the scene. It flooded his mind with the memories of his family. He knew what Galvez was going through.

As Galvez lifted the cloth above the lid of the container, it was now visible to Manuel and John.

"Uh!" Manuel gasped. He was expecting to see a test tube with blood or a piece of skin, bone or preserved flesh. He wasn't at all expecting to see a cloth. It looked old, fragile. Perhaps made of cotton linen.

"Maybe there's some tissue wrapped in the cloth," Manuel thought to himself. Hans had noticed their surprise. He had been expecting it.

"This cloth was used to wash the wounds of Mr Galvez's little boy. Unfortunately someone washed the cloth after that. So the blood stains are not obvious to the naked eye!" Hans explained. Manuel and John nodded in unison.

"If there is blood there, we'll be able to see and isolate those cells under our microscope." John chipped in.

"Yes" Manuel concurred. "That shouldn't pose too much of a problem" he went on to add.

"Thank you gentleman. Thank you" Galvez was genuinely appreciative and he was happy that he didn't have to use any coercive force.

"You don't know how much this means to me, Manuel and John" Galvez went on. This caught Manuel and John off guard as Galvez had addressed by their first names. It added a personnel touch to an already emotional scene. If they had any doubts about their commitment to Galvez and this endeavour, this personal plea from Mr Galvez erased them. John, in particular, felt for the first time that he had been addressed as an equal and only then did he manage to escape the nightmare of his high school past. In that one sentence and plea, Galvez had transformed himself from that bastard of a headmaster John remembered with so much fear, to a loving father grieving the death of his sons.

"Consider it done Sir!' was Manuel's pledge to Galvez.

"Si. Thank you once again. Gracias. Thank you" Galvez added.

"When do we start?" asked Manuel. He was now eager to rise to the occasion and meet the challenge head on.

"You start on the Cloth tomorrow. First you must make sure that all is ready in the laboratory, that you have all you need. You will have only one go at this. We must not fail!". It was Hans now. He'd taken over and was now directing the chronology of the play, of the events to follow.

"Manuel...and John, if you succeed in bringing back my son to me, I will personally reward you with anything that you desire!" Galvez had resumed that flat serious tone again. "I must remind you all that this, this project, this Cloth and all that we have discussed here today, must never be divulged elsewhere. Do I make myself understood?" Galvez raised his voice this time. John was back on edge again.

"Yes Sir!" was his spontaneous response. John had regressed again to his boarding high school days. Suddenly old "Puttapoof" was back in the office again.

"So don't be surprised to see some of my men around here until the project is complete. They are here to guard the project, to guard my sons' remains and to make sure that you are not disturbed," added Galvez.

"I have arranged that you move into the guest quarters until this project is through. I suggest that you collect all that you'll need for the next few weeks, or for however long you think this will take you, from your apartments. Once we begin no one will be allowed to leave the research premises!" Hans was now filling in the practicalities of what was required. This last exchange of words worried Manuel somewhat. Up to that point he was enthusiastic about the project. This, this incarceration of sorts worried him a little.

"Will that be all then Sir?" asked John. He was eager to leave the office now.

"Yes...and thank you once again!" Galvez had softened his tone again.

As John walked out of Hans's office and passed all the other baddies lining the walls of the passageway, he reached for his butt and rubbed it. Manuel noticed it and John realising the surprised gaze from Manuel, shrugged his shoulders. It was no use trying to explain all this to Manuel. How would he explain the "Puttapoof" caning, the queues outside the headmasters office on Friday night and now him rubbing his butt. He always rubbed his butt after being given six of "Puttapoof's" best on his bum. It helped to ease the pain by distributing the pain throughout the whole butt, rather than having only one half of his butt absorbing all the trauma.

"Surely" John thought to himself that if he tried to tie all this up with the events of the morning, "Manuel would think he was losing it". "Huh" John sighed to himself
and I wouldn't blame him!"

"You ok John?" asked a frowning Manuel.

"Oh just fine! My ass was a little itchy that's all" John tried to explain.

"I didn't ask about your ass John, I asked if you were fine!" Manuel was teasing now.

"Oh fuck off Manuel!" John hit back and tried to kick Manuel, who skipped a step ahead to avoid making contact with John's boot.

Dr Brock had just finished a delivery in the private maternity hospital in London. It was a healthy little girl, 3.4-kg and she was announcing to the rest of the world that she had arrived. Her screams of protest at being rudely removed from the warm environment of her mother's womb to a harsh world with funny, strange noises and bright lights, could be heard throughout the corridor of the Labour ward wing. She had an Apgar score of at least 10 at five minutes. This was medical jargon to say that she was a perfectly fine baby.

"Congratulations Mrs Banda" Dr Brock said as he handed the lovely bundle of screaming joy to her mother.

"Thank you very much Dr Brock…Thank you so much. You have been very kind to us" it was Mr Banda, the Malawian Ambassador to the United Kingdom.

"Oh the pleasure was all mine, believe me!" Dr Brock responded and shook Ambassador Banda's right hand. Mr Banda was shaking with excitement and nervousness. He was an emotional wreck. This was the first time that he'd attended the birth of his child. Their first born, a little boy was born back home in Malawi, while he was in London on business. This time he had been with his wife from the time that her water had broken till their daughter was born. It was a total of twelve hours of anxiety, of not knowing what to do to help his wife each time the pain came. This was worsened by the fact that his wife had refused any form of analgesia or pain relief. She wanted to have a natural birth. This meant of course that each time she had a contraction, she would hold on to him and ask him to rub her back. At times at the height of a contraction, her nails would sink into his skin and it would really hurt.

So when their daughter finally decided to come out, he was finished, drained of all energy. Although he was happy now, he felt that for the first time in his life, he felt completely useless. There was nothing he could do to ease the pain his wife was going through, nothing. He had to simply wait and let time and nature play out its course. Being an important and powerful man, he wasn't used to being so helpless, so vulnerable and weak.

For Dr Brock this was the norm. He had developed a clientele of women that read from a who's who in business, politics and entertainment. Many of the so-called shakers and movers had been ushered into the world by him, royalty included. He didn't come cheaply either. But then for his clientele, money wasn't exactly the problem. He managed to keep such a high-quality practice by restricting the number of pregnant women he looked after at any one time. He made sure that he was available all the time when they went into labour, from the beginning to the end. He also insisted on working with one sister alone. It was better for his clients that way. Confidentiality was very important to him. He needed to rely on only one person. And that person was Sister Lucile. A close friend, companion and confidant. He paid her well, so that she didn't have to look for another job. There was really no need for that though. She loved working for him. In fact Sister Lucile had developed a soft spot for Dr Brock. She loved his gleaming white patch of hair and his dangerously intelligent mind. And oh, those blue piercing eyes that revealed more about him than he was prepared to articulate.

"Ok Mrs Banda, I'm just going to clean you up with some warm and soothing water!" said Sister Lucile as she placed the receiver with the warm soapy water between Mrs Banda's legs. The after birth had been removed and inspected by Dr Brock and it was in a silver dish on the delivery trolley.

"Oh thank you Sister Lucile!" Mrs Banda felt the soothing water splashing over her vulva. It was a bloody mess. Mr Banda had moved to his wife's head and they were both admiring their daughter. Mr Banda was not too keen to see what Sister Lucile was doing. He had seen enough. At one time just before the delivery of the head, he wondered whether his wife's anatomy would regain the look and feel he knew.

"There you are love, all clean and dry now" Sister Lucile was through. She then put two sanitary pads between Mrs Banda's legs and covered her with a warm blanket. Then she and Dr Brock left the parents and their new baby, so they could start discovering each other.

When Dr Brock reached his consulting rooms and office it was 14h30. He had one more appointment for the day. It said Mr Bell, for 15h00.

"Huh…Interesting?" he thought to himself. He found it rather curious that the appointment was a Mr Bell without Mrs Bell. He had been in this business for more than two decades now and he had learnt to take things as they came. It wasn't uncommon, particularly amongst the very rich and secretive clientele that he dealt with, for the husband to consult alone first. Dr Brock felt that some of them wanted to scout his practice first, size him up and then decide whether he was good enough for their wife. At times it would be an impotent male partner, wanting to discuss these sensitive issues man to man first, before the wife came into the picture. At times it would be a married man wanting to bring a mistress for consultation. There were many possible combinations.

He took his shirt off and changed into a fresh one. The he put on his bow tie and jacket. He was ready to see Mr Bell.

"Sister Lucile, could you kindly make me a cup of tea my dear. And oh do please bring Mr Bell's file in with you when come with the tea" He'd worked up a thirst and the winter was still casting its grey shadow over London. The tea would warm him up he thought to himself.

"The tea will be ready in about five minutes Dr Brock" answered Sister Lucile via the intercom phone. "And Mr Bell has just walked in. I'll bring him through as soon as you are ready!"

Dr Brock preferred going to the reception and collecting the patient himself, particularly on the first visit. He was convinced that most patients felt uncomfortable about visiting their doctor for the first time. By going out to them, he felt that he was meeting them in a neutral territory and this allowed them to retain some of the confidence they usually lost on their visit. It seemed to work all the time. He noticed that when he did this that the patients would settle down much earlier. Once they had become used to him and their relationship was now based on them being equals as humans, he would sometimes skip going out to collect them from the reception. But even then, he would always be waiting to usher them in at the door.

"You must be Mr Bell?" Dr Brock asked as he put out his right hand to greet Senator Bell.

"Yes I am and thank you for seeing me on such a short notice" Senator Bell replied and shook Dr Brock's hand.

Dr Brock immediately picked up the East Coast American accent. "Must be one of the diplomats," he thought to himself. "Rather old to start fathering a child". Brock had learned to use all his skill of observation to assess people. It was a skill he honed in on in while practising his profession over the decades. He learnt that you could tell more by what people didn't say, how they dressed, the yellow cigarette stains on their fingers, etc, than by what they said. This he found to be more so with the husbands who accompanied their wives to his consultation rooms. The women, who were his primary patients, usually did most of the talking, so it was easier to gauge what they were really like.

"Please Mr Bell, do come in. How about some tea or coffee to make you nice and warm?" Brock was ushering Bell into his office. He always followed the patient.

"Coffee would be great!" responded Bell.

"I have Arabic and Kenyan, which one would your like to indulge your taste buds with Mr Bell?"

"I'll try the Kenyan" Bell replied.

"Good choice if you ask me!" Brock added. "Oh Mr Bell do have a seat please". Brock had three large, leather seats in the centre of his office. An oak wooden table separated them. That was another of his trademarks. The consultations always started there first. With him and his patient seated on the leather chairs as if they were in his lounge. He never rushed to go behind his desk. That he felt only increased the gulf between him and his patients. His job was to narrow that gulf, shorten the bridge and quickly gain their trust and confidence.

Bell was already impressed. There was none of the brashness and cockiness he was used to back home in the States. He liked Brock and decided within the first five minutes of their meeting that he was the right man to do the job. Of course he had been highly recommended by his colleagues in London and even amongst the diplomatic core in Washington. But Bell being the obsessive man that he was, knowing that this project was far too important to have anybody whose credibility was questionable involved in it, wanted to see for himself. He was so taken by Brock's manner and calmness that he even wished that his son who was practising on the West Coast as a plastic surgeon, had been with him, so that some of the sublime communication skills Brock had would rub off into him.

Brock waited for Bell to settle down to his coffee first before he prodded.

"How can help I you Mr Bell?" Brock asked with a smile on his face.

"Well I must start by saying that you come highly recommended in your field as a fertility specialist. Both here in London and amongst my colleagues in Washington" said Bell.

"Oh people always like to say nice thinks about me. You know when you get older and your hair is all silver and white like mine, people assume that you've become the wiser!" Brock responded and laughed. He was being at his usual modest best. Bell appreciated the modesty, so he nodded his head and smiled to acknowledge it.

"I'll come straight to the point Dr Brock, because I'm sure you are a busy man."

"Oh no Mr Bell, do take your time. There is no rush!" Brock interjected. As a man who loved Shakespeare he couldn't resist to add.

"As Shakespeare would say 'wisely and slowly, they stumble that run fast!'"

"Thank you Dr Brock. I have a niece that has been having problems falling pregnant. We have shopped around and all the doctors we've been to, advise that she have in-vitro fertilisation (IVF). From what we have been told, you are the person she needs to see" Bell paused waiting for Brock's response.

"Oh the pleasure would really be all mine. Is this niece with you in London at the moment?" Bell wasn't trying to be nosy. He simply wanted to get the ball rolling.

"If you don't mind, perhaps I can arrange with your secretary for an appointment so that you can examine her yourself when she comes up to London" Bell wasn't giving away too much at the moment.

"That would be fantastic. So I shall hear from you soon then?" Brock said as he stood up.

"Yes and thanks once again" Bell meant it. He shook Brock's hand and then was escorted to the door by Brock.

Bell was now convinced that Brock was the right man. He had no doubt in his mind. They had him under surveillance for the last eight months and he had come out clean. His phones had all been tapped and even his rooms had a secret camera placed in one of the air vents. There was nothing Brock had said or done in the last eight months that would jeopardise their plan. Bell felt sure that the other members of the Millennium Club would be impressed and glad to hear that Brock had passed the test.

Thirteen

Manuel and John had been incarcerated in the MIRC research institute now. They'd moved all their necessary clothing and other essentials to their new residential quarters. The MRC facility was turned into a fortress of sorts.

"I wonder whether it's to keep people out or in?" Manuel thought to himself. Galvez had left behind at least a dozen or so of his men. He could see that they were armed and they made it clear that they would go wherever the cloth that Galvez had left behind was. To say that Manuel and John were anxious is an understatement. They worried about whether they could isolate the proper cells from Galvez's son's blood. They were concerned that some of the genetic material could have been damaged and more importantly, they hadn't been given the eggs from the woman who was supposed to carry Galvez's son.

"Shit this looks like it's going to be more difficult than we thought mate!" John was looking at the bloodstains on the cloth under the microscope. Manuel was also looking at the cloth. They had joined their high focus microscopes together so that they could work on the same material together.

"Damn…these cells are so few and…Don't they look rather old to you?" asked a puzzled Manuel.

"Definitely older than I thought. They should have been only a month or so old shouldn't they?" John had raised his head and was looking at Manuel directly in front of him. Manuel took his focus away from the microscope and looked at John, then he shrugged his shoulders. He paused for a moment then went back to staring down the lens of his microscope. John did the same.

"I think if we can find a decent white blood cell, we might be able to take the nucleus out and then remove the chromosomes from it!" said Manuel. The white blood cells had the chromosomes, 23 pairs that coded for a full human. If they could get them, all they need do after that was to make sure that the genetic material in the chromosomes was not damaged. John read Manuel's mind.

"Well, if there are any damaged portions we'll have to fix them first before we put the chromosomes back into the donor egg!" This was John's speciality. He had been recruited for this because he'd spent three years at Cambridge unravelling the human genome. This was part of an International collaboration that was set up to unravel the human genome. Once the human genome was unravelled, it would be the genetic blueprint of man. John had done a lot of work on chromosome number 21 in particular.

"So…John, it looks like you're going to have your work cut out for you!" added Manuel. John was relishing the challenge.

"No problem!" he quipped.

"Ok let's start systematically and go through all the stains on the cloth. We must collect as many of the white blood cells as we can." Manuel suggested.

'Fine." replied John.

It was a trying procedure. The white blood cells were few and far between and were very fragile. It was much easier finding and collecting the red blood cells, the cells that carry the oxygen in the blood to the rest of the body's organs. Manuel and John decided to first collect all the cells, both the red ones and the white ones together. After that they would use a cell separation technique, using immunofloresence to separate the white cells from the red ones. They had a machine they called the 'cell-sorter' to do this. The red cells were of no use for cloning because they are one of the very few types of cells in the human body that have no nucleus, no chromosomes or the genetic material that was needed for the cloning.

By the third day, they had enough cells to work with. The cell sorter then separated the cells into two. Red blood cells and white blood cells on their own.

"Send the read blood cells for typing and cross matching" Manuel instructed John.

"Why?" asked a curious John.

"Just curious to know what blood group Galvez's son was. Besides if the mother is blood group rhesus negative and Galvez son is positive for rhesus, this might cause a problem with the pregnancy". Manuel was thinking ahead.

"You right again there mate!" John acknowledged the wisdom of finding the blood group.

Rhesus (Rh) blood grouping was important if the mother was Rh negative and the baby Rh positive. Essentially the mother's immune system would recognise the baby's blood group as different to hers. She would, in some cases, than make antibodies, chemicals to destroy her own unborn child's blood. If she made plenty of these antibodies, she could eventually kill her own baby even before it was born.

"Right…now let's look at what we have here!" They were looking at the reaction of the blood group test.

"AB positive…the boy was rhesus group positive" John chipped in.

"Well, let's hope that our mother is also Rh positive," added Manuel. "Why don't we start working on the white cells tomorrow. I don't know about you but I'm bushed!"

"I'll second that" John replied. It was now 22h00 and they had been pushing twelve hours a day since Monday the 15th of February. It was now Thursday the 18th and they were both knackered.

"How about a cold beer at the canteen?" asked John.

"Yeah why not, let's first store these cells in the incubator".

After Manuel had put the cells away, he gave the cloth back to Hans. Hans always took the cloth away with him at the end of the day. Manuel and John speculated that Mr Galvez probably placed a lot of sentimental value on that piece of cloth.

"I guess he'll only discard it once we bring back his son!" John quipped.

Patricia and Jos were packing their bags in Cape Town. It had been a hectic few days since their wedding. They were excited about leaving for London the next day. They had both been there before but not as husband and wife. Patricia noticed that her period had now completely stopped. She wondered whether she should actually take the lead tonight, to show Jos that she was ready for him to break her virginity and deflower her. She wanted it to be a special event, a night they would both remember and cherish forever. Patricia was beginning to worry that perhaps Jos didn't really find her sexually attractive. It was a strange sense of guilt, almost as if she felt ashamed of her body. She wanted Jos to find her physical attractive. "After all" she thought to herself "it's my duty as a wife to satisfy my husband". So that evening she decided to wear a skimpy nightdress, even though it was still a little chilly. She put some logs into the fireplace and had a good fire going before Jos had come up to the suite. Jos was downstairs in the bath. After waiting for ten or so minutes she decided to go downstairs and join him in the bath. She had become bold now that her period had stopped.

She didn't knock as she opened the bathroom door. She should have. But she wanted to surprise her husband and reveal her nakedness to him.

"Oh my God…Jos. What are you doing to yourself?" Jos was caught totally unaware. The needle and syringe fell to the floor. His pants were around his ankles and he was sitting on the toilet seat. His aim had been to inject his right thigh before he was disturbed by Maria.

His first reaction was to try and hide it from her, but it was too late. She'd seen the needle and syringe!

"God…Maria my love…I should have told you this before!" he mumbled.

"Tell me what Jos. Jos are you sick?" Maria was alarmed. She was shocked and had no clue what to think or what was going on.

"Maria can we talk about this in the bedroom?" Jos was buying time, trying to get his facts and story straight. Maria followed Jos numbly up the stairs to the bedroom. They both set on the bed. Jos with his head buried in his hands. Maria staring in disbelieve at him.

"Jos what's going on? Why were you injecting yourself?" She was a little calmer now, her voice more controlled.

"I'm sorry Maria, I should have told you this before, but I was so afraid of losing you" Jos turned and looked at Maria. He'd managed to bring some tears into his eyes. This softened Maria a little.

"Are you a drug addict? Is that what you're trying to tell me?" Maria raised her voice this time. She was bewildered and upset.

"No Maria. I swear to you I'm not a drug addict." Jos was sounding like a wounded dog.

"Then what were you injecting into your thigh then huh?"

"I'm diabetic!" Jos finally blurted out.

There was a moment's silence. Maria didn't know what to say. Suddenly she felt a wave of immense guilt overcoming her. "How could she have assumed that he was a drug abuser?" She thought of the personal torture that Jos must have gone through, hiding the fact that he was diabetic, having to sneak and hide each time he needed an injection.

"Oh Jos I'm so sorry to have judged you so harshly!" Maria turned towards him and embraced him. "Please forgive me Jos…I'm sorry" Jos felt a little more relaxed. This was not exactly how he planned to explain things to her. But it appeared as things had actually worked for the better this way.

"There is nothing wrong with you being diabetic, that will never change my love for you!" added Maria as she looked into Jos eyes. "Don't cry my darling" She wiped the tears that had welled in Jos's eyes.

"The problem…uh" Jos cleared his throat, his voice was still hoarse. "The problem is that since I've been injecting myself with insulin for the last twenty five years…the problem is that it has begun to affect my manhood." he looked down and away from Maria as if he was embarrassed and ashamed of what he'd just said. Maria in her naivety hadn't understood what Jos had just told her.

"You're all the man I need!" she responded lovingly and hugged him again. Jos sensed that she hadn't got the message clearly. So he decided to be blunt about it. It was the only chance he had to bring this out to the open once and for all.

"I have erectile dysfunction Maria. I don't know if I can make love to you, as a man should. I'm sorry and I know I should have told you this before" Jos felt relieved now that he'd brought this out to the open. Maria didn't know how to respond to Jos's confession. She knew that sex was the least of her worries. But children, she wanted to have her own children. The thought of not having her own children panicked her.

"Does it mean…I mean you and I can't have children of our own?" She tried to ask the question without bringing more hurt to Jos than she felt that he was already going through.

"I mean sex isn't the most important thing in our life. We can work that out if we love each other like we do. But I really would like to have my own baby…our baby!" she quickly corrected herself, again trying not to sound selfish.

"Oh me too Maria. I want us so much to have our own baby. We will have our baby that I promise you. I'll do everything in my power to make sure we have our own baby!" Jos was nodding his head and stroking Maria's hair, trying desperately to reassure Maria.

"OK" Maria, said rather sheepishly. She was shocked by the intensity of her desire to have a baby, not just any baby but her own. She'd never thought about this before. She hadn't even formed an opinion of it before, but now when she was faced with the possibility of not carrying and giving birth to a baby of her own, she knew she couldn't take that.

"What will we do then? She asked. She wanted to get this clear once and for all.

"Well we can see a fertility specialist, the two of us together!" Jos suggested as he held Maria's hands in his.

"Ok Jos, anything you say, but I really want us to have our own baby" Maria had now fitted snugly into Jos's broad chest as he hugged her. It all appeared to make sense now. The fact that Jos never not once hinted that they have sex. It always ended with the cuddling. 'Come to think of it, she mused she hadn't even noticed whether Jos had an erection at any of the times they petted heavily. No he definitely didn't. I would have felt it. My poor Jos!'

That night they fell asleep in each other's arms. They kissed for a while and then reaffirmed their matrimonial vows of love. Maria meant it when she repeated to Jos, "till death do us apart!"

Father Khumalo wanted to make sure that he said goodbye to his little Patricia before she and Jos left for Cape Town International airport. They'd said that their flight was leaving at nine in the morning. So he decided to go to their cottage at 06h30 hoping that they'd be up by then. If they were not, then he would do them a favour and wake them up. As he was knocking on their door, he smiled to himself. He imagined that the newly-weds must have spent the whole night making love to each other.

"Patricia it's me, can I come in?" He announced his arrival after he'd knocked on the door twice.

"Oh Father Khumalo, come in, the door is open. We'll be downstairs in a minute or two!" Patricia added. Her voice was bright and merry. It was the visit of her dear friend that brought out the joy in her. Father Khumalo thought it was the night's activities of newly-weds that was the reason for the joy and song in Patricia's speech. He let himself in and sat on one of the chairs. After a minute or so he decided to use the toilet before Patricia and Jos came down.

He lifted the toilet seat so that he could take a leak. He aimed his flow of urine towards the side of the toilet bowel so that his urine didn't make that hollow noise when it hit the water. He felt embarrassed wondering how Patricia would react hearing that all too familiar sound of urination. He couldn't bare the thought of her imagining what he was holding in his hands. So he managed to let it flow on the side without splashing some of it on the seat or the floor, well just about. As the last flow came, he swerved ever so slightly but that was enough to soil the floor. "Damn!" he thought to himself. "That's why most men in his village preferred to go behind a bush. You don't have to aim, pissing should be a relaxing pleasure!" That thought brought a grin to his face. "There is no way I'm going to sit on the toilet like a woman just to catch a leak!" he shook his head.

"Boys will be boys!" he whispered to himself and zipped back his plumbing equipment.

Since he'd piddled on the floor, he rolled down some toilet paper and snapped a chunk off. Then he bent down to wipe the little puddle of urine.

"What the hell is this?" he asked softly. Father Khumalo had bumped into the needle and syringe that Jos had dropped the previous night. Next to it was a vial of medicine. He picked the vial up and read the label. He was alarmed. He knew very well that Patricia was healthy and wasn't on any medication, particularly injections.

"It must be Jos!" he concluded. "But why would any man be taking oestrogen's?" he asked himself. "If I remember oestrogen's are female hormones!"

Father Khumalo was perplexed. He didn't know what to make of it.

"Father Khumalo where are you?" It was Patricia. He left the syringe and needle were he'd found them but he slipped the oestrogen bottle into his pocket.

"Oh I'll be with you soon my child!" He flushed the toilet and then came out, hoping that Patricia was not waiting for him at the door. "That would be embarrassing!" he thought. And, of course, she was waiting right at the door.

"Oh my child you mustn't stalk an old man like me......I might just drop dead and have a heart attack!" he joked. She laughed in response and gave him a long hug. Father Khumalo felt that her embrace was a little more in tense than usual. She held on to him as if she wanted to be saved. He also noticed that she had stopped laughing.

"Travel well my child...Hamba khale!" Father Khumalo said softly rubbing her back.

Patricia was sniffing and starting crying. This surprised Father Khumalo somewhat. She was only going away for a month at the most he thought.

Patricia wanted to tell him about what happened the previous night, about Jos's diabetes and her fear of not having her own child. Father Khumalo had always been her spiritual mentor and friend. She wanted so much to off load all this on him, but there was no time.

"Hi Father Khumalo, you're up bright and early!" said Jos as he came down the stairs. Patricia quickly wiped away her tears as if she were embarrassed and went to the kitchen. Her eyes stayed focussed on the floor. Father Khumalo noticed that too. He noticed these small things. "Something is wrong with my little girl," he thought to himself. But then again everybody thought that he was still crazy!

Fourteen

Early March, 1999. MIRC, Honolulu, Hawaii.

Manuel and John had been at it for more than a week now. They'd managed to isolate enough white blood cells to provide them with the full complement of chromosomes. Yes 23 pairs, all 46 chromosomes.

"I think we have a major problem with chromosomes number 1, 14, 19 and 21!" John sounded excited. It was as if he'd worked out a jigsaw puzzle.

"What problem? What does that all add up to?" asked Manuel.

"Well all those four chromosomes seem to have had one of their genes mutated or altered from the normal!" added John. He was prolonging Manuel's anxiety.

"Go on John, tell me what it means and will it be a problem?" Manuel was getting a little impatient. This was no time for games or intellectual sparring. The sooner they completed their task, the quicker they could get out of this incarceration.

"Me says that Galvez's son would have developed Alzheimer's Disease (AD) in his sixties!" John actually had a victorious grin on his face. He'd cracked the puzzle. The changes or mutations on those four chromosomes were now known to be associated with Alzheimer's.

"Can we fix those genes then?" asked Manuel.

"Well we could but what's the point. I mean I'm sure Galvez would just be happy to have a healthy boy!" John was serious. He didn't see the point of spending another day or two trying to correct a gene that would only manifest itself long after Galvez had become a grandfather and died.

"Fix it!" Hans interjected. He surprised the two of them as they had been peering through their microscopes and they hadn't heard or seen him arrive in the main lab.

"What?" asked John. "All the four chromosomes. It would take us weeks?" he added.

"Fix the mutation on chromosome 21 only then!" Hans ordered.

Manuel was actually impressed by Hans. He'd always doubted his scientific credibility. But how did he know that the mutation on chromosome 21 was the main one. He looked at John for confirmation. This was John's speciality.

"Actually you're correct Hans. We think it's mainly the mutation on chromosome 21 that is responsible for AD" John said nodding his head. He too was surprised that Hans was aware of this.

"But how can we sort it out then?" Manuel was looking for practical answers and wasn't really keen to go into the details. John, however, wanted to impress.

"The problem with Alzheimer's Disease is that that there is an increase in the protein material called amyloid. The body makes too much of this stuff and with age deposits the excess material in the brain!" John was giving the two of them a tutorial. "After a while it messes with the memory section of the brain and then first, you can't remember facts and events. Sooner or later you can't even remember your own family!"

"So John how do we slow down this problem?" Manuel kept pushing for the practical solutions.

"Easy. We stop the production of the enzyme that makes too much of that amyloid stuff that clogs the wires in the brain!" said John triumphantly.

"Well let's do that then. Let's sort that gene out, so we can get the hell out of here!" said Manuel.

By the following day Manuel and John had three white cells they had fixed with perfect chromosomes in them. All that was required now was to get the egg from the surrogate mother and then remove the chromosomes from her egg. When the egg was empty, they would remove the 46 chromosomes from the white cells and place them into the egg cell. The egg would then have the exact chromosomes as Galvez's son. It would be clone of Galvez's son, or rather a delayed twin.

"Hans we're ready on our side, all we need now is the egg from the woman that will carry this baby!" Manuel announced. There was an air of relief and success. It had been a long slog but they were now almost through. Soon they could hit the pubs again. Who knows Manuel thought, they might even give us a week's vacation. Both of them felt that they deserved that. Hans felt the same way too.

"Well done and congratulations guys! The egg will be arriving in a day or two. Congratulations again!" He shook each one of them's hands.

"Formal as usual." thought John.

"Must be his German nature" Manuel whispered to John as Hans left the lab. They had all been thinking about the same thing. None of them could have guessed how happy they had made Hans. Hans went into his office, opened his liquor cabinet and poured himself some Cognac. Then he sat down and raised his glass and made a toast.

"To the coming of the Son of Man!"

He took a gulp of the fine champagne cognac and allowed his mind to drift to his childhood days in the village of Oberammergau in Germany. He grew up there.

He recalled the last time he watched the Oberammergau Passion Play being performed. It was in 1990.

The history behind the play dates as far back as the 17th century. The story is that his village had been decimated by the plague and the people that survived the plague turned to Jesus for salvation and protection. The inhabitants of the village made a promise to Jesus to perform the Passion play every ten years. This was their expression of gratitude to Jesus for saving them from the plague. It was also gratitude to Jesus for his sacrifice on the cross. Even today the people in his home village still believe and express their feelings through their Passion Play.

To them "In the Cross is salvation, in the Cross is life, in the Cross is hope". That was the message in the Passion Play in the 17th Century and that was the same message that came out to him as a spectator in 1990. He recalled how moved he was by the performance as it traced the suffering, the death and the resurrection of Jesus Christ. Nothing much had changed in the Play since his childhood. The same rules were still followed. Only the inhabitants of the village could participate in the Play. So he could recognise almost all of them. The only change was that the Play was now performed in the 'Passion Theatre' rather than in the graveyard next to the church.

The Passion Play was divided into 14 acts, mixed with soft music and prologues. Hans felt as if he were reliving the suffering of Jesus as the scribes and priests mocked him. He felt the terrible blow of betrayal when Judas sold Jesus out. By the time they enacted the crucifixion, Hans recalled that he shed a tear. It saddened him that one man could go through so much pain and suffering all in aid of saving mankind. The climax of the Play for him was the resurrection. It was the saving grace. It lifted the dark cloud of depression that he felt when they murdered Jesus. For Hans the resurrection meant that there was always hope. That there was light at the end of the tunnel. He knew that eventhough the world had become an evil place, Jesus would eventually come back and save them all.

This in 1999 was even more meaningful to him for two reasons. Europe was back at war again. The end of the Century was being punctuated by a terrible war in Yugoslavia and Kosovo. The systematic ethnic cleansing of the Kosovo Muslims reminded him of what his own countryman had tried to do to the Jews during the Second World War. He could never identify with such brutality. As a village boy who grew up in the lovely village of Oberammergau, this ran against everything that Jesus had suffered and died for. Jesus had gone through all this so that all man could be free. Today he could see that Europe was at war with itself again. Men were raping women, killing the children and the old men. The young men were being systematically rounded up and then slaughtered like animals just like Jesus had been slaughtered.

Hans was shocked when on the February 1999, there was talk of nuclear weapons being retargeted at human sites again. This he felt was the beginning of the end. Man was not capable of living in peace with another. Man needed Jesus again. And that's why he was feeling so happy and proud today. He'd played his part and now they were almost there. He felt confident that come Christmas this year, the Son of Man would be here on earth again.

"Hans we are knocking off now!" it was John. He jolted Hans out from his dream visit to the Passion Play of Oberammergau.

"Oh…OK, see you guys tomorrow!" he shouted. Hans raised his glass again and toasted.

"To the coming of The Son of Man!". Then he gulped the remaining cognac in his glass.

Patricia was with Jos in Dr Brock's consulting room in London. Her dad's friend Senator Bell was also there. She thought that perhaps it was logical that they see a fertility specialist, but she was a bit confused why it all had to happen on their honeymoon. She felt that honeymoons were meant for the newly-weds to discover themselves. But Jos had been so embarrassed about his failure to achieve an erection that he had convinced her that they should use the opportunity to see the best fertility specialist in Europe. When she showed a bit of reluctance at being rushed into all this, Jos politely reminded her that most couples tried to conceive during their honey moon. He reminded her that he was doing it for her and that she needed to have her own child. This made her feel guilty and after a few days in London she accepted that they see Dr Brock.

"Wouldn't it be really nice Maria, for us to go back home to Cape Town with you being pregnant?" Jos asked her. In fact it was more of a suggestion.

"Actually that would be wonderful" Maria replied. The thought of having her own baby was beginning to excite her the more she thought of it. After all she agreed with Jos that that's what honeymoons were for, to procreate and fulfil God's wish. She was nervous at the thought of visiting a doctor she had never met before and having to undress in front of him. She would have been more comfortable with a female gynaecologist. "Sr. Lucile is great," Maria thought to herself as she watched her going about her business in the rooms. Sr. Lucile was ever so gentle and always had this motherly and warm smile.

"Uncle Bell…it's nice of you to have made all the arrangements for me and Jos!" Maria spoke softly. They were in the waiting room and a Muslim couple had just come out of Dr Brock's consultation room. Maria wondered why she was whispering. She found it strange that people always whispered when they were waiting to see the doctor. It was probably because they all imagined that if they were noisy, no one would take their illness seriously. Sick people were supposed to be quiet, to keep still and conserve their energy. A moan in pain was more acceptable if you wanted to elicit the right response of sympathy. "But I'm not ill, I'm not sick!" Maria reminded herself.

"Oh it's a real pleasure to help such an angel as yourself. Besides I got to meet your lovely husband Jos!" Senator Bell wasn't whispering. He spoke with that typical loud and confident East Coast accent. Maria almost told him to shoosh. She felt embarrassed by his loudness and he kept sighing, trying, she supposed to get some oxygen into in to his 100kg frame. She wondered if Uncle Bell knew that he reminded her of Charles Dickens character, Mr Pickwick. Maria was sure that Uncle Bell had the Pickwickian syndrome.

She hadn't quite figured it out how he happened to be in London when they arrived. When she asked him, he told her that it was a mere coincidence; that her father had informed him that they would be coming to the States to stay with them, but that they would go via London. Since he too was in London he decided to surprise them and met them at Heathrow airport. He asked if they needed anything while they were in London and she found it rather strange that Jos had opened up to Uncle Bell, whom at that time had been a complete stranger to him.

"I know the best fertility doctor around. I'll give him a call and see if you can jump the queue!" he responded when Jos opened up to him. Maria was glad because at least they were going to see the best doctor in London, but she was saddened by the fact that their honeymoon had been converted into some reproductive consultative pilgrimage. Somehow the fondness and closeness Jos felt towards her before she caught him with the injection, had given way to the preoccupation of her conceiving. The intimacy had gone. Maria put it to Jos feeling guilty about his inability to have and maintain an erection. So she decided to play along and not hurt his feelings more than they already had.

"Morning Mr Bell!" It was Dr Brock. He'd come out of his rooms to meet Maria and Jos. Maria liked him immediately. There was this calmness about him, this reassuring and kind demeanour that he had.

"This must be your lovely niece Patricia Maria and her husband Jos!" he added and greeted them both. "Coffee or tea?" he asked.

"No I'm fine" both Maria and Jos responded almost simultaneously. They were both a little too anxious to enjoy a cup of tea. Because she was so anxious, Maria had been to the ladies twice in the twenty minutes that they'd been there to empty her bladder. "Fluids are definitely out for me!" she thought to herself. She imagined having a full bladder and then having to possibly undergo an internal vaginal examination. "I'd probably wee on him," she thought to herself.

"Oh come in then Maria and Jos," said Dr Brock. Senator Bell remained in the reception, being entertained by Sister Lucile and indulging in some of the Kenyan coffee he had now acquired a taste for.

The three of them settled on the leather couches. Maria liked that. Jos was sitting next to her and Dr Brock was to her other side. It didn't feel as if she was having a consultation. Well not just yet. After the usual 'get to know each other' chat Dr Brock started to lead the conversation, with some direct questioning.

"Now Maria…which name would you like me to call you by…Maria or Patricia?" he asked politely. Maria hesitated for a while. She was used to Patricia, but now that she was with Jos and she was his wife, she decided to let her preference become second to Jos's. She reasoned that that's what true love was all about.

"Maria" she answered and looked at Jos. He smiled in approval.

"Lovely name if you ask me. You know you are just as lovely as Mary, mother of Jesus!" Dr Brock added. He meant it though. Because of his experience he could sense the beautiful warmth and honesty that lay deep in Maria's heart. He also realised that she was nervous and that Jos seemed to be the more dominant of the two. He'd learnt over the years to shift the balance of power and responsibility during the consultation process to the woman, always. He was after all a gynaecologist and although he appreciated the fact that pregnancy and raising a child was a couple's joint responsibility, he felt strongly that the decisions be centred on what the woman wanted. So he always allowed them to lead the discussion. If they didn't come out, he would lead them by asking the right questions.

"Maria…I'm going to ask you some very basic and silly questions, so bear with me because I am an old man!" he smiled and peered at her above the rims of his rimless glasses.

"Ok" Maria responded and fidgeted in her seat.

Brock went through the usual questions about her age, previous illnesses, allergies and so on. Kind of standard medical history data questions.

"Now I know that the next questions might make you feel a little embarrassed, but believe me I ask all the women I meet the same questions. Even those that I bump into on the streets!" Maria giggled. She found him funny but it also allowed her to release some of the tension that she had stored up in her.

"When was the first day of your last period Maria?" Brock asked.

"Oh it was last week…well ten days ago to be exact, on the 18th of March!" she remembered the date quite easily. She had to. It was her wedding day.

"And how many days do you usually bleed for?"

"Four to five days at most!"

"Any pain or cramps?" Brock asked.

"Mild ones. Mainly on the day before I start bleeding" Maria was now more relaxed

"Excellent Maria. Now I'll ask your loving husband a question or two then I think we can proceed to the examination room" said Brock shifting his intense gaze to Jos.

"Any medical problems or medication that you're on Jos?" Jos was hesitant and even more fidgety than Maria had been. Realising this Maria stretched her left hand and took Jos's right hand into hers. She squeezed it gently, trying to give him support.

"Well yes Dr Brock…that's why we are here. There is nothing wrong with Maria. The problem is with me." Jos blurted out. Maria gave his hand another squeeze, telling him to answer the question. Brock simply nodded and waited for Jos to go on.

"I have been an Insulin dependant diabetic since I was five or six years old. The problem is that I now have difficulty in getting an erection…and maintaining it. I mean, I love my wife and I find her extremely attractive…" Jos was being apologetic.

"Oh I do understand" Brock intervened. "I'm sure that you have a physician who's been looking after you?" Brock asked.

"Yes in the States! My sugar is really not a problem. I manage to control it all right." Brock sensed that Jos was not keen to see another doctor in London. He seemed to be happy with his Insulin therapy. He was about to suggest that he should try Viagra, but since he was happy with his physician in the States, he assumed that he'd already tried the medication.

"Fine then…Maria if you step into the examining room, you'll find a gown. You don't have take everything off, just enough for me to examine your tummy my dear" Brock said as he stood up and showed her were to go. "You can cover yourself with the sheet and when you're are nice and comfortable give me a shout!" he added with a smile.

Maria undressed and slipped under the cotton sheet. She noticed that there was a scan next to the bed and a lamp at the end of the bed.

"I'm ready Dr Brock!" she announced loudly. Brock had closed the door so that she could undress in private. Brock knocked before he came in. "It's all right you can come in she repeated!" this time a little more softly.

"Lovely, Maria. Just relax and we'll take this step by step…Ok?"
Maria nodded.

"First things first, I don't mind if you want your husband here if it makes you feel more at ease." Brock suggested.

"Yes…You can call him." She really didn't mean that though. This wasn't an intimate occasion. It was embarrassing to say the least and she hadn't exactly got used to Jos seeing her naked and exposed. But again she thought that it would give Dr Brock a bad impression of their relationship if she'd said no.

"Ok Jos, if you can stand there you'll be able to get a good view of the screen." Brock made way for Jos to stand at the head of the bed, next to Maria.

"I'll do a general examination first, you know listen to your chest to hear if your heart is still beating and so on…"Brock examined her as he spoke. He was meticulous and explained his findings as he went along.

"Fantastic heart and lungs you have there Maria. I'm sure you've never smoked in your life hey?" He couldn't hear her response. His stethoscope was still plugged into his ears.

"Nice soft tummy you have. No pain when I press there?"

"No." Maria responded.

"Excellent then. We'll do the scan now…perfectly harmless…jelly is a bit cold though." Maria gasped when the cold jelly touched her abdomen.

"Lovely womb and you see those black dots?" Brock was pointing on the scan to an area that was to the right side of the uterus.

"Yes!" Maria and Jos responded in unison.

"Those Maria, are your eggs in the right ovary. You'll be ovulating in a few days time!"

"Oh!" Maria didn't know whether to be happy or not. At least, she thought to herself, she could have her own baby.

"That means I can have my own baby then?" She wanted to hear the doctor saying it. "Oh yes. It looks like everything is fine here. How soon were you planning on falling pregnant?" asked Brock.

"We thought that it would be nice if she could be pregnant during our honeymoon." Jos interjected. He looked excited.

"You mean this month?" Brock asked Maria, stopping his scanning to gauge her response.

"Yes…this month if it's possible" she added trying to sound as enthusiastic as Jos.

"Well we'll have to act soon. What we need to do is get hold of some of those eggs of yours."

"How do we that? "Maria was a bit nervous now. This was the real thing.

"Quite easy my dear. We'll do it tomorrow if it's ok with the two of you. I'll give you something just to calm you. Then we'll retrieve some of those eggs via the vagina under ultrasound guidance." Brock spoke as if it was a routine procedure. That calmed Maria somewhat.

"Will tomorrow be fine then?" he asked for confirmation.

"Yes." Maria responded nodding her head.

"Well you can dress now and when you're through please join us." Brock concluded and led the way out of the examination room.

Maria put on her clothes and joined Jos and Dr Brock. She felt much more at ease now that she had met Dr Brock. He first impressions had been correct. He was a lovely man.

"Well we'll see you at 10hr00 then tomorrow!" Brock summarised as they were leaving his office. Senator Bell was still chatting with Sister Lucile. When he saw Maria and Jos he approached them.

"I'm sure you agree with me that he's a fine doctor eh…my little angel?" he asked. "She was a little doubtful before she met you!" he added talking to Brock.

"Uncle!" Maria pleaded. She just wasn't used to his brashness. It was so un-African. Where she came from such boisterousness was usually associated with drunken behaviour or madness. It was not on!

"Dr Brock and I will just have a little word about the payment and so on. I'll meet you guys in the restaurant downstairs for lunch…howz that? The Senator added.

"That will be great" Jos replied "I'm starving. I think my sugar must be low!"

Senator Bell spent the next thirty minutes behind closed doors with Dr Brock. At first Dr Brock took offence at the suggestion but after thinking about for a while he agreed.

"On one condition though Bell!"

"And what condition is that?" Bell asked tentatively.

"I'll have to explain to Maria myself, alone and if it's OK with her, that I have no problem with that!" Brock was not about to let his patient lose control over decisions that affected her health. Bell hesitated for a while then he stood up and shook Dr Brock's hand.

"It's a deal. And let me express my sincere gratitude for arranging everything at such short notice!" Bell then left and joined Jos and Maria for lunch. He decided to indulge the honeymoon couple by ordering a large seafood platter. Seeing the seafood platter his thoughts drifted to Galvez and the night his bodyguard was shot.

"The never did catch the bastards who did it!" he thought to himself. That's why he'd come to London himself, to make sure that Maria was safe.

He nodded to the three gentlemen sitting at the table a few paces behind them. They acknowledged and nodded back. All his men where in place and he felt confident that nothing would go wrong now. This brought back memories of Nicky. He felt pissed off and was still upset about. So many things were pissing him off. His mind started wondering back to Bill and he kept asking himself why the hell the guy couldn't send in the army into Yugoslavia!

"Problem is we're being ruled by some baby boomers who don't want to die but are prepared to kill!" Bell had regressed again into the Bill and Al bashing mode. He simply couldn't let the failed impeachment pass.

"Uncle are you ok?" asked Maria. She'd noticed that Bell's mind was drifting somewhere else and for a man his size he had hardly done justice to his food.

"Oh I'm fine. Jetlag I think!" Bell sighed heavily. For a moment again Maria recalled Mr Pickwick, her favourite Charles Dickens character.

The following day Maria and Jos arrived at Dr Brock's surgery. Everything had been set. She undressed, this time taking her panties off and then waited for Dr Brock after covering herself with the cotton sheet. Maria felt the needle piecing her skin as it found the soft wall of the vein in her right forearm. That was about as much pain as she could remember.

"I'm going to give your some Pethidine just to make you relax and it will drive all the pain away!" said Dr Brock. Sister Lucile was stroking Maria's forehead, comforting her. Maria's legs were up on the leg stirrups exposing her vulva. She felt the warm soothing sterilising solution as Dr Brock washed her. Then he covered her with a sterile green cloth. She couldn't see what he was doing and after the Pethidine her mind drifted far away from Dr Brock's surgery. She thought of her friend Father Khumalo and hoped that he was well. She was feeling a little dizzy and could feel Dr Brock fidgeting below her. He kept talking to her, trying to keep her calm and relax. Inbetween he'd talk to Sr. Lucile.

"Speculum?" he asked and Sr. Lucile handed him the stainless steel speculum, which had been warmed to body temperature in the sterile incubator.

"Ok Maria, I'm going to put this into you, it will be a little uncomfortable. If you do feel too much pain, please say so. Dr Brock parted the lips of her vagina and he hesitated. He looked at Sr. Lucile and frowned. She had a look too and frowned in disbelief. Maria's hymen was still intact. She was a virgin and that had taken both of them by surprise. It was rare for Brock to see an intact hymen, in someone that age in his practice. He had to change his management plan. Instead of using the normal adult size speculum to open her vagina, he asked Sr. Lucile for the one he used in young girls. It was much smaller. Almost the same size as the ones that are used to look up the nose. He gently pushed that in and just managed to do so without tearing Maria's hymen.

"Ultrasound scan?" Sr. Lucile handed him the one with the vaginal probe, and then she realised that it too wouldn't fit into Maria's vagina. Brock realised that too and decided to surgically cut part of the hymen so he could have more space.

"Knife!" He took the surgical blade and with one stroke made a cut through the hymen. Maria flinched a little then she settled. She was too drugged to have felt anything.

"Swabs" Brock ordered. The bleeding was a little more than he had anticipated. He had to swab the area and he applied some pressure on the small bleeding vessels of the hymen. That was enough to stem the blood flow.

"Needle!" Sr. Lucile gave him the long needle. It was a special kind of needle that he then inserted in Maria's vagina via the speculum. Using the scan for guidance he directed the needle towards the right ovary, dodging the major vessels of the pelvis. He punctured the largest cyst in the ovary and sucked out the egg. Sr. Lucile put the fluid material that contained the egg into a special medium and container.

Brock moved to the microscope to look at what was in the cyst.

"Wonderful!" he exclaimed. He had seen the egg in the fluid. He was happy that he'd succeeded at the first attempt. Sometimes he would have to do it two or three times before he got the egg. This would have been difficult in Maria's case because he had very little space in which to work through.

"That's it, Maria…we are through here!" he shouted. He knew that she was still a little drowsy.

"Is it over…is that all?" she asked in a slurry voice. "I didn't feel a thing," she added.

"Well, you have been the most patient person I've done this to!" Brock replied. He then nodded to Sr. Lucile who was ready to clean Maria and remove the remaining stains of blood. She then put her legs down and helped her dress.

Brock, in the meantime, had put the egg in the special medium to preserve it and handed it to Senator Bell. He noticed that two other men had accompanied Bell. He knew instinctively that they were hired security.

"Thanks…You'll have it back in two days then you can go ahead and put it back into her womb!" said Bell. He and his gang then left for Heathrow Airport and took the first flight out to Honolulu, Hawaii.

Maria had now fully recovered and Jos was supporting her. She was glad it was over and that she didn't feel too much pain. In fact, she'd hardly felt a thing.

"Now Mr Bell informed me that you have your sperms stored in Hawaii?" Brock asked Jos. He had been through this with Maria and she had given written consent.

"Yes…I was advised by my physician in the States that because of my condition, that it would be wise to store some of my sperms while I still could ejaculate!"

"Fine…they'll do the fertilisation there and return the fertilised egg in two days. By that time Maria your womb should be ready to accept your fertilised egg!" Brock added looking at Maria.

"An by the way the results of the blood tests we did yesterday were all normal. Your blood group is O Rhesus positive!"

Maria knew that already as she was a regular blood donor in Cape Town. He then gave them a run down as to what to expect during the next visit in two days and then bade them good bye.

When they had left he called Sr. Lucile into his rooms. There were no other patients booked for the day, so he asked her to bring some tea and chocolate cake.

"That feels refreshing" Brock said after taking a sip of his tea. "Strange case there don't you think?" he asked Lucile.

"Yes…you mean the virginity?" she asked.

"Well yes, but more so the need to have the egg moved and fertilised in the States first…really strange. I thought I'd seen it all, but by God this must be a first!" Something was bothering Brock. Something didn't fit.

"She gave written consent…I mean both Jos and Maria?" asked Lucile.

"Oh yes…oh yes" Brock was still distant, trying to tie things together. He wondered about the hired security, but Sr. Lucile gave him a logical explanation.

"Well, Bell is a Senator and he should have security personal around him all the time!" she said,

"Yes…yes." Brock was still distant and not too satisfied with it all.

"What's really bothering you Dr Brock?" Sr. Lucile asked. She knew him well enough to know that there was something else that he was aware of that bothered him.

"Well I asked Jos whether he was still having morning erections… and he said yes!" Brock offered to explain.

"So what does that have to do with this?" Sr. Lucile hadn't quiet put two and two together.

"Morning erections are the first to go in Diabetics with vascular disease!" Brock answered and looked at her again with that frown on his face.

"So you think he was lying about his failure to have an erection and ejaculate?" Lucile asked. She looked surprised. Jos and Maria had appeared as the perfect loving couple.

"Well, I don't know. What I can tell you is that we could have made him ejaculate here. John has been doing that for us with all the husbands and partners we have sent to him. It wouldn't have been a problem at all!" Brock stood up and stretched his body, unwinding his tired muscles. John was the urologist that Brock referred all his male clients too.

"Anyway, it's none of our business. Both of them seemed happy with the arrangement and have signed consent!" he concluded.

"And they have already settled the bill up front in cash!" added Sr. Lucile. She had no problem with the arrangement as long as the bill had been paid and Maria had signed an informed consent.

Fifteen

March 31st 1999, MRC Laboratory. Honolulu, Hawaii.

"Perfect egg!" Manuel commented. Hans had given them the egg. It was the egg from the woman that was to carry Galvez's son.

"Well what are waiting for…let's take all the 23 chromosomes out from the egg!" John suggested. He was looking through the other microscope. Because they were connected they were able to view the same field. Manuel would be sucking the chromosomes out, while he watched.

"Fine…let's start!" Manuel took the fibre thin suction device that was called a micropipette. It was almost invisible to the naked eye. But under the magnifying glare of the microscope it was like a fine needle next to the egg. Manuel guided the pipette towards the egg's wall. Because of the magnification it appeared as if Manuel had a tremor. He was as cool as ice though. Practising with the chimps had given him a lot of confidence and experience.

The micropipette went through the wall of the egg and Manuel guided it to the centre, where the nucleus and the chromosomes lay. Again he punctured the surrounding membrane and entered the nucleus. Then he gently sucked out all the twenty three chromosomes until the nucleus was empty. There were only twenty-three chromosomes in the egg, the same number found in the sperm. Combined together at fertilisation that made a total of forty-six, the normal number for all human cells.

"Well done!" said John.

"Thanks…now it's your turn with the white blood cell from Galvez's son!" Manuel responded and nodded to acknowledge the praise.

"Now let's see what we have here…fine I'm ready to roll!" John said. He followed basically the same procedure as Manuel had performed and extracted the chromosomal material they'd been working on for the last few days.

"Fantastic John…now let me have your pipette" Manuel said and he took John's pipette with the chromosomes from the cells of the Cloth, all forty six of them and proceeded to place them in the nucleus of the egg donated by the surrogate mother.

"Magic!" shouted an elated John as Manuel completed the task. It was all over now.

"I'll take that!" It was Hans who had been biting his nails. Manuel had never seen him so nervous before. Even Galvez's baddies to seemed a little more edgy that day.

"Hold on Hans…I need to vacuum seal the container first then you can take it back" advised Manuel. He was glad that this was over.

"Now it's ready!" Manuel said and handed it over to Hans. Hans turned to leave the laboratory immediately.

"Hey Hans…can we leave the premises and go back to our apartments?" John shouted.

"Yes! Yes!" Hans didn't even look back as he hurried out of the lab and was accompanied by some of Galvez's men.

Manuel and John did a high five to celebrate their success and to ease the stress they had developed over the last few weeks. Now they could go back to their normal daily routine. Hans had even agreed that they take the week off.

"I'm going to take all my junk back to my place…then why don't we meet at the pub at 19hr00!" Manuel suggested.

"Sure thing!" John was visibly excited. He was looking forward to a beer and sex. He hadn't slept with a woman for the last two or more weeks. He was feeling really horny now and he was clear that tonight he was going to fuck some woman.

"Aye Manuel…why don't we make it for 2030 hrs instead!" John added.

Manuel paused for a second.

"Ok…20h30 then" he added as he left the lab leaving John still inside. He wondered why John needed so much more time but decided to shrug it off. "Maybe his place is really a mess and needs some thorough cleaning!" he concluded.

Manuel went via the Chromatography and Dating Laboratory to check on some results that he had been waiting for.

"Mike do you have the printout for me yet?" he asked. Mike was one of the junior research fellows in the Centre. His speciality was dating organic tissues.

"Sure thing Manuel…I don't know where you got these fibres from but they are very old. And I mean very old!" added Mike. Manuel looked at the printout and his heart thumped his rib cage instantly.

"You sure about this?" he asked Mike. Manuel couldn't believe what he saw. The fibres were at least 2000 years old.

"You bet I'm sure. I ran the test three times just to be a hundred per cent certain, and the same results kept popping up!" added Mike.

"Ok thanks Mike." said Manuel as he folded the paper with the data on the age analysis and put it into his pocket.

"No problem!" Mike said as he was walking away.

"Aye Mike…Can you keep this between me and you…as a favour?" Manuel interrupted.

"Sure, if you say so. You're the boss!" Mike couldn't understand what all the fuss was about. He dated plenty of old stuff and this was nothing special. Some of the stuff he had dated went back a million or two years back. Like the human fossil that had been found in South Africa in February, this year. So he was a little surprised at the reaction from his senior.

"Hi sweetheart…are you looking for some fun tonight?" asked the petit skimpily dressed blond. She was about twenty with a 'Baywatch' body.

"Yeah…how much for everything?" John asked as he lowered the passenger seat window so that he could hear her clearly.

"For a blow job twenty dollars…for a blow and sex thirty dollars. And I don't do anal!" she added, chewing on her gum and rubbing her exposed shoulders. It was 19h00 and cold out on the street. She had to dress to attract customers, so she felt the chill.

"Fine…come on in, I live just down the road!" John responded excitedly. He figured that he would fuck her then still manage to meet Manuel at 20h30. That's why he'd asked Manuel to postpone their meeting time.

"Sorry honey, I only go to hotels or my place. It's not safe anymore…you know what I mean. Plenty of weirdo's around these days!" she replied. John hesitated for a second then decided to agree. He already had a hard on and he really fancied that she was going to be a good fuck.

"Ok your place!" he added and opened the passenger door for her.

"Thanks honey…you're not going to regret this. If you like my service maybe you can tip me hey?" she asked.

"Well we'll have to wait and see!" John knew her type, promising things they sometimes couldn't deliver. He was only going to pay for exactly what he'd bargained for. If she really was that good, maybe he'd tip her and even ask her out again. Perhaps even for the whole night.

"What's your name honey?" she asked trying to create some conversation as they drove to her apartment. She knew very well that most if not all her customers lied about their names.

"Peter…and what should I call you?" John asked with a grin on his face.

"People call me Madonna…you can call me any name you like though" she replied, pouting her lips and used her left hand to massage John's thighs and then when she found his dick, she started to slowly rub back and forth. John already had a hard-on and this excited him even more.

"Ok honey…turn left at the next corner then it's the first apartment on the right." Madonna was now whispering in a sexy bewitching voice. "Don't worry it's safe out here and that guy over there will keep an eye on your car!" she added as she noted that John was feeling a little unsafe in that neighbourhood.

They went into the apartment. It was well decorated apartment but there was the distinct smell of sex about it. There were at least two other bedrooms.

"OK honey…Peter did you say?"

"Yeah" John replied as he was hurriedly taking off his clothes. He couldn't wait any longer.

"Money first Peter." she said, standing still at the end of the bed.

"Ten, twenty, thirty dollars!" John counted and handed the money to her.

"Thanks honey…Peter." She put the money into her drawer. Reached for a candle and lit it with a match. Then she switched off the lights so that the room wasn't too bright. There was just enough light from the candle for John to see her tits and when she undressed and turned to put her jeans and underwear on to the table, John could just about make out the fine hair that covered that soft part that was between her thighs. She had her back towards him and he peeped lustfully at the gap between her thighs. She had a perfect body. John decided to get off the bed and joined her at the table, which had a mirror in front of her. He grabbed her tits from behind and started rubbing them in a slow, circular motion, until he felt her nipples harden.

"Oh, I see you like the view from the back…you can come into me from behind but first things first!" Madonna turned around and went on her knees and with the condom already in her mouth she glided it over John's erect manhood. Then she slid it into her mouth, in and out, slowly. John was amazed. That condom trick in her mouth was a first for him. It really turned him on. After a few minutes John was ready and wanted to enter her. She sensed it. She felt from the throbbing of his penis that if she continued for any longer John would come even before he had fucked her.

"You want to enter me now honey?" she asked knowing very well that, that was what he wanted. She got up and turned her back towards John and bent forward, holding the table. They could both see each other in the mirror in front of them. Watching their naked bodies entwined together like that was a real turn on for John. For him this was eroticism at its best.

"It's OK honey, you can take me from the back" she said and took John's dick and guided it into her. John groaned when he felt her warmth and held on tightly to her breasts as he moved rhythmically in and out of her. She quickly caught up with his rhythm and in no time they were moving as though they were one. John could feel the intensity building up in him. He closed his eyes and tensed his facial muscles. The pleasure was so intense that he knew that he was about to come any time. At the same tine he wanted to delay his orgasm, so that he could enjoy Madonna more.

"Tell me you like it!" she screamed.

"I like it…!" John didn't have time to finish his sentence. The rope around his neck was tightened so quickly and violently that he heard his own vocal chords crack. The gloved hand over his mouth and nose prevented him from screaming or breathing. He tried to kick but he felt his feet leave the ground. He was helpless. His head was throbbing, short of oxygen and his bluish tongue was peering through his teeth against the glove hand. Through his bloodshot and congested eyes, he thought he saw Hans. But after a minute, it didn't matter any more. It was 19h45 and John was dead.

It was 21h30 and Manuel was getting worried about his friend John. He tried his cellular phone but it was off. He didn't have a line at home. By the time it got to 22h30 he was now really worried. It was so unlike John to be so late. Manuel couldn't think of any reason why John would be so late. He'd already downed his fourth whisky and was feeling tipsy.

"Bar man can I have one more for the road!" he called. He decided that after this double he would grab a cab and head for John's apartment. "I hope he didn't get drunk in the afternoon and then pass out" Manuel thought to himself.

"Look I was expecting to meet a friend of mine…Yeah, you remember John?" he asked the barman. The barman remembered John.

"You mean that small fellow with a foreign accent?"

"English accent." Manuel corrected him. "Anyway if he does get here tell him that I was around and that he can reach me on my mobile!" He added.

"Will do!" the barman responded. He liked Manuel. Manuel had just left him a ten-dollar tip. Not every customer was that generous. But he had noted that Manuel and John always tipped him well and they were always respectful and orderly.

Manuel was outside the bar and saw a cab across the street. He decided to cross the street so that he could reach for the cab. He went to a pedestrian crossing, pressed the button to control the traffic lights. Although it was chilly outside, the whiskeys he had downed made him feel warm inside. This had been a wonderful day, if only John hadn't spoiled it. "I'm going to kick his butt when I find him" he murmured to himself. The light turned green and he proceeded to cross the road. He looked to his right, where this noise was coming from, and it was too late! He just about saw the grill of the car and the driver, the driver…His body was swung into the air as the car crushed his hips and ribs. He landed on his head and the force it generated snapped his neck. His body lay on the road with blood spurting from his neck veins. Someone immediately jumped out of the car and emptied his pockets, jumped into the car and sped off.

The barman and the rest of the patrons rushed out after hearing the thud and Manuel's final scream. They were just in time to see the car that hit him, screeching away. No one managed to see the plates of the car.

They found Manuel alone on the road, his face buried in the ground and the rest of his body facing up. His neck had been twisted around such that his head was now back to front. His stomach not knowing what was going on decided to empty the whisky out on to the tar. The vomit was mixed with blood. The last of the Manuel Diaz clan was gone. What Hurricane Mitch had failed to complete, was now done.

Sixteen

April 1st 1999, London, England.

Maria was lying on her back with her legs supported on the poles by stirrups. She didn't require any sedation this time because all that Dr Brock was going to do was to replace her fertilised egg into her womb. She felt the small speculum as it opened her vagina. Dr Brock was extremely gentle.

"Are you alright my dear?" he asked.

"Oh I'm fine!" Sister Lucile was at her side holding her right hand and talking to her all the time. It helped her relax. Jos was waiting inside the consulting room and Senator Bell and a few other men Dr Brock hadn't met before were waiting n the reception area.

"You're going to feel a little funny sensation when I put the fine syringe I showed you with the egg into your cervix!" explained Dr Brock. He was now transferring her fertilised egg that had just arrived from Honolulu into her womb. He did this by pushing the fine syringe via the opening of her womb.

"That's it…finished my dear. You'll have to lie on your side just for about thirty minutes then you can go home and enjoy the rest of your holiday!" said Dr Brock as he ungloved and motioned to Sister Lucile to help him lower Maria's legs. He had every reason to be hopeful that this pregnancy would catch. The timing had just been perfect and Maria had all the signs on the scan that her womb was ready to support the fertilised egg. Since her last period was on the 18th of March, she was now going through the secretory phase of her cycle. The time when the inner lining of the womb develops a thick inner lining of blood vessels to support the fertilised egg and pregnancy. He'd seen the thick layer on the scan before he performed the procedure. He'd also checked her blood hormonal status and all her hormones indicated that the time was just right.

Jos and Maria spent the following two weeks in Amsterdam on holiday. She was only due to see Dr Brock after three weeks when her next period would have been due. They had both never been to Amsterdam and when Uncle Bell had bought them tickets to cross the English Channel for Holland they were both more than delighted. Maria loved the arts and coming from South Africa, for her it was sort of a pilgrimage. After all most of the Afrikaners in South Africa had Dutch ancestors.

They visited the Rijks Museum, the Van Gogh Museum and the Royal Palace. Then they spent some time up country and stayed the last few days in The Haig. On one occasion while they were in a restaurant in Amsterdam, Maria pointed out a man she felt sure she had seen in London to Jos. But Jos brushed her suggestion aside.

"Oh Maria we have seen far too many people on this trip. How could you possibly remember?" He asked almost in a patronising manner. Maria agreed that perhaps she was just imagining things.

It was now the 20th of April and they were both at Schiphol Airport waiting for their flight to London.

"Can you feel anything yet?" asked Jos. It was rather a naïve and clumsy question. What he wanted to know was whether Maria was having her periods yet.

"No nothing yet. Just a little discomfort in my tummy." Maria was also anxious now. She was worried that the cramps she was feeling in her tummy were the beginning of her period. That would mean that her pregnancy had failed to take. She really wanted this pregnancy now and the thought of her having to undergo the same procedure all over again made her very anxious.

"Are you feeling OK though?" Jos asked.

"I'm just fine!" Maria snapped back. Even she was surprised at her reaction. She wasn't sure whether this was pre-menstrual tension or that deep down she'd developed some resentment for Jos. "Why couldn't she have fallen pregnant the natural way like most women?" she thought. Maria felt that perhaps if Jos had been forthright to her from the very beginning, maybe she wouldn't have agreed to marry him. She was having all these negative emotions towards him at that moment so she wasn't in the mood for any lengthy conversation. Jos picked the hint and decided to keep quiet too. Once they were on the plane Maria pretended to sleep so that she wouldn't have to converse with Jos or the elderly fat lady sitting next to her. She was in the middle seat.

Halfway through the flight Maria felt a wave of nausea overcoming her. Her mouth filled up with saliva and she felt her stomach twist into a knot.

"Jos…move!" she waved to him to let her through and showed him her closed mouth and her cheeks that had suddenly ballooned filled with vomit. She just about made it in time. When she was in the toilet she knelt on the floor and wretched bile stained vomitus into the toilet bowel. Her stomach continued with these waves of cramps until her stomach was empty and her nose was running from all the straining.

When the cramps had subsided she got up, took some tissue and wiped the mess she had made on the floor and toilet seat. Then she blew her noise and looked at her self in the mirror. She looked like shit. Her eyes were congested and red from all the straining and vomiting. Her hair was a total mess. She also felt like shit.

"Are you OK Maria?" there was a knock on the door. It was Jos.

"I'm fine...just fine...I'll be out in a minute!" again she snapped back at him. She rinsed her mouth, combed her hair and then went back to her seat. Jos had that concerned look about him as she sat down.

"I'm fine," she said this time with less venom. "It must have been the burger I had this afternoon!" she added.

"Ok" Jos, said sheepishly. He was disappointed but he didn't want to show it to Maria. He thought that Maria was hiding the fact that her periods had started. For him that explained why she was so moody and the abdominal cramps. The fat woman next to Maria nudged Maria gently.

"You should try black tea in the mornings and don't take any oily foods for the next three months." she whispered.

"What?" Maria asked also keeping her voice down. She didn't know whether she had heard clearly what the old lady had said. The old lady simply nodded her head, as if to say yes. The old lady took out her rosary and started praying quietly. Her eyes were shut and only her lips moved. She did this for the entire journey. Maria was perplexed but decided to leave her alone. She assumed that either she was insane or else she had recently suffered a loss and was seeking solace. As they approached Heathrow the old lady's prayers were just about audible to Maria. She wasn't sure at first, but after the second verse she recognised what she was saying.

"Blessed art thou among women,
and blessed is the fruit of thy womb!"

"Blessed art thou among women,
and blessed is the fruit of thy womb!"
"Blessed art though among women,

and blessed is the fruit of thy womb!"

"Blessed art though among women,
and blessed is the fruit of thy womb!"

She went on repeating this until the Captain had announced that they had landed at Heathrow. Maria still didn't quite know what to make of all this. When she stood up to leave, the old lady Reached for her hand and kissed it gently. Then she went into the full prayer...It was the "Hail Mary!"

"Hail Mary full of Grace
The Lord is with thee,
Blessed art though among women,
And blessed is the fruit of thy womb.

Holy mother, mother of God,
Pray for us sinners
Now and until the hour of our death!"

Maria shook her head and said good bye to the old lady, who put her hands together, continued with her prayer and moved her head slowly back and forth as if she was in a trance.

Maria and Jos were sitting in Dr Brock's office. He was sitting on the phone waiting for the results. He'd taken a blood sample from Maria to check if she was pregnant since she still hadn't received her period. The tension both in the office and outside in the waiting room was almost palpable. Dr Brock and Sister Lucile were amazed at the entourage, besides Senator Bell and his security men that had accompanied Maria for her check up. Even Father James, Father Khumalo, other clerics from London who belonged to the same Parish had come along. There was literally standing room only in the reception room.

This was getting all rather dramatic for Sister Lucile and Dr Brock. But then again they were used to dealing with high profile cases. So they took it in their stride.

Maria was just happy to see Father Khumalo, someone from home; someone she could identify with and confide in. She wondered why she was getting all this support and attention. Although she appreciated everyone's concern she felt it was all becoming a little too much. He private life, her pregnancy was now becoming part of the public domain. She felt she was slowly losing control over her body and her life.

"Well, well, well…"said Dr Brock with a smile on his face as he walked towards Maria and Jos, who were holding hands in nervous anticipation, "Your hormone beta-HCG is positive!"

"What does that mean?" asked Jos immediately. Maria knew by now that she was pregnant.

"It means that you, Jos Leon, can expect to be a father soon!" pronounced a happy Dr Brock.

"Oh God!" shouted Jos and he immediately went on his knees in front of Maria and kissed her tummy. "Thank you God…Thank you God!" Jos went on. The noise that Jos had created in the office filtered to the reception room and even before Dr Brock could say come in, Father James had opened the door.

"Is it true my dear Maria?" he asked walking slowly as if in disbelieve. The others followed behind him. Only Father Khumalo remained in the reception area. He sat down quietly and buried his head into his hands and shook his head in sorrow. He had come along only because Father James had insisted, saying that Maria would appreciate his being there.

"Yes Father James…yes I am pregnant!" Maria responded. There was instant jubilation and prayer from the crowd that had now filled up Dr Brock's office. Dr Brock was disturbed by this all but kept his anger in check. He had witnessed how the control over this pregnancy had been wrested from his patient and taken over by a whole entourage of people. He could see the panic and resignation in Maria's eyes and he felt for her.

The humming and prayers from the entourage in his office had now eclipsed the private and tender moment this was usually meant to be for the couple. What he couldn't understand was that even Jos seemed to be more with the crowd than with his wife in this bizarre reaction or was it a celebration? It occurred to Dr Brock that the only people, who were still sitting in his office, were Maria and himself. The rest were on their hands and knees, chanting prayers.

"Oh my God…what have we got ourselves into?" Brock asked an equally shocked Sister Lucile when the crowd had left.

Seventeen

April 19th 1999, Baltimore, USA.

Maria and Jos were at last in the States and having a relaxing holiday. Senator Bell had offered them one of his condo's in Fells Point. Maria loved it there. Fathers James and Khumalo had returned to South Africa from London. She never got the opportunity to be alone with Father Khumalo, so she decided that evening or the next day she would call him. The vomiting and nausea was still a problem, so on that score she wasn't feeling too good. The only benefit was that once the morning was over she felt much better during the latter part of the day. Her relationship with Jos was also on the mend now that the tension and drama of the in-vitro fertilisation was over. They started to get to know each other and Maria felt that she'd been a little harsh on him the past few weeks.

"I'm sorry for being so moody the past few weeks!" she said. They were having dinner at one of the restaurants at the harbour in Baltimore.

"I know you were going through a lot of stress my angel. After all if I'd been a normal man, you wouldn't have had to go through all this!" Jos was still being apologetic. It invoked the desired response though.

"Oh Jos…you're all the man I'll ever want or need. I love you so much" she stretched her arms wide trying to give him some indication of the vastness and depth of her love. "And you have given me what I really wanted…my own baby! How can I ever thank you for that?" she asked as she held his hands into hers, kissing them softly, trying to express her gratitude.

"We must thank God…it's God's wish and blessing, that you are pregnant my Maria!" Jos was serious now. He looked into her eyes and wondered whether this was the right time to tell her the truth. Father James had advised him to wait until she was at least four to five months pregnant. By then she would have felt the baby moving and if she were appalled by all this betrayal, it would be too late for her to terminate the pregnancy. She would have bonded with the baby by then. It was not that Maria believed in abortion, but Father James wasn't leaving anything to chance. So Jos decided that he should wait before he told her the truth.

"Hello…can I speak to Father Khumalo please?" Maria was phoning from a public phone. She was trying to get her friend in Cape Town, South Africa. She decided to use the public phone instead of the phone in their apartment because she wanted this to be confidential. There was no way she could speak freely with him if Jos was in the same room.

"Oh Maria, how are you?" it was Cynthia one of the helpers at the church.

"I'm fine Esther, is…"

"Congratulations on the baby!" Cynthia interrupted her excitedly. The news had spread around her community already.

"Thanks Esther, but where is Father Khumalo?" Maria pressed. She wanted to keep the conversation as short as possible.

"Oh…Father has gone into town. He says he'll be back in the evening around eight!"

"Ok thanks Cynthia, give my love to everyone…Goodbye!" Maria put the receiver down. She was going to send Father Khumalo an e-mail and tell him to expect her call the next day in the evening at seven. She found an Internet Café, ordered some tea, and settled down to writing a message to Father Khumalo.

"Hello my dear friend,
It was nice seeing you in London. I was sad because we couldn't spend more time together. There is so much I want to tell you. So much has happened to me in such a short time.
You know that I'm expecting a baby of course. I'm so excited about that. The morning sickness is so awful, but I think that it's getting better every day. There are other things I want to tell you, but I'll wait until our return there in May. Please be waiting at your phone tomorrow at seven, I'll give you a call.
Missing you a lot and hope that you are doing well.
Sala Kahle
Patricia."
Maria then returned to their apartment to join Jos, oblivious to the fact that she was being followed wherever she went.

The following day, Tuesday the 20th of April, turned out to be a depressing day for Maria. In fact, it turned out to be a day that could only be described as horrible, a day when insanity and Satan held sway for a full five hours in America. Maria had decided not to go out that day. She was feeling rather weak after having vomited quite a lot that morning. So she decided to lie in and watch TV. At first she thought it was a joke when CNN interrupted its regular broadcast to go live to a high school in Littleton, Colorado. But as the horror unfolded, Maria felt sick. She had witnessed violence in South Africa, but this was different. It was America's worst and deadliest school massacre.

The school that had to bear this satanic invasion on that day was Columbine High School. Eric Harris and Dylan Klebold, both students at Columbine high, went on a senseless and mindless orgy of murder and destruction. It was around 11h30 when Maria tuned in to the life news.

Dressed in dark, Gothic-style clothing, long black coats and ski masks, Eric and Dylan walked through the school slowly and systematically hunted down their fellow classmates and teachers. Lucifer had possessed their minds and hearts, as they alternated between firing their automatic weapons and throwing explosives at their fellow human beings. A teenager that had managed to escape the carnage stated in an interview that Eric and Dylan walked around "with that devilish, half-dead, half-alive look". Maria wept as they brought the lifeless bodies of the innocent children out and placed them into body bags. Their lives gone, taken away by what Governor Bill Owens of Colorado could only label as "this cultural virus!"

Everyone that day was trying to find some logical explanation for all this insanity. President Clinton came on CNN and stated, in Maria's mind, perhaps the most logical conclusion, "we don't know yet all the how's or whys of this tragedy; perhaps we may never fully understand it. St Paul reminds us that we all see things in this life through a glass darkly, that we only partly understand what is happening."

Maria had seen enough of the madness after five or so hours of being glued to the set. She was about to turn the TV off when they interviewed another teenage girl who had also escaped with her life. Her horror account of the events proved to Maria that something was horribly wrong within Eric and Dylan. She said, "Everyone around me got shot and I begged him for ten minutes not to shoot me. And he just put the gun in my face and started laughing and saying it was all because people were mean to him last year. I thought I was going to die, I really didn't think I was going to make it. We would hear shots, then we heard crying!"

Maria got up to collect a box of tissues. She wiped the tears from her eyes and blew her nose. When these "half-dead, half-alive' boys had finished their work, they shot themselves. In all more than a dozen young lives had been ended and many more had lost their loved ones. In Littleton, Colorado, Maria thought to herself on that night, surely the devil himself must have walked through the corridors of Columbine High.

Maria was so shaken after witnessing this devilish saga that she decided to call Father Khumalo. Perhaps it was because she was now carrying life within her, that she took this so badly. She had witnessed sporadic human violence on TV in South Africa, but nothing so cold, so evil and calculated. And she was single then, with no one but herself to look after. It amazed her how her attitude to life had changed once she had a baby growing within her. She felt sure that she would do anything in her power to protect her baby. Her heart ached not only for those kids who'd lost their lives, but now the parents who had to live a life emptied of the sweet voices of laughter of their children.

"Father Khumalo it's me…" Maria broke down again. The day had been emotionally taxing. She missed home and had been systematically denied her freedom and individuality the moment she arrived in London. Now that she'd got through to someone she really felt one with spiritually, she downloaded her burden. Father Khumalo was expecting this, but the magnitude of her heartache shocked him.

"My child what is making you so unhappy, what has happened?" he asked.

"Did you see the massacre on TV? Did you get my e-mail? I want to come home!" she was rambling on and on. She didn't know what the problem was exactly, but she knew that she was unhappy and that she now wanted to go home were she would be amongst family and friends.

"OK my child…It's ok. You're going to be fine. First you must calm down and not cause your heart to ache so much!" Father Khumalo understood suffering and personal torment. He could identify with the crisis Maria was going through. "Your baby is fine isn't it?" he asked.

"Yes…yes the baby is fine!" Maria was beginning to calm down.

"Then don't worry my child. I'm going to speak to Father James and your parents tonight. I'm sure they will all agree that you come back home now!" added Father Khumalo firmly.

"OK Father!" sniffed Maria.

"Now listen my child, you have to be strong. You are the mother of that baby. You must make your own decisions. Tonight you will tell Jos that you want to come back home…OK!"

"Yes father!"

Maria felt much better by the time she had replaced the receiver. She was going to tell Jos tonight that they should go back home. If he refused, she was going to go back alone. Her knew found confidence and assertiveness came from her inherent desire to protect her unborn baby. Everything she did now was driven by this biological maternal instinct that was so strong and so very protective of her own.

"Jos we have to go back to Cape Town tomorrow!" Maria blurted it out during dinner. But this time it wasn't some emotional outburst. She said it with a calm and confident tone. She was no longer asking Jos, she was telling him. Jos sensed the change.

"I thought…I thought we were having a good time here Maria…"

"Yes, but this is not home for me and I want to go home now. It's been more than a month now!" Maria interrupted Jos. Jos kept quiet for a moment. He was weighing which approach to take. The agreement with Senator Bell and Galvez was that the longer they could stay in the States the better, because it was easier for them to provide the necessary security. Maria wasn't aware that the doorman, the maids that cleaned their apartment, the various 'taxi drivers' that chauffeured them around were all security provided by Galvez.

"Does it have anything to do with the shooting at Colorado?" Jos asked after a while. Maria stopped eating and put her fork down.

"Yes…well partly. Jos it was so terrible" she almost broke down again. He voice had become hoarse and teary, but she decided she would not. She remembered what Father Khumalo had told her about taking charge of her life and her unborn baby.

"I wonder how all this could have happened?" she asked.

"It's just a freak occurrence Maria, you're perfectly safe here in Baltimore" Jos tried to calm her.

"No Jos, this wasn't a freak occurrence. What about the shooting at the high school in Springfield on the 21st of May in 1998? What about the shooting of the science teacher in front of his eighth-grade students at a banquet Hall in Edinboro, Pennsylvania on the 24th of April 1998?" Jos was silent. It was clear that Maria had done her research into "this cultural virus" that was infecting young kids at schools across America.

"What about the four girls and the teacher that were shot at middle school in Jonesboro, Ark, on the 24th of March 1997?"

Maria went on to list all the mindless acts of school violence including the murder of the three students in the hallway at Heath High School in West Paducah, Kentucky. She reminded Jos that one of the girls was left paralysed for life.

"OK…I'll talk to Uncle Bell." Jos replied timidly.

"What did you say?" Maria asked in a rage. Jos realised that he had blundered.

"I mean I'll inform Uncle Bell" he tried to correct himself. But Maria had just about had enough of people making decisions about her life.

"Jos…You're my husband and the father of my child. I want to go back home tomorrow and I don't expect you to ask Uncle Bell for permission!" she snapped. "You can stay if you want, but I'm catching the plane at Baltimore-Washington International (BWI) airport tomorrow!" she added and left the table. Jos realised the futility of trying to change her mind.

"Maria you know that all I want is your happiness. I meant that we should just inform Uncle Bell that we're leaving, otherwise he'll worry. After all he's been very kind and supportive to us. Right from London, Amsterdam and now here in Baltimore!" Jos was trying to salvage the situation.

"Well call him now then!" Maria demanded. Jos hesitated then decided to go ahead.

"Uncle Bell Sir, thank you for all your kindness, but Maria is feeling homesick. So we will be leaving from BWI airport via London for Cape Town tomorrow at 18H30!" Jos was expecting Bell to explode, order him to convince her otherwise etc. But to his surprise, Bell didn't. They'd made contingency planes in the event that Maria demanded to go back home. Instead he simply asked to speak to Maria.

"Maria my little Angel, I hope you've had a wonderful honeymoon!" Even Maria was caught off guard by the kindness and understanding in Bell's voice.

"Yes Uncle, thanks to you. You have been so kind to us!" she replied. Then he said goodbye to them both and promised that he would be visiting them in South Africa soon. It had been almost a year since he had been to his wine farm in Stellenbosch, so he would use that opportunity to 'kill two birds' with one stone.

"Galvez, it's Bell here. Maria and Jos are leaving BWI for London at 18h30 tomorrow. They connect for Cape Town on South African Airways the following day at 12h00 GMT!"

"Fine" said Galvez, "I'll get the team ready and I'll warn the others in London and Cape Town to expect them!"

It was now Thursday the 22nd of April and Jos and Maria were on the Virgin Atlantic Airlines flight to London. Maria was trying to doze off, but the images of the students who had been killed in Columbine kept coming back to her. It haunted and tormented her brain as she tried to find some rational explanation for 'this cultural virus'. She had heard many possible explanations debated at length on TV. Some blamed it on the easily available and abundant guns in America. But this too her was almost a lost cause because the right to own a gun was enshrined in the American constitution. Others tried to blame the parents of these "half-dead, half-alive" kids. But again to her this was too simple an explanation. The most alarming argument she heard and had not thought about, was the role the violent video games played in training kids to kill. She herself had tried one of the games before but shrieked at the goryness of the game and was appalled at the fact that points were actually awarded according to the number of kills you made. That surely must be part of the problem she thought to herself. That young minds were subjected to such violent games that were addictive and that hero-worshipped and rewarded the murder of other humans was surely evil in itself. And it had turned out that a lot of the kids that walked around "half-dead, half-alive" actually did spend a lot of time playing these killer video games.

"Jos…did you know that the American Army and the police actually use those violent, killer video games to condition their soldiers mentally to be prepared to kill without remorse?" she asked a dozing Jos. He wasn't in the mood for some academic discussion.

"No honey I didn't know that!" he mumbled than he dozed off again.

"Perhaps it's also due to the violent movies that the kids see these days, like 'Natural Born Killers' and 'Basket Ball Diaries'" she tried Jos again.

"Honey I'm sure you're right" and he dozed off again.

Maria was left confused by all this. Confused about a society that was prepared to expose their young to so much violence. Any child could easily log into the Internet and find themselves in a 'whore house', watch acts of child pornography or bestiality. At the tap of the mouse they could enter into 'school' that taught them how to make bombs. Bombs to kill other humans. It occurred to Maria that with all the benefits that the Internet had brought to society, it had also opened up the 'neigh-bourhood' in which all children lived. For her that could explain at least why middle class children that were brought up by 'God fearing' parents and lived in nice neighbourhoods, attending good schools, suddenly became obsessed 'with this cultural virus'. The parents were no longer in control of which neighbourhood their children grew up in. This gener-ation belonged to the 'virtual world neighbourhood' of the Internet, with all its images of the slaughter in Kosovo and Rwanda only a click of the mouse away!

"My baby is not going to touch one of those games." she mumbled to herself.

"Did you say something?" asked Jos, still halfway between sleep and awake.

"I said they should ban those violent video games. That's where the virus really is. The devil is in that software, in those games and we have given him carte blanche with our kids' minds! Not with mine, never!" She had raised her voice and Jos decided to wake up and calm her.

"Don't worry Maria, we'll make sure that he stays away from those games!" Jos blundered again unknowingly. Maria frowned. She had become very perceptive and had always been intellectually more alert than Jos.

"He?" she asked with a frown.

"I mean I wish it's a boy that's all but if it's a girl, it would still be a blessing!" he added quickly. Maria simply frowned and then turned to the window and starred blankly into the night outside. Then she fell asleep.

"Ladies and gentleman, it's a good morning to you all. We will be commencing our descent for London in about 40 minutes. For those who might be interested if you look to your left in a few minutes you'll see the coast of Scotland." said the Captain. Maria had already been to the ladies to empty her bladder, but this time fortunately she didn't vomit. She was reading the in-flight magazine when the Captain made the announcement. She looked through the window and saw the shores of Scotland. Then it hit her again, "Dunblane, Scotland in 1997!" She recalled the tragic day the primary school in the village of Dunblane was invaded by another 'half-dead, half-alive' man, who killed sixteen kids and their teacher.

"Oh God this virus has spread much further than I realised." she whispered.

"What honey?" asked Jos who was digging into his breakfast.

"Nothing Jos…nothing Jos!" she whispered back and starred blankly at the shores of Scotland and prayed for the parents of the Dunblane kids. She was now beginning to understand why Father Khumalo had been so affected by it all. His experience in Rwanda, in KwaZulu Natal, South Africa. The Ethnic cleansing in Kosvo and now the war in Kosovo. She recalled Father Khumalo telling her that on one particular occasion, when he walked amongst the dead in Rwanda, sprawled all over the fields, he felt the presence of a spirit so evil, so frightening, he knew that it had to be Satan himself!

"Jos I've seen that man before in Baltimore!" Maria said as she recognised the man who was walking down the aisle towards the toilet.

"Are you sure honey?" he asked.

"Yes I'm sure it's the same man!" she responded confidently.

"Well, perhaps he's also on holiday." Jos added. Maria kept quiet. This was now the second time she was having this déjà vu feeling.

"Strange." she murmured.

Jos decided not to comment, in case he gave anything away. He wondered how he was going to inform Galvez that Maria had recognised one of them. Galvez would have to remove that guy and make sure that he doesn't come to Cape Town, or else their cover would be blown.

When they arrived in Cape Town Maria's family, Fathers Khumalo and James were all at the airport to meet them. Maria and Jos moved into one of the cottages on Maria's parent's farm. At last she was getting control over her life again.

"You know Jos before I left South Africa I used to always mourn about how violent and unsafe this country is. Now I realise that there is no escaping the violence. It's spread all over the world!" Maria and Jos were watching the sun set from the porch of their cottage.

"Africa may have her problems, but this must be the most beautiful place on earth!" she added as she took a sip of tea.

"Oh Jos look what's happening in Oklahoma!" Maria was calling Jos to come and watch the live coverage on CNN. It was May the 5th 1999 and a few monster-twister Tornadoes had just ravaged the State and city of Oklahoma. When it was through more than 43 people had been killed, at least 600 injured and thousands more left homeless.

"My God, how much does one city have to take?" Maria asked a quiet Jos. He was trying to hear all the details of the disaster. Maria was referring to the bombing of the Federal Building in Oklahoma City in April 1995. On that day the city lost 168 of its inhabitants in one act of shear evil and madness. And now this again! The news went on to broadcast that President Clinton had declared Oklahoma a Federal disaster area and went on to add" The people of Oklahoma City, in particular, have suffered too much devastation in recent years and they have been hit very, very hard by this!"

"Jos what is going on in the World these days? I wonder if it will be safe to bring up our child in?" Maria mumbled as she watched the sniffer-rescue dogs and volunteers searching for bodies under the brick and metal rubble.

"I'm sure our child will be safe Maria, stop worrying about that now." Jos answered, still glued on to the TV. He himself had noticed how violence, war, destruction and disease had become so rampant in the last ten years. AIDS had devastated entire families, villages, communities and countries in Africa and Asia. Africa was engulfed in war. There was war in Congo, in Eritrea, in Sudan, in Lesotho and the never-ending civil wars in Angola and Sierra Leone that the rest of the world had conveniently forgotten. Then there was the major war in Kosovo that was slowly engulfing all of Europe like a cancer. Displacing almost a million people overnight and thousands, thousands simply being butchered and buried in makeshift mass graves. And just when everyone thought that they'd seen the worst of 'this virus' that had infected society, someone in London decided to go on a bombing spree; killing Jews, blacks and gays! And again in Atlanta, Georgia, more' half dead, half alive' kids stalked another high school in May.

These were ominous signs as the New Millennium approached. That's why he was going to make sure that Maria remained safe. That the child she was carrying would live and one day save the world from all this death!

"Well I must say that I fell much safer now that we are back on the wine farm here in Stellenbosch!" Maria concluded as the transmission from Oklahoma ended.

Eighteen

May 1999, Washington DC, USA.

The Millennium Club (MC) had gathered at Wilt's residence once more. They were there to celebrate their success and also to decide on where to have Maria deliver the Child from the Cloth. They had plenty of time. Their planning had been spot on as Maria's last menstrual period had been on the 18th of March 1999. That meant that she'd be exactly forty weeks; nine months pregnant on the 25th of December 1999. Their timing and attention to detail couldn't have been more perfect!

"Before we start Gentlemen, this is to Nicky Thomas!" Wilt raised a silver goblet and toasted to Nicky. They all responded by repeating Nicky's name. Then Wilt passed around the silver goblet with the port in it. All four of them Galvez, Wilt, Bell and William O'Niel took a gulp of the port. By Christmas of 99, with the new Millennium beginning, they would be the most powerful men in the world. It would be the beginning of a new era! The mention of Nicky's name brought them back to reality and dampened their celebratory mood. None as yet had any clue as to who could have been responsible for the death of Nicky and Bells' bodyguard.

"Hey Bell…any clues from the Bureau?" Galvez was hoping that Bells' contacts within the FBI would have provided them with some leads.

"No! Nothing. No finger prints, no tips…not a fucking word!" This topic upset Bell each time it came up. It reminded him of this enemy that lay in wait, hiding and striking only when he saw it fit, only to disappear into the darkness again.

"Fucking yellow bastards!" he cursed under his breath.

"What?" Galvez hadn't quite heard what Bell had said. He heard the word yellow and he wasn't sure what yellow had to do with all this.

"Oh nothing" responded a startled Bell. For Bell to have described it as nothing was a gross understatement. Bell had regressed back to his Vietnam days when the Vietnamese guerrillas' would hide in the thick jungle, attacking them when they least expected and before they knew what had happened, they would disappear back into the jungle. To the naked eye it appeared as if they would merge with the vegetation. And just as much as the plants and thick lush vegetation in the jungle needed their breathe to stay alive, those "yellow bastards" would take away with them the breath and souls of his fellow platoon members. Each time the jungle vomited those "yellow" bastards, they would systematically reduce the size of his platoon. Decades had passed since Vietnam but every now and again it would return to haunt Bell. And now another member of his platoon had just been whisked away from him. Again by an enemy he could not see. This both irritated and frightened him.

"How the fuck do you fight an enemy you can't see?" he mumbled again.

"What's that?" Galvez asked again. He noticed that Bell's lower lip was quivering, his nostrils flaring and he had a blank stare; as if he was staring into a thick bush, his eyes darting from place to place, searching for something that he knew was out there. Bell looked really scared shit for he knew that although he couldn't see the enemy, it could see him. It was strange how the role of predator and prey was so easily reversed in Nam.

"Bell...you OK?" Galvez asked, giving his right shoulder a warm and supportive squeeze. That startled Bell. Wilt noticed the stare. He knew where Bell's mind was. They'd been there together. Wilt considered it hell. As opposed to Bell he had no romantic memories about Vietnam. He had no nationalistic feelings about the time he'd spent there. He thought it was a fucking stupid war; a waste of his fucking time and it damn near got him killed before his 23rd birthday. But he understood what it felt like to be hunted down like prey. He knew what it meant to be shit scared, so he moved in to rescue his friend's mind from the evil that the Vietnam and all wars really are.

"OK gentleman, we'll have to stay on the alert until we get a break-through" Wilt added. He needed to bring back that air of control and power they'd had before Nicky was murdered.

"I'll increase the bounty to 2million on the street. Someone out there must have seen or heard something. We'll get them eventually!" Galvez concluded. While Bell was going to use the state's resources to get some information, he'd work on the other side of the law and the dark side of society where he ruled as he pleased. That was his territory. They spent the rest of the day ironing out details and by the time the meeting ended, the mood was a little more upbeat again.

"That's it then amigos'...I'll be gone now!" he said as he rose from his chair to leave.

"Galvez...I have some news you might want to know," said Bell.

"Your scientists in Honolulu were murdered last month!" Bell said.

"What?" Galvez was shocked. He hadn't put out a hit on them. In fact he'd instructed Hans to reward them for all their hard work! It would have been stupid to do so anyway because that would only have attracted the attention of the local police and eventually the FBI to his research Institute. That meant that sooner or later the FBI would come knocking on his door.

"I thought you arranged that Paulo!" Wilt chipped in. He was visibly taken aback by the fact that Galvez had no clue what had happened to his scientists. This put a different complexion on things again.

"No! For God sake which idiot would want to attract attention now that we are almost through with our project?" Galvez was now on his feet, pacing up and down the room. He was fuming.

"I talked to Hans two days ago, while I was in London and he told me that everything was fine!" Galvez added. "Bastard!" Galvez cursed. "The bastard lied to me! He must have been involved in their murders… Maybe even Nicky's!" As Galvez started to put his criminal mind to work, the improbable all of a sudden became the possible. Over the years his mind had been trained to strike at his enemies first; before they got to him. He knew when Nicky had been killed with the Viagra overdose that someone else was on to them. He blamed himself for not being as diligent as he normally was. But he'd been caught up in the excitement of this endeavour and then the death of his family had laid his mind to waste for a few weeks. Now he was paying for that lapse in concentration.

"I'll deal with Hans personally, my way!" Galvez swore. "No one, absolutely no one fucks with me and lives to tell the tale!" He wiped the froth and saliva that had escaped from his mouth and settled half way down his chin. Galvez was livid. How could not have seen this coming. How was it possible that he could have trusted someone like Hans and not even have a slight hint of his duplicity. He felt that he was losing it. In his line of business that meant disaster. If any of the cartel got word that he was losing his touch, he would be history!

"Whatever you do Galvez, make sure that he tells you who he's working with!" added Wilt.

"And please don't create a trail that leads back to our project!" Bell was worried that Galvez might become careless and ruin all that they had worked for.

"Don't worry…when I'm through with him, they'll be no trace of him and he'll have talked alright!" Galvez concluded.

"OK gentlemen…everything seems to be all right in Cape Town. There hasn't been anything unusual reported from the team there." Bell updated the MC. "If things remain as they are, we can keep her there until she is seven to eight months pregnant. Then we must move her to London so that she can be delivered by Brock. I have discussed this with him and he has agreed to visit Maria in Cape Town once a month just to make sure that everything is fine."

"Well at least there is some good news!" O'Neal interjected. "We can't have too many people involved in looking after her. We have Brock under surveillance and he hasn't cottoned on to anything yet, although he was rather surprised at all the excitement when the pregnancy test came back positive!". O'Neal and the rest of the MC had reviewed the surveillance cameras' and tapes that were hidden in Brock's surgery.

"Fine then gentleman, we will hear from Galvez how his interview with Hans pans out and in the meantime, let's all be vigilant. We are almost there. We must not fail him now!" concluded Wilt.

Back in Cape Town, Maria felt at ease there and her morning sickness was now a thing of the past. It was May 1999 and the South African elections where due at the end of the month. Nelson Mandela had already made it clear that this would be the last time that he'd vote as president. It was Thabo Mbekis' turn now. And is it turned out, the results were announced by the electoral commission on the 7th of June, the ANC had won. Thabo Mbeki was to be President of South Africa. And Kosovo…there appeared the first glimmer of peace that month. The sight of Sir Jackson reading the surrender agreement on the 9th of June was a welcome one. And when Clinton announced on international TV that the war for now was over, Maria felt for the first time that perhaps her baby would grow up in a world with out conflict. She recalled his exact words.

"Think of all the millions of innocent people who have died in this century because democracies reacted too late to evil and aggression. Because of our resolve in the 20th century is ending not with helpless indignation but with a hopeful affirmation of human dignity and human rights for the 21st century!"

"I do hope you're right…I really do hope you're correct" Father Khumalo mumbled to himself. He didn't want to infect Maria with his pessimistic soul. Maria and Father Khumalo spent that evening at the fireplace celebrating in prayer. Another futile war appeared to be coming to an end.

"Perhaps Father…this will be the last ethnic war the world will ever have to re live" she commented.

"I hope so my child…how I really do hope so!" This time he said it louder so that Maria could hear. But Father Khumalo didn't sound very optimistic. Ethnic and religious wars were part of man's history. We were the only animal species on earth that systematically made an effort to eliminate others of its kind. This century alone had seen two of the worst wars on earth, the brutal assault on the people of Jewish descent by the Nazi's, the genocide in Rwanda, the endemic civil wars in Angola and a new war in Congo. Then there was the continuous and relentless assault on the Croatians, then the Bosnians and finally the Kosovo Albanians by Milosevic; the list went on and on. He had every reason to be doubtful. But for Maria, who was now with child, he had to show confidence in the goodness of mankind. He knew that hope was the only thing she could hold on to and he had no right to deny her that. "For wasn't hope after all the gift of youth?" he thought to him self.

The Cape winter was slowly chasing away the sun. The rainy season had started. This brought relief to their neighbours on the wine farms in Stellenbosch and Franschoek. For in February and March of 99, they had become victims to the worst fires ever to engulf the Cape. Thousands of hectares of fruit trees and grapes had been razed to the ground. The animals were not spared either. It was only after a month of concerted effort that the fires had been put out. And just when everyone was sure that the fires from hell had gone, Table Mountain was ablaze in March while she was in Baltimore.

"It was as if the Mountain had changed into a volcano! Ironically there was something magical and beautiful about the way the mountain glowed at night!" said Father Khumalo. He was briefing Maria on all the goings on that had occurred during her absence.

"Maria, I have a personal question…you don't have to answer it if you think I'm prying and it's none of my business" Father Khumalo simply had to bring this up. He felt that his loyalty was to Patricia. She was his friend and he had been upset by the way that she'd been disempowered in London.

"Father you know that you can ask me anything you want!" she responded. She kind of suspected that he was going to ask about her relationship with Jos. Although they were now getting on well together, the spark had died. There's was now more a friendship rather than a passionate affair so typical of newly weds.

"Is Jos ok? I mean is he healthy, not sick?" Father Khumalo was hesitant. If Jos was a sick man then this would be bothering Patricia and he didn't want her worrying on her own, more so now that she was with child.

"Jos…healthy!" Maria wasn't expecting that line of questioning.

"Yes, he's not sick is he?" Father Khumalo persisted realising that Patricia was trying to hide something. "If you don't want to discuss this, that's perfectly all right. As long as you are aware that you do have a shoulder to cry on, my little Angel."

"He's ok. It's just that he's diabetic but his sugar is well under control!" Patricia wasn't about to tell Father Khumalo about the impotence. She was too shy.

"Diabetes?" asked a shocked Father Khumalo.

"Oh diabetes is a common condition, Father. Plenty of people suffer from it and as long as they take their insulin injections, they ok!" Patricia was hoping that her answer and explanation would be enough to end the topic there.

"You're sure he's diabetic?"

"Yes I'm sure father. I even saw him injecting himself the day before we left for London!" Patricia was a little annoyed that Father Khumalo was doubting her." Why do you look as if you doubt my story Father?" she asked.

"No my angel…I've never doubted you. You're the most honest person that I know!" he said and turned away from Patricia's gaze. He pretended to be tidying up his desk. The problem though was that his desk was already tidy. And Patricia knew him better.

"Father, is there something you know that I should know?" Patricia held his forearm so that he could stop fidgeting around and look her in the eye.

"I don't know my child…it could be nothing. But the morning I came to bid you farewell and you surprised me as I was coming out of the toilet…you remember?" he paused.

"Yes I do…go on father!" Their eyes were both searching each other's. Lying wasn't an option anymore. It would have been too obvious and it would have created more pain than if it were not told.

"Well I found a bottle, a medicine bottle."

"So?" asked Patricia frowning, imploring father to come clean.

"It was an oestrogen vial. You were not on any hormone injections…I mean for this fertility program?" asked Father Khumalo. When he saw her at the fertility expert in London, he assumed that perhaps the vial was Patricia's. But the more he thought of it the more he realised that it couldn't have been. He'd known her since she was a little girl. He knew that she was perfectly healthy. She had even confided in him that she was still a virgin and he'd given her counsel on that issue each time a boyfriend tried to force her into a sexual relationship. He'd eventually taken the vial with him to Dr Carl Matthew, his psychiatrist. For a moment Dr Matthew's thought that Father Khumalo was inject-ing himself with the oestrogens.

"That's a female hormone father…it will change your voice, make you gain in weight and make you impotent!" he recalled was the response from Dr Mathew. Father laughed when he heard the concern in Dr Mathew's voice.

"No doctor…I love my voice and weight just the way they are!" he replied. He had laughed then because he noted that Dr Mathew had turned away when he mentioned the issue of impotence. He looked like an altar boy at confession, trying not to say anything embarrassing to his priest. Father realised that for that split second, the roles had been reversed between him and Dr Mathew.

"Oestrogen vial?" Maria asked in disbelief.

"Yes my child!" Father Khumalo could read what was going on his angel's mind. She was now putting the pieces of the puzzle together. The impotence, the 'test-tube' baby and so on.

"I'm sure there must be a logical explanation to all this my child" he said trying to comfort her soul." You are pregnant after all!" he added.

"Yes…" Patricia was now distant. She looked down at bulge of her belly. The baby kicked and she reacted.

"Are you OK?" Father Khumalo was concerned.

"Oh I'm fine…the baby just kicked!" she said and forced a smile. "The problem father…is that I'm no longer sure who the father is of my baby!" She was now totally confused by it all. She felt for the first time in her life that she was not in control of her destiny.

"Oh my child, Jos must be the father. He is after all your husband…remember?" Father John Khumalo was trying his best to con-sole his friend. But he was finding it difficult to sound convincing. For he too had his own doubts. However he was pleased that the baby was well. New birth of a child was something special to him. The meaning of life took on a whole new dimension after Rwanda. The creation and birth of a human life was something that was to be cherished and celebrated.

In the jungle of Armenia, Colombo, however, a life was slowly but surely ebbing away. Hans Schmidt had never felt so much pain in his entire life. But he was clear that he'd rather die than talk.

"OK dip him in again!" ordered Galvez. As Hans's feet touched the acid he screamed out in pain. His scream was heart piercing. It was loud. But it fell on deaf ears. They were in a warehouse, in the middle of a forest somewhere in Galvez's backyard. Galvez had decided to work on him in his own backyard, in Colombia. Here he could take his time and not worry about being disturbed by the police or passers by.

"OK" he gave the signal to one of his men to raise Hans naked body up. Hans had been tied to a rope naked. He was dangling in the air and below him was an industrial container big and deep enough to fit four adults comfortably. Hans had filled it up with sulphuric acid.

"I want to know who the fuck you work for? If you tell me that I'll let you live!" Galvez said. He was sitting a few metres from the acid container that was slowly chewing up Hans's feet. He didn't want to be too close because each time they lowered Hans's feet in to the acid, a few drops would splash out on to the wooden floor and the wood would sizzle and smoke as the acid made holes into it.

"Fuck you!" Hans replied. He knew that he was going to die. He knew the look in Galvez eyes. It was the look of death. He'd prepared himself for death and he would rather embrace the arms of death than sell his cause out. Galvez nodded to his man to lower Hans again. Hans screamed again. The flesh and skin around his feet had fallen off and dropped into the acid. His bones were now exposed and the acid was beginning to chew them. His right big toe was the first to fall. His feet were now a bundle of blisters, dissolved flesh and bones. There was no blood. It coagulated and formed brown clots as it mixed with the acid.

Galvez gave the sign to lift him up again. He was beginning to lose his patience. They'd been going on with this for the last three hours. But Hans hadn't given in. He would scream from the pain. That was the only consolation that he was prepared to indulge Galvez with.

"Who killed Nicky and my men? Who else knows about our project?" Galvez was literally begging Hans for answers.

As Hans's body swung and rotated on the rope and ended up facing Galvez, he collected as much saliva as he had left and spat at Galvez in a show of defiance and disdain.

"Mother fucking fool!" Galvez screamed as he jumped backwards from his stool, just about managing to escape the slime that had been aimed at him. In a rage he got up and slammed the chair he was sitting on against the wall. Then he took the rope that was supporting Hans away from one of his thugs. Then he slowly lowered Hans, feet first, then to his knees and thighs. Hans was screaming and crying. But not once did he beg for mercy or shed some light on the barrage of questions Galvez kept asking.

By the time balls had been dissolved in the acid, he passed out.

"Shit! Shit! Shit!" Galvez was mad. He wanted to see Hans scream with pain as his whole body entered the acid bath. He was clear that Hans was not going to deny him that pleasure.

"Pull him up!" he ordered his men." OK dump him on the deck there and tie him by his legs this time!" Galvez watched as Hans twitched with agony as he slowly came back from the dead." Pour some cold water over his face…I want him awake!"

Galvez waited for at least forty minutes to make sure that Hans was now as fully conscious as he could possibly be in that state.

"Your last chance…tell me who else did you work with?" he asked looking at Hans straight in the eye. Hans simply shut his eyes. He knew that there was no going back now. Half of his body was on fire, dissolving as the acid chewed first through the skin, then his muscles and finally into his bones.

"You can kill me now," he said softly as he opened his weary eyes to look at Galvez for the last time.

"Fool…you'll die when I say you die!" Galvez spat at him." Leave him there…I'll be back!" Galvez left the shed as Hans' bound, disfigured and naked body lay on the floor, groaning in agony. Galvez wanted Hans to experience the living hell, eternal burning and pain beyond human comprehension. He went to the kitchen and ordered a tuna sandwich from a frightened chef. He opened the fridge and took out a cold beer, sat on a stool and had his lunch. There were at least five of his men in the kitchen with him. None of then said a word. After ten minutes he had finished his sandwich, he gulped the beer down and when he was through he let out a loud burp.

"OK…now Hans can die!" he said as a matter of fact, using his tongue to clear some of the tuna that had got stuck inbetween his teeth. Walking calmly he traced his way back to the warehouse, his troop following behind.

"Hey Hans, Hans!" he shouted to make sure that he was still conscious. He didn't want to kill a man who was unconscious. He saw no fun, no point to that. Hans tried to open his eyes again, but he was too weak. For Galvez that was good enough, he was awake.

"OK give me the rope!" Galvez ordered his man after they had hoisted him up again, only this time he was in the head down position, hanging from his legs. Galvez lowered him slowly until Hans blond hair had dissolved, and then he dipped his head into the acid until it covered his head, up to his chin. Hans bubbled and made a chilling gurgling sound. The more he fought for air, the more he filled his mouth, nostrils and his lungs with the burning acid. Galvez watched for the full four minutes it took before Hans became still, completely still.

"Bastard!" Galvez fumed as he let the rope go. The men around him had to scatter as Hans's body dunked into and under the acid. The fumes were acrid and smelt of human flesh. Hans' burning flesh sizzled into a smoke that mixed with the bubbles from his lungs as the acid replaced the air and life that was once in his body. His body sunk to the bottom as the acid chewed the rope that was tied around his feet up.

Galvez had this strange and devilish look of satisfaction on his face. It had been almost three years since he'd last killed a man and in his sick mind, this filled him with immense pleasure. He'd forgotten how it felt. The beads of sweat ran down his baldhead. His eyes were shut; trying to capture and retain those last moments as Hans struggled to stay alive. He wanted to make sure that, that picture remained permanently imprinted in his memory. So he kept his eyes closed for another two minutes. He was afraid that if he opened them too early, that picture might just escape and deny him the pleasure that was now embedded in his memory and his alone to keep! He would replay it, that moment when death overcomes life, when evil overcomes good, whenever he felt the need for that adrenaline rush and orgasmic pleasure that it gave him.

"Bell…the fucker didn't snitch. He was willing to die with his secrets. It's the first time that I've had someone not talking!" Galvez was both furious and rather embarrassed. He felt as if he'd let the team down. Hans was dead but they were still no closer to finding out who was stalking them.

"He didn't say a damn thing?" asked Bell. He couldn't believe it. He knew what Galvez was capable of. If Hans had refused to talk even in those circumstances meant that he was a professional. It meant that they were dealing with a formidable opponent. Again that sense of being hunted by an invisible enemy came rushing back to him, engulfing his mind in a chilly embrace.

"Don't worry Bell, who ever Hans was working for doesn't know that Hans didn't talk. They are probably assuming that we know who they are. It's all a mind game. They've probably taken cover, worried that we will be coming for them. Rest assured Bell, even I would be scarred shit if I was in their boots!" added Galvez. This seemed to have the calming effect that Galvez intended it to have, because even though they were using cellphones, he could feel the tension in Bell. Bell was out of his league in this game of cat and mouse, of predator and prey.

"Well I hope to God you're right" Bell answered with a hint of relief in his voice.

"Amigo…Don't worry. Once they resurface again, I'll be waiting for whoever they are!" Galvez concluded. He'd done all he could for the moment. He had called all the pimps, drug dealers and prostitutes that were part of his industry, and put out the word of the two million reward. He knew that on the streets of life, money like that was bound to produce a snitch. Money did that all the time. It was only a matter of time. Someone would talk. They always did!

Nineteen

September 1999, Cape Town, South Africa.

Jos had now become completely subservient to Maria. When Father Khumalo had told her about the oestrogen, she had initially gone into denial. She refused to confront Jos about it. Dr Brock had been to see her at least once every month. She was seven months pregnant and as her baby grew, she became more and more protective of her baby as the last few months had seen some of the worst crimes committed in Cape Town. It was too close to home, to frightening to contemplate. It all started with the rape and murder of a lovely fourteen-year-old girl called farmer in Cape Town in June. Yes at least six men raped he, stabbed her forty two times and then slit her throat, leaving her for dead. Only through Gods will did she manage to crawl out from the house she'd been raped and stabbed, and find help in the street outside that had been covered with the evil darkness that guided the men that killed her. Although she lived to tell her tale, God relieved her pain and took her back the following day and left her family and the community numb with anger, anguish and fear. Instead of this sending a clear message to Lucifer, more young women were sodomised, raped and murdered after that. It appeared to Maria, that Lucifer still roamed the streets of Cape Town. She and her Son were not safe! However that still didn't explain the barricade of security around her home, as if they were living in a lagger again.

This violence was everywhere though. There was the mysterious fire that killed 23 South Korean children in a dormitory as they attended summer school at the end of June. Hiroshima in Japan was also visited by Lucifer's bile as more than 30 people died in floods and landslides. New York was experiencing one of its worst heat waves that picked on and took away the week and the old. But why was she a prisoner in her own home?

So as time went by, she now wanted answers to her questions. Dr Brock and Father Khumalo had been very supportive. Her own parents seemed rather timid whenever she asked them for advice. They kept referring her to Father James. She had slowly begun to distrust Father James. In fact she felt that the only person she could trust was Father Khumalo. Maria had noticed how the security around her parent's farmhouse and the church had been beefed up. She had virtually become a prisoner. She was not allowed to leave the farm without an armed escort. It looked more like a private army to Maria. And when she asked Jos why this was happening he'd refer her back to Father James. Finally last month she had plucked up enough courage to confront Father James. She waited until he was in church, taking confessions.

"Forgive me father for I have sinned!" she said as she settled into the confession box. Even Maria hadn't anticipated Father James' response. She heard a loud noise and then some shuffling. Father James had fallen off his chair when he heard Maria's voice. He hadn't heard her confess for almost four years. She was always a good person and for her to have come for confession now, while she was carrying the Son of Man frightened him. What possible evil could she have done while she was with child, with Jesus growing inside her, he worried.

"Forgive me father for I have sinned!" Maria repeated after she had allowed Father James to settle down again. She knew that he'd fallen down, because he wasn't expecting her! He knew that she knew that he must have been hiding something from her.

"Yes…yes my child. Go on what have you done?" he asked. He hadn't quite regained his composure.

"I have lied to my husband!" she said. Maria was choosing her words carefully.

"Yes my child and what lie did you tell your husband?" Father James wasn't quite sure whether to relax or not. A simple lie, wasn't much of a problem for him, or God he imagined. But he wasn't quiet sure were all this was leading. He knew that Maria was a smart woman and he held his breath hoping that she was not setting him up and leading him up a path he wasn't aware off and would later regret.

"I have not lied in word father but in deed," she added. Father James shifted about again and banged his head on the wall.

"What deed…what deed did you commit?" he had raised his voice and there was an urgency in his tone. He was beginning to panic. Every sort of evil deed crossed his mind. He knew that Maria and Jos were not having sexual relations. "Could she?…Could she?" he thought. He didn't want to ask the question. He knew that she and Father Khumalo spent a lot of time together, even late at night. He knew that father Khumalo was still on medication. But surely even he in his insanity would not have violated a girl half his age! The thoughts were too ghastly to even contemplate.

"I have lied to my husband about the baby I'm carrying…" Before she could continue Father James had left his box and was shouting.

"What have you done, Maria? What in heavens name have you done? What evil have you brought unto yourself?" he shouted as he came to her and held her by her shoulders and shook her vigorously. He was enraged, livid and his eyes had ballooned into massive red marbles, wanting to leave their sockets. Father Khumalo who was in the church office heard this altercation in the church and rushed out. Visions and echoes of the chilling screams in the churches of Rwanda as women and children were carved with machetes flashed through his mind. Who was this, who was bringing back this nightmare, called Rwanda, to him again? This time he was not afraid and he went out ready to confront his haunting past.

"Father James! Father James!" he shouted as he ran towards them" Let her go now!" Throughout Maria had remained silent. She had developed a calmness and confidence that even she never thought possible. She was going to extract the truth from Father James whether he liked it or not.

"Father...leave her! Let Maria go!" Father Khumalo had held Father James in a vice grip from behind.

"You...you...you Kaffir!" he shouted trying to kick and hit Father Khumalo. "You mad black man from hell...don't you see what you have done? Don't you see what you have done?"

To say that Father Khumalo was shocked by Father James' outburst is a gross understatement. He was torn between retaliating and beating the older Father into the ground and to hold on to his sanity. Because his Maria was Father James's target of verbal and physical abuse, he held on to him with all his might. By doing so he succeeded in holding on to his own sanity.

"How could you have slept with her when she was supposed to be carrying the Son Man in her...Oh God no!" Father James, stopped fighting back, slumped to the floor and broke down in tears. Beads of sweat glistened and moistened his forehead and nose. It was all over for him. How could he have let this happen right in front of his eyes? He'd noticed that just before she left for London, she'd spent too much time with Father Khumalo at night. How was he to explain to the others that the child in Maria was possibly halfwhite and halfblack? A nigger, a halfcast and impure. He lay prostrate and wept on the floor of the church like a wounded animal.

Father Khumalo let him go and allowed him to crawl on the floor of the church. He felt sorry for him as it reminded him of the many who had crawled into God's churches across Rwanda in 1994, seeking his protection and salvation, only to be followed into the church and butchered in front of Jesus Christ as he hung on the cross. He decided instead to move away from Father James and moved towards Maria who had tears streaming down her cheeks. He understood now. The IVF, Jos injecting himself with female hormones, the increased security and so on.

"What did you say?" Maria asked, her voice trembling as she walked towards a helpless Father James.

"What did you say about my baby?" she screamed and grabbed Father James by his white collar and tried to rip it off him. Father Khumalo jumped and pulled Maria away.

"Don't my child…Please don't," he said in a calming and soothing voice.

"What did he mean by me carrying the Son of Man?" she turned to Father Khumalo and curled up into his warm and supportive embrace.

Father Khumalo didn't want to answer that question. He didn't want to believe that they had actually done it, that they had used his Maria to do it, that they had defied God and Christ. He burst into tears. The noise from the three of them wailing echoed in the church. Father Khumalo wondered how much longer he could hold on to his sanity. Just when he thought he had seen the worst mankind was capable of, now this, this grand defiance of God. He guided Maria to sit on the front bench. Then he grabbed Father James' right hand and pulled him up to his feet.

"Sit down!" he ordered. Father James did as he was told. He sat next to Maria, but his eyes were focused far away. He looked straight ahead as if in a trance, in a total state of shock. He looked a wreck and he felt that surely now, it was too late to save the world. The new Millennium would be the end. He was now convinced that with this change in

Millennium, that it would be Lucifer instead of Gabriel that would reign supreme!

"Now you are going to tell Maria…and I who the father of her baby is!" Father Khumalo was firm. His hands pinned Father James' shoulders to the bench. He wasn't going to let him go until he had answered the question.

"You mean…" Father James slowly turned his eyes to meet Father Khumalo's. He wasn't sure he had heard correctly. He was confused. "You mean you have not deflowered…?" he couldn't finish the question as he slowly realised that he had made a horrible mistake." Oh God what have I done?" he asked as his chin fell to his chest in resignation.

"Answer the question!" Father Khumalo raised his voice. This startled Father James and he realised that he had to now come out with the truth. She had to know sometime. They had changed their initial plan and decided to tell her when the Boy was a teenager, when he'd become a little more independent of his mother. Now there was no way out. At least he'd been wrong about Father Khumalo and Maria. She was still carrying the Son of Man, and not some mixed race bastard.

"It all started five years ago…" he started narrating the events as they had occurred. He told them everything, about how Jos was a set up, about the Cloth and the Boy from the Cloth that she was now carrying. He told them about how Senator Bell had approached him five years back on one of his visits to his wine farm in Stellenbosch. The Senator convinced him about the nobility of the plan. As an incentive, the Senator had provided funding for the church and all the charities that Father James supported. Initially he had doubts about the holiness of the plan. But after weeks of meditation and prayer, he came to the conclusion that the world needed the messiah. He saw all the violence in his own country, the rapes, robberies and murders. He saw the saw the uncontrollable devastation caused by AIDS in Africa and that man was helpless. And he went on and on, trying in some way to explain why he had done all this. His voice was monotonous and he went on uninterrupted for almost an hour. When he was through, he stood up slowly, knelt before the life-size wooden cross with Jesus crucified on it. He bowed his head and shut his eyes for a minute in silent prayer. Then he got up and took a step towards a numb Maria, knelt before her and kissed her feet. Then he left the church quietly.

Maria and Father Khumalo must have sat huddled together on the church bench, in total silence for at least another hour. They each needed time to absorb what they had just heard from Father James. Maria went through the most torment. As she catalogued the events of the past few years, she realised how everything in her life had been stage-managed. Her parents had been involved; Jos, Uncle Bell and the list went on. The faces that she would see in the streets that gave her a sense of déjà vu. All the time she was being used and she didn't even know it. Only her friend Father Khumalo had been honest to her. "And to think all along they all thought that he was crazy!" she thought to herself. How wrong they'd all been. "He was the only sane one amongst them."

"Patricia my child…" Father Khumalo cleared his groggy voice.

"Patricia my child, I think we should go home now. It's getting late!"

So much had been said that day. And Father James…"What could have possessed the heart of such a good man?" Father Khumalo wondered as he walked down the aisle, hugging and supporting Patricia as they moved towards the exit.

When Jos saw the look in Maria's eyes that night, he immediately knew that she now knew the truth. She was silent and completely calm as she walked into the lounge area. There was a log fire burning.

"Jos I don't want you to ever touch me again! You will sleep in the guest bedroom from now on!" she added, not raising her voice. She had decided that she was going to have things done her way from now on. Having realised that Jos had been 'planted' to marry her, that he didn't love her and that he'd lied to her all along, she saw no reason to pretend that they were husband and wife.

"Maria...I know you'll find this difficult to understand" he started speaking cautiously, afraid to provoke an outburst from Maria. "At first I was doing as I was told...But I have really grown to love you..."

"Shoosh...don't say a thing!" she snapped at him, putting her right index finger to her lips to indicate to him to shut up.

"I'm so sorry" Jos replied as he stood up, went into their bedroom and emptied his clothes. He so much wanted to tell her that not everything was a lie. He really didn't have any parents. The Bell's had supported him through college and he felt that he owed them everything. They were the parents he never had. They had provided for him when no one else was prepared to. If it weren't for them, he would have ended up in the streets of Washington, probably as an addict. Mrs Bell had befriended him in 1997, when he'd volunteered to join the Senator Bells' re-election campaign committee. She had taken to him almost immediately.

After Bell had succeeded in securing his seat in the Senate, she suggested to Bell that they assist him when they found out about his impoverished and lonely background. Their own boys had long left home so Mrs Bell took him in as one of her own sons. It made her feel good again having a 'son' around. The Senator saw things differently. This had coincided with the scheme that the M.C had hatched up. So when the need for a man to woo and marry Patricia Maria Oppenheimer came up, he had just the right man in mind. Convincing Jos was the least of his problems. Jos was so frightened of losing the only 'family' he'd ever had that he saw no problem with this. After all it was not as if he was required to rape Maria. He wasn't even required to have sex with her.

"Surely" he thought to himself" there can be no real evil in that!" By the time he'd discovered who the actually "sperm donor" was, it was too late. Maria was already pregnant and although he wanted to protest...it really was too late. There was nothing he could do but play along. He also felt betrayed and lonely. But he knew in his heart that he had no moral right to complain as he had done the same to Maria.

Maria made herself some soup and ate it with some fresh bread, Cynthia had baked during the day. She sat alone in the lounge slowly consuming her soup, staring blankly at the wall and pictures in front of her. At times she was so absent minded that she would spill some of the soup on to the table as the spoon missed her mouth.

"Oh Father in heaven…why me? Why me?" she whispered. She couldn't withhold her tears any longer so she started to sob quietly. She didn't want Jos to hear her crying. The last thing she wanted was him trying to comfort her.

Maria lamented her whole life, the people she loved, people she regarded as family and friends all her life had grossly deceived her. She had always spoke against cloning at school and amongst her friends. It seemed ironic to her, that a few months ago, in June, she had read about how researchers from Hawaii University had eventually cloned the first male mammal. It was a mouse they called 'Fibro' because it came from cells taken from its tail, called fibroblasts. By all accounts she recalled, they even boasted in the journal Nature Genetics, that Fibro was normal in all respects and had already fathered two litters. She recalled discussing this with Father Khumalo.

"Father did you see that article in the Argus newspaper?" it was on a Wednesday evening on the 2nd of June 1999.

"Which one my dear?"

"This one!" Maria responded by showing him the piece of paper she had torn from the newspaper. It was obvious to Father Khumalo that Maria was alarmed, well actually, enraged by it. Father Khumalo read it slowly. When he was through he started shaking his head.

"Do these people know where they are taking us to?" Father Khumalo and Maria had discussed cloning in passing before. But they never for once thought that science would move so fast and without consulting the rest of mankind. He gave the example of the atomic and nuclear bombs. No government had asked whether we as citizens of this earth, or as taxpayers, wanted to live in a world now teaming with nuclear weapons, some of them in the hands of trigger-happy lunatics.

"This must surely be the beginning of the end!" Father John Khumalo concluded that day. The only good news that month was the end of the war in Kosovo.

But now here she was in this predicament and there was nothing she could do. Her baby, the Boy, the Son of Man, growing inside of her was now perceptive of her feelings. They had started to communicate with each other. When he was hungry he would nudge her womb with his hands and that would trigger a hunger pang within her. When she laughed or sang him his favourite tune, he'd stay still as if he was trying to capture all the words or listen to her sweet voice in laughter. And when she was depressed or sad, she would feel him continuously massaging her womb. It was a different kind of feeling. Different from the hunger pangs' nudge. And each time he did that her depression would float away, her heart would sing again and the smile would return to her face. Then he would stop the massaging movement. They had bonded completely as a mother and a baby normally would. But this was more. She had become so very protective of him. He became the driving force in her last four or so months of pregnancy. So this deception was something she was going to have to come to terms with. There was no choice. She would nurture and nourish her boy until he was strong enough to come out into the world. Then she would guard him like a hawk, with all the maternal instinct and skills at her disposal.

"No one is going to use or deceive you my son…You will make your own choices when the time comes!" she said. She realised that she was talking to herself and that it was now past midnight. It really was time to sleep. Strangely now that she knew the truth, she slept soundly for the first time since she had married Jos. She stretched her right hand across the bed in the darkness, just to make sure that Jos wasn't there. Then she slept.

For Father Khumalo sleep was hard to come by that night. At first he found it difficult to drift into deep sleep and when he got there, he kept being woken up by recurrent nightmares. Nightmares of all kinds, Rwanda included, but even worse ones. He tried praying and that seemed to help ease the torment in his heart, but still he felt that that wasn't enough to reach God. He needed to ask for his mercy. He was doing this on behalf of mankind. After several attempts at trying to connect with God and failing he decided to get out of bed. Normally he would connect spiritually with God within a very short time. But not tonight. So he put on the light in his bedroom took off his collar and went into his kitchen.

"I'm sure they'll understand" he mumbled to himself as he took out a bottle of port. After opening the port he poured it all into a one of the large African clay pots that lay scattered around as decoration in his cottage. He found his favourite reed mat that had been hand woven in KwaZulu Natal, and pushed the chairs in the lounge away from the centre of the room towards the wall. Then he neatly rolled the mat down, covering the floor in the centre of the lounge. He took the African clay pot that had the Port in it and placed it in the middle of the reed mat. Father Khumalo then squatted on to his haunches, scooped some off the port with a big soupspoon and spilled it carefully onto the ground over the reed mat. Then Khumalo started clapping his hands together slowly, in a deliberate, rhythmic movement like all African men would. He proceeded to call out the names and totems in Zulu, of his father, his grandfather, his great grandfather and all the Khumalo clan that had long departed from this earth.

"Khumalo…" each time following it up with the rhythmic hand clapping.

"Mtungwa…" (clap, clap, clap!)

"Mbulase…" (clap, clap, clap!)

"Mzilikazi…" (clap, clap, clap!)

"Kwamashobane…"(clap, clap, clap!)

"Ndabezitha…" (clap, clap, clap!)

"Mqumane…"(clap, clap, clap!)

"Wen'ondl 'umuntu umyenga ngendaba!" and he clapped again rhythmically for the last time. Khumalo felt his heart stir and was overcome with a sense of peace and security he hadn't felt for decades. He'd managed to awaken his ancestors and they were now willing to listen to his request. Father Khumalo took the African clay pot in his hands and brought it to his lips. He took a sip of the rich port and then placed the African clay pot down.

All along he kept speaking in Zulu, in his mother tongue. He started by asking them to forgive him as he had neglected them and had last appeased them many, many years ago before he'd become a priest. He asked that they hear him…Mandla Khumalo. Mandla was the name his father had given him after his birth. It means power in Zulu. He had stopped using it when he was Christened and baptised as John. He had asked to be named John because as a young man as he read the bible, he admired John the Baptist most.

So Mandla Khumalo went on to make his request, still in fluent Zulu.

"You who are in heaven, you who sit next to him the great one…I am asking for your help. I'm asking that you deliver this message to him, God, that we have committed the greatest sin of all. Please ask him to forgive us, that we are human and weak in mind, spirit and faith!" Mandla Khumalo paused for a minute then continued.

"Please ask him to give me the strength to look after U-Patricia Maria Oppenheimer…and ask him to help me watch over her and his son!"

Then he repeated their names again and threw some more of the port onto the mat. This was done as a symbolic gesture to them, so that they could also partake in the drinking of the port together.

After putting everything away he went back to his bedroom, got into his bed and like Patricia he slept like he'd never slept before ever since the evil in Rwanda had taken a hold over his soul.

For Father James that evening was the worst ever in his six plus decades on earth. He had sworn at Father Khumalo, using language he felt sure he was not part of. It disturbed him that perhaps deep down, this was the real him. That besides all those years of Christian upbringing, of helping the people that worked and lived on the farms of Stellenbosch, he had used such a derogatory racial term to describe his colleague. But that was nothing compared to the mess he'd created. Now Maria and Father Khumalo knew that she was carrying the Son of Man, that everything else had been a hoax. He knew that this deception of Maria that they'd orchestrated for years, since she was in primary school, must now be hurting her immensely.

But there was nothing else he could do now, he thought to himself. They were all at the mercy of Maria. He tried to pray but the words failed to come from his heart. For the first time he wondered whether what they'd done was really right.

"How can wanting to worship you in the flesh be wrong? How can wanting the Lord to rescue us from all this evil, death and destruction that had become the norm in the 90's be wrong?" he asked himself. He was confused and lost like a lamb that had strayed from the rest of the flock. That night he failed to sleep and he had to listen to his clock tick and tock, as he starred at the ceiling. Strangely, for the first time in his life, he was afraid of the darkness, so he left the light in his bedroom on.

He almost jumped off the bed when his alarm went off at 05h30. His instinct was to get up and get ready for morning church prayers, but when the reality hit him again he sat down on his bed and started sobbing again.

"Can I come in?" Father James hadn't heard the knock on his door. He was tired and his mind was floating around aimlessly. He looked at his clock, it was 07h45 now.

"Come in" he answered half heartdely. He was caught off guard. It was Patricia and he still hadn't washed or dressed. He was still in his pyjamas, his chin was rough, covered with sprouts of prickly white hair trying to start a beard going. His eyes were droopy and red from the lack of sleep and crying. Maria realised that he was a total mess and looked ten years older, than the day before. When she entered he got off his bed and started to kneel down on his knees.

"Stop that!" she ordered him as she touched his shoulder. Maria was firm, unsmiling but not hostile. There wasn't a trace of anger left in her. In fact she had nothing but pity for Father James. He had proved to be a weak and mentally unstable man. She realised though that she was now in great danger. That many people for many reasons, would want to either kidnap her baby or have him killed. Father James and his sponsors had the money to protect her. She now understood the reason for all the security and the familiar faces she kept bumping in to wherever she went. She decided to use Father James and Uncle Bell for her own benefit. She was determined to start taking control of her destiny and that of her unborn baby!

"I will carry my child to nine months and I want Dr Brock to deliver me in London. Father Khumalo will come with me to London!" She said calmly. "After my Son is born, I will decide were he will live and I will bring him up as my son, until he is old enough to make decisions for himself!" she added.

"Thank you." Father James responded humbly. He was grateful that she was going to co-operate. Now all he had to do was to inform the others that the situation had changed. Maria was now aware of the deception.

"And Father James…clean yourself up please!" she said as turned to head for the door.

Twenty

"Uri…pass me some off that cognac!" Uri poured the cognac carefully into the glass. Then he gave it to him as he sat in the steam bath. They were alone, naked and enjoying the warmth. Moscow was in a chilly winter grip. They'd been together for the last twenty years. They had both done their time for the KGB and when he'd decided to quit the KGB, he'd reached the top. He was in charge of the intelligence section. That was now almost ten years ago. When prestroika and glasnost came into being during Gorbachev's time, he decided to start his own enterprise. He saw it as a golden opportunity to expand their business. He knew then that there would be chances to move their business outside the USSR. With their contacts in the KGB, the world was their oyster.

Uri was his head of personal security then, so when he went into the commercial world and joined the free enterprise boom in the global economy, he followed his boss. He was his right hand man. Now Sasha Nikoliovic's empire spanned the globe and was worth at least 30billion US dollars. None of the core business was legitimate at first. So he wasn't the sort of fellow that featured in the Forbes Fortune bean count magazine.

"Uri…where are they now?" Sasha asked as he stared blankly at the walls of the vana (sauna). He liked to take his time. The only noise in the vana was the sound of the water as it splashed and waved lazily against the walls.

"In London Gaspadina Nikoliovic" Uri always addressed Sasha that way. It was a sign of respect. He always used his surname. Gaspadina was the Russian equivalent of sir.

"London…and the other two?"

"They're in Washington. They will be spending their Christmas with their families. We have our men tailing them at all times Gaspadina Nikoliovic!"

Sasha was now in his mid fifties and had a well formed muscular body. This was due to the mental and physical discipline he'd learnt and administered during his time at the KGB. His trademark was his bald-head. He had it shaved with a razor twice a week. He was a Serb by birth.

"The Kaiser…we owe him to finish the deal, no!" It wasn't a question really. Sasha was merely stating a business fact. They had a contract. They'd been paid a billion dollars by the 'Kaiser' to complete the job. And Sasha always delivered. It was a pity that Hans had been killed but then again, Hans wasn't under his command. He was answerable to the 'Kaiser'.

"Yes Gaspadina Nikoliovic. We are ready at your command." Uri joined him in the water. He poured himself a glass of the cognac and took a sip.

"Bloody Nazis…when are they ever going to learn?" Sasha had agreed to the job offer from the 'Kaiser' but he disliked the old man. He hated the Nazis and he hadn't forgotten the misery they had tried to impose on mother Russia during the Second World War. But this was business. If the Nazis were prepared to pay a billion US$ for the kid, who was he to complain. Still, sleeping in the same bed with the devil left a sour taste in his mouth.

"And the cargo…is it on its way to Serbia?" Sasha was keen to conclude the two business deals. He was more sympathetic to Mihalovic's request. After all they were both of Slovak origin and he was upset at the treatment they received in Kosovo by NATO at the beginning of the year.

"It should be arriving in Serbia right now as we speak Gaspadina Nikoliovic!" Uri answered just as calmly. They went about their discussion as if they were deciding which Christmas present to buy for their kids. Mihalovic's group of right wing Serbs had never forgiven NATO for the bombing of their Holy Land of Kosovo. Sasha had used his connections in the army to get what their requested. In return they had deposited US$30 million into his account. He felt that he had actually given them a bargain.

"Uri…play some Tchakovsky please" Uri knew what that meant. He reached for the remote control and selected the third track. It was "Waltz from serenade for strings", Sasha's favourite. He loved to listen to it whenever he went for the kill. He closed his eyes as the music played, as if he was in some sort of trance and swayed his head from side to side; imagining himself in the middle of a waltz or rather…a hunt. In between he opened his eyes slowly and looked into Uri's eyes, nodded and then closed his eyes again and moved to the waltz; back in to the hunt. Uri reached for his cellphone and gave the man on the other side of the world the go ahead.

"Gaspadina…everything is fine" Uri whispered. He didn't want to disturb the trance that Sasha was in. Both submerged their bodies slowly into the water until it reached their chins and allowed Tchakovsky to waltz them through the gruesome events they'd just triggered.
Washington, DC. 24th December 1999. Christmas Eve

Wilt was busy doing his last minute shopping. He was excited and anxious at the same time. He was aware that in London, England, the birth of The Son of Man was in progress. He hadn't told his wife a thing about their project. She'd noticed though that he'd become a little edgy the last few weeks. She put it to stress. He wanted to make it up to her and so he bought her the most exquisite diamond bracelet. As he got into the elevator, he pressed the P1 button. He'd left his car there. The excitement and tension during the last two weeks had become unbearable. His stomach hurt. His ulcer had flared up during the last few days. As the elevator door opened, he flicked a Zantac into his mouth. "That should do the trick," he thought to himself.

The lights of his silver Volvo C70 flicked twice as he pressed the remote control. He started humming 'Silent Night' to himself. It was Christmas Eve and wherever he went the tune was echoing everywhere, including in his mind. He mused at the irony. It was Christmas and he was one of the very privileged few that knew that The Son of Man was being born on the same day. The call from Bell and Galvez in London had settled him that morning. Things were on track and his mind was somewhere in London, with them. He reached for his door. Then he felt the pain. At first he thought it was his ulcer playing up. But no, the pain he felt as the knife sunk into his heart felt more like burning hot oil. He tried to scream but the gloved hand around his mouth stopped him. He saw the steel blade in front of him. It had blood all over it, his blood. It went back into his heart swiftly, this time crushing one of his ribs in the process. His eyes remained opened, pupils dilated. It was a weird sensation. He was witnessing a murder; his own murder and he couldn't stop it. As the knife came out of his chest the second time, it made a sucking, sloshing sound as the air rushed in to fill the space that it had created. Again the blade went into his heart. This time it stayed there. He felt the blade twist and turn, twist and turn…twist and then turn again, tearing all the muscles of his heart and entering all its 4 chambers. Wilt knew it was over. Flashes of Vietnam filled his mind…knifes and bayonets and death. He knew this was it. His legs twitched uncontrollably as the knife finally reached his spinal cord, cutting it in half. Then his legs went limp. In the background, Silent Night played on, oblivious to Wilt's fate.

When Wilt's body stopped twitching, his executioner gently allowed him to settle down on to the flow. Wilt lay there, silent. His nose and face starring into the ground and the pool of blood that had started to cake as it clotted.

O'Neal was on his way home. It was probably around 21h00. He lived a few kilometres out of town. He steered his Buick around the corners with ease. He loved listening to Eric Clapton. 'I shot the Sheriff' was blasting from his CD. He liked his music load. At the traffic light, he reached over to press the forward button. He was looking for his favourite song. He found it and as it played he started singing along. The traffic lights were still red. It reminded him of his days in the seventies. He also liked Bob Marley's version.

"Shit it's along time since I've had a joint" he whispered to himself. He mused how strange this music made him crave for a joint. It also made him horny. O'Neal was sure he saw some one at his window. But the shadow had engulfed him before he could stare into its eyes. It was that swift, that quick. He definitely heard the sound as the bullet went through the window, into his left ear, through his brain and out through the passenger window. Pieces of his memory were sent splashing onto the passenger window. Some of it found itself on the snow, trying to figure out what on earth it was doing there. And as Clapton belted his favourite song "Knocking on Heavens door", O'Neal slumped on to the steering wheel. Even the blaring of the hooter failed to wake him up.

25th December, 1999.Rio de Janeiro, Brazil.

When the 'Kaiser' heard the news, his wrinkled face broke into a faint evil smile. He was now 89 years old. He had spent the last four to five decades in hiding. He'd made a promise to Adolf that he would get the Cloth and that they'd control the world again. With the Son of Man in his reach, this time they would not fail. There would be no war, no bombings. They would control from within the heart of the free demo-cratic world itself. He put the phone down. He was sitting in front of a log fire in his stately home in Rio. A blanket covered his frail legs. The room was quiet. The other members of the Revived Nazi Movement (RNM) were silent as they waited for the news. The Kaiser took his time.

"We're on track. The boy will be born tomorrow. Our friends in Moscow say that the MC has been reduced to two. Now all we have to do is to tell them when to take The Boy!" The clapping was spontaneous.

"Hail Hitler!"

"Hail Hitler!"

CIA headquarters. 25th December 1999.

"Sir I think you should have a look at these pictures!". Mike had just received the latest pictures from the satellite orbiting over Europe. They scared the shit out of him. So he called for his commanding officer.

"Shit…by God that's a SAM 66 missile. What the fuck is it doing in Serbia?" Mike went pale. How had they missed it? Could this really be true? He asked himself. How could his have happened when they had all those NATO troops stationed there?

"Call the Chief of Staff…Number one needs to be informed and move that satellite nearer to Serbia. This better not be true!"

"Yes sir" Mike reacted. The whole room, the nerve centre, was silent. A missile in Serbia, in the hands of a disgruntled right wing movement was definitely cause for concern.

The satellite made a swift turn and passed over England, then France, and Belgium and eventually it was stationed over Serbia. As the pictures started coming in, their worst nightmare was confirmed. The Serbs had the missile. It was a Russian one. Gaspadina Nikoliovic had delivered his cargo.

"Shit…It must have been slipped in via the Russian controlled part of Kosovo" mumbled the Chief of Staff.

"Sir if you ask me sir…we should never have allowed them to take the airport in Kosovo after Milosovic had given up!" Mike added. He was upset and pissed of. This changed the politics of power in the Balkans all over again. The new millennium was promising to be a difficult one, not one of peace and prosperity for Europe.

Twenty-one

24th December, London. 1999.

"And there shall be signs in the sun, and in the moon, and in the stars; and upon the earth distress of nations, with perplexity; the sea and the waves roaring; men's hearts failing them for fear, and for looking after those things which are coming on the earth: for the powers of heaven shall be shaken. And then shall they see the Son of man coming in a cloud with power and glory. And when these things begin to come to pass, then look up, and lift up your heads; for your redemption draweth nigh."

The coming of the Son of Man. (Mt.24: 29-35, 42-44; Mk 13:24-37)

Maria was in London now. She was happy that at least she had spent the last two months of her pregnancy where she'd always wanted to be, in Stellenbosch with Father Khumalo watching over her. Her relationship with Jos had also changed now. She began to understand how he'd also been made into a victim, an unwilling participant in her deception. Gradually she opened up her barricaded heart and allowed him to be a friend. She realised that Jos was just a simple man. Besides Father Khumalo, she had failed to rekindle the trust and friendship with her parents, let alone with Father James. So she took Jos on board. He'd learnt his lesson and was genuine in his repentance.

During the month of November her stomach was so big, she found it difficult to walk without resting. The heartburn had also become unbearable, so she had to use at least three pillows when she was sleeping. She spent most of her time with Father Khumalo, discussing philosophy, politics, religion and yes, her son. She was sure it was a boy now because Dr Brock had scanned her the last month and although he didn't say it, it was so obvious on the scan. Her Boy had opened his legs and there in the middle she saw it. He was definitely a boy. By the end of November they consulted with her and decided to move her to London as the time was near. She agreed with them that her son would be safer there and if he did require any extra medical care, it would be immediately available. She now understood the real danger her son was in and the need for extra security!

It was now the 24th of December 1999 and Maria still hadn't felt any contractions yet. It was ten in the evening. Her stomach was huge and she could feel the kicks and nudges from her little boy. She was anxious because they'd told her that her due date was the 25th of December. Dr Brock her gynaecologist had said that if she didn't go into spontaneous labour by the 24th, he would have to induce the labour, to start the process going. She was anxious because it was her first pregnancy and, more so, she was carrying God's child. But being comfortable in the private residence in London, which had been turned into a fully-fledged maternity and paediatric hospital, helped to ease her anxiety. She also felt safe because there was 24-hour security cover here. She was determined that now that she had come this far, she would protect her son with her life.

Outside her room though, if you put your hand out carefully into the air, you could almost feel the tension. The entourage of religious purists, the security personal and Galvez's pack were pacing the corridors. The priests were huddled in corners; prayers and verses were being recited. Candles, dozens of them, had been lit, fresh flowers were in abundance, and the smell of incense filled the atmosphere, mixing with the smoke from the candles like a thick blanket. The lights had been dimmed and one had to acclimatise to the dim light before you could find your way around.

Father James was huddled on a chair in one of the rooms. He had been waiting for this day for a long time. His little Patricia Maria Oppenheimer was now going to bring forth the Son of Man. He was proud of her although she had scant respect for him now. He felt confident that with time she would understand, in fact she would be grateful that he'd picked her amongst the many girls in Cape Town that attended his Church.

He felt humbled by the fact that the good Lord had chosen him to look after this girl. He'd tried his best from the time of her birth, through kindergarten, and her teenage and adult life. Now she was ready with child and in a day's time, she would give birth to God's own son. He felt confident that all the problems of the world, both natural and manmade disasters would now pass. The new Millennium was nigh and it was right that the Messiah should once again lead mankind through the path of righteousness. He believed strongly that this was mankind's last chance and hope. Man was in desperate need of salvation.

The last decade had seen the full hand of Lucifer's cards on the deck. This all started with the terrible and savage human slaughter in Rwanda, the ethnic cleansing and wars in Kosovo and Burundi. The relentless civil war in Natal in his country and the earthquake in Nicaragua. The rampant high school shootings all over America and the freak monster tornadoes of Oklahoma. The list of disasters was endless.

There were also the flash fires in his hometown of Stellenbosch in South Africa and the massive poverty and hunger caused by the global financial crises triggered by the collapse the Asian economic miracle.

Further, this decade had witnessed the worst epidemic in modern human history. AIDS had wreaked so much havoc, caused untold human suffering and deaths in his continent and elsewhere. There were now hoards of pitiful orphaned children, roaming the streets naked and alone. Their stomachs empty, their souls broken and with no spiritual or moral guidance. But now the Son of Man was coming again to give us all hope and end all this pain. So he joined the other religious men prayed and repeated with them;

"Blessed be the King
that cometh in the name of the Lord:
peace in heaven,
and glory in the highest."

This had been going on for the last week or so ever since Maria was confined to bed, when the first signs of contractions had started. This was repeated ad nauseam and the humming could be heard all along the corridor a few metres from Maria's room.

Paulo Galvez, Bell and their gang of close confidants were in the main lounge. Wilt and O'Neal had opted to stay away. They'd concluded that it wasn't safe to have all of the M.C in one place. And went they right!

They were all sitting around the table, smoking cigars, and drinking Remy Martin cognac, with plenty of crayfish and fresh fruit to devour. For them this was a time to celebrate and delve into their bankrupt and megalomaniac egos.

Paulo Galvez was now convinced that within a few days he would rule the earth. All its inhabitants would bow to his command. His plan had worked perfectly. He was here not only to witness the birth of the Boy from the Cloth, but also to protect and guard his investment, the investment of the Millennium Club. He had to be there because he was still concerned about the people Hans had been working with. They had failed to uncover any leads as to who possibly could have been behind those murders. So as far as he was concerned the enemy was still out there and when it came to protecting his money or investment, he trusted only himself and his deceased mother.

Galvez had invested a lot of his money and time to see this project come to fruition. He would have killed several times in the situation required it to protect the Boy from The Cloth. He'd done so already and with such ease. He'd killed because this was his idea, his creation. He had killed because he knew that once the Boy from the Cloth was born, he would answer to no one on earth. America would be his including the FBI and those narcotics guys that kept breathing down his neck. The whole Christian world would be his to govern as he saw fit. Heads of State would beg him for his audience and favour. He would be the father of the Son of Man on earth. That would make him the most powerful man next to God. But on earth for now, as the Boy grew, he would be God to all other humans. Finally the painful memory of the loss of his two sons in the earthquake that devastated Colombia, was beginning to subside. The ache in his heart didn't hurt as much now. He was going to have his own son again. So when he took a puff on his Havana cigar and blew the rich thick smoke into the air, he smiled contentedly. The time was nigh.

Father Khumalo knew better though. He was a sad man because of what man had done in defiance of God…He'd previously witnessed all the evil man was capable of in Rwanda and in Natal, South Africa. This had destroyed his soul. Perhaps it is true that he was psychotic. But what he had now been made party to and now about to witness was the greatest evil man had committed against his Father in Heaven. That any man, made from the earth in God's own image, could now want to make God's son, was to him too evil to even contemplate. But no one listened to him. They all thought that the trauma of Rwanda and KwaZulu Natal had left his mind barren of any intellectual thought process. He had come along with Father James, although he'd lost all respect for his mentor, because he had pledged to God and Maria he would protect her and watch over the Boy. While the others recited their prayer, he continued to beg the Lord for forgiveness. He prayed that the Lord have mercy on all of mankind for this sacriligious and heinous act that they were about to complete. So as the others prayed and repeated their verse;

"Blessed be the King
that cometh in the name of the Lord;
peace in heaven,
and glory in the highest."

Father Khumalo hummed a different verse and tune. He recited Genesis 17, 18 instead;

"And God saw that the wickedness of man was great in the earth,
and that every imagination of the thoughts of his heart was only evil
continually
And it repented the Lord that he had made man on the earth,
And it grieved him at his heart.
And the Lord said, I will destroy man whom I have created

from the face of the earth;
both man, and beast, and the creeping thing, and the fowls of the air;
for it repenteth me that I have made them."

And for the second time now in his Christian life as a priest, he said a prayer to his ancestors, hoping that perhaps they could relay his request again and again to God for mercy as the hour of his coming approached. After the ceremony he'd performed for them in Stellenbosch he knew that they would be his only bet for an audience with God. Having passed on to God's Kingdom, he felt confident in his heart that God would have more time for them and what they had to say.

So again he started by asking his forefathers to forgive him for having ignored them in mind and ceremony, because of his chosen path as a Christian. He asked them to forgive his lack of wisdom and strength, in this time of need. He asked that they kindly relay his prayers to God Almighty for mercy. Father Khumalo even promised them that if they did that, and God heard his prayers, he would on his return to his home village in the Natal Midlands, slaughter a cow to appease and thank them according to the great Zulu Nation's, traditions and custom. That he'd forever be indebted to them and live by those traditions for the rest of his life on earth.

Jos was at Maria's side, kind and supportive as he had become in the last two months as their friendship had grown. She was lying in her bed, facing Jos who was sitting on her left. The room was a light blue colour. It had been decorated with fine paintings depicting the Angels, Heaven and God. Directly opposite her, stuck on the wall, was a life sized bronze piece of Jesus Christ on the cross. She smiled and thought to herself how ironic it was, that in his moment of death on earth, Jesus was now supposed to watch and guard over his own birth.

There was a TV set mounted on the wall and she had her own bathroom and toilet. A few leather chairs were scattered around the room. Jos was sitting on the one next to her bed on the left. She looked into his eyes and he smiled.

"How are you Maria?" he asked softly and with a genuine air of concern. He was visibly anxious and looked tired. The last few months had been very emotional and traumatic for both of them. They both missed Stellenbosch and Maria now missed her parents sorely, even though they had colluded in her deception. She forgave them and assumed that they thought that it was the right thing to do.

Maria wished that her mother were with her now. She could have done with her warm support and love. As great as this occasion was supposed to be for the rest of the Christian world, she couldn't help but still wish that her parents were here. To her the birth of this Boy, her son, was also an addition to the Oppenheimer family, the first of the grandchildren.

"I'm fine Jos." she replied. "I am still feeling those vague contractions that started three weeks ago. Dr Brock said that they're false labour pains, Braxton-Hicks contractions he called them. But don't worry yourself, I'll be fine". Maria was now by far the stronger of the two. Her maternal instinct spurred by the hormones of pregnancy and her baby growing inside her had transformed her. She was going to be a mother by the 25th and she was ready; emotionally, physically and physiologically.

"How is the baby?" Jos asked with a smile.

"Well you can hear from the foetal monitor. His heart is nice and strong!" she replied. Maria had been hooked onto the foetal monitor, called a cardiotocograph (CTG) for the last twelve hours. The CTG measured her son's heart rate and so far everything was fine. It also showed that her uterus or womb was having mild contractions. These were the Braxton-Hicks contractions and she was having one contraction every thirty minutes now.

"Are you feeling any pain, my dear, I mean with the contractions?" Jos was concerned.

"No Jos. I feel a little tightening below that's all. It's like there is something pressing down. And each time that happens, I feel like going to the toilet." she smiled.

"I love you very much Maria and I'm sorry". Jos had stood up and was holding Maria's left hand in both his palms. He kissed her hands and hugged her tenderly.

"I understand Jos and stop worrying, everything is going to be OK!" whispered Maria. They hugged each other for about a minute and stopped only when Maria felt her baby kick.

"Feel Jos, feel him. He's saying that I must tell you not to worry and that everything will be fine".

"He is a strong little boy. He is God's child." Father Khumalo interjected. He had walked into Maria's room unnoticed. "I know Maria that you can't wait to hold him in your arms and look into his eyes!" he smiled as he walked towards Maria. Jos moved away slightly. He and Father Khumalo still hadn't made their peace. Father Khumalo was still suspicious of him and Jos would sometimes catch him glaring at him. It was always enough to scare Jos.

"Father!" Maria responded. There was excitement in her voice and her eyes lit up when he walked over to her bed.

"Are you fine my child?' he asked.

"As strong as a mule!" she answered with a smile." But please don't leave me." she added and her voice changed as she said that.

"I'll always be here for you and your son!" Father Khumalo gave her right hand a firm squeeze of reassurance.

"Maria my dear, any pain yet?" It was Dr Brock. He surprised them both as he entered with Sister Lucile, Maria's midwife.

"No Dr Brock. It looks like baby is in no rush to come out yet." replied Maria.

"Well, well…I'm sure he's finding it more comfortable and safer there in your tummy. Which baby wouldn't be in your tummy? You are such a wonderful woman and soon to be, mother". Dr Brock was always so gentle and kind to Maria. He had sensed that something was going on during her pregnancy but he never pressed her for the details. He'd witnessed the metamorphosis in her character and resolve in the last few months and that pleased him greatly. He'd been very unhappy about the invasion of her privacy and erosion of her will that had happened during the early months of her pregnancy. At one time on one of his many visits to Cape Town, she considered telling him the truth about the baby. But she decided against it, not wanting to burden him with the enormity of the responsibility that had been dropped on his lap. She felt sure that if he knew what he'd been conned into doing, it would tear his heart apart. He was a good man. So after consulting with Father Khumalo, she decided to leave him in the dark as to the true identity of the boy that was growing in her.

Dr Brock was now looking his age and to Maria he seemed to have aged quicker during the last few months. He was now at least fifty-five, with white hair and a hairline that was receding in a hurry to form a central bald patch at the top of his head. He still had those warm eyes she first saw in March behind his thin, rimless glasses. Although he was looking older and tired he always had a smile on his face.

"Maria, would you be so kind again, as you were this afternoon and lie on your back. Let's feel your tummy and see how baby is doing?" Dr Brock added.

"OK, but you will have to assist me, because I feel like an elephant when I try to turn from one side to another." Maria joked.

Father Khumalo and Jos rushed to her sides. They grabbed her arms and assisted in turning her.

"Thanks." said Maria.

Dr Block went on to expose her pregnant belly, by gently pulling the sheets down. It was huge and the dark line that ran from her belly button down was standing out as if someone had used a pen marker on her white tummy. Her navel was inverted like the navel of a ripe orange. Her flanks had the typical hyper-pigmented stretch marks.

"Hmm…nice size boy we have here. I think he's now keen to see the world. His head is now well into your pelvis" he added as his right hand felt for the baby's head above her pubis. "I can't feel much of his head now. That's a good sign and I'm sure we will be in business very soon my dear." Dr Block went on.

"Do you think I will deliver by the 25th then doctor?" asked an excited Maria. Although she had initially decided to refuse the induction as an act of defiance, she had changed her mind as time dragged its lazy hands and her tummy became impossible to carry.

"Well, well, well Maria, I don't think baby has much of a choice on that decision. He will be born on the 25th all right. The question is whether he's going to come out on his own or we might have to encourage him along." Dr Brock had that kind, warm and supportive smile on his face.

"Now Maria, I know that this you will find a little uncomfortable, but I must do an internal examination to assess your cervix, the opening of your womb, as we did this afternoon. I will be very gentle of course my dear."

"That's fine Dr Brock, I never felt a thing this afternoon." replied Maria bravely, trying to disguise her anxiety.

"Well that's because you are the most wonderful patient I've ever had Maria"

"That's not true Dr Brock, it's because you are so gentle." added Maria.

"Oh you do flatter an old man, Maria. Sister Lucile if you don't mind…"

Sister Lucile had brought the vaginal examination sterile pack already. She had placed it on a trolley next to Maria's bed on the right hand side. Father Khumalo and Jos went behind the screen so that Maria could have some privacy and not feel too exposed.

Sister Lucile had been working with Dr Brock for the past twelve years and she knew what to have ready for him, even before he asked for it. She had no children of her own, as her husband had died in a car accident before they could start a family. She never found another partner after that and concentrated on her job as a midwife. She loved her job and was the best in her class when she completed the midwifery diploma at St Mary's hospital in Paddington, London. She soon rose in the ranks and was the matron in charge of the labour ward for ten years.

That's where she and Dr Brock met. In fact she trained in his department and when he was Professor of Maternal-Fetal Medicine there, they developed a very close relationship. When he moved out into full-time private practice, she went with him. Rumour at the hospital, was that they had more than a working professional relationship. Besides the rumours they had a genuine bond of Christian fellowship. They attended the same church and often attended prayer meetings together.

"If you would kindly open your thighs and bend your legs at the knees…that's perfect Maria. Now just relax…as you did this afternoon," added Dr Brock.

"I'm going to pull the sheet over your legs, so that you don't feel too exposed my dear." he went on and then he put on some sterile gloves.

"Oh no I'm fine doctor!" Maria replied. Sister Lucile was holding her left hand and standing next to her head and shoulders.

"I'm going to clean your vulval area now Maria, so it's going to feel a little cold and wet. That's perfect my dear. Some jelly please Sister Lucile!" Dr Brock said turning to Sister Lucile who had the jelly in her hands already, waiting.

"Fine, now I'm going to do the internal examination. Take a deep breath if you find it a little painful, we'll take our time. There's no rush, so just relax Maria".

"Umm…" Maria responded as she felt Dr Brock's two right fingers separating the lips of her vagina and slowly enter her. It wasn't painful as such; it felt rather cold and clinical. She felt some mild discomfort.

"Fine…Maria, you are doing well. I'll be through in a second my dear," said Dr Brock.

"Well your baby's head is well down in your pelvis. Your cervix is now much softer. It must be because of those prostaglandin tablets that we put in this morning. I'd say that you're cervix is at least two to three centimetres dilated now," he added.

"What does that mean doctor?" asked Maria.

"Well, let's first finish the examination down here then you can relax and we can all discuss…Maria I'm withdrawing my fingers now. Excellent, you were wonderful as always. Sister Lucile, some swabs if you may…"

"They are on the trolley Dr Brock" Lucile replied.

"Wonderful!" Brock said. He proceeded to clean and dry Maria's vulva and vagina.

"There…you can put your legs down and relax now. Fine that's it, remember to try and spend as much time on your left side, as is possible. That way your baby will get the perfect blood supply and nourishment from you." Dr Brock then pulled the sheet to cover Maria's legs and tummy, and then he went to the basin and washed his hands, after lathering them with some fresh smelling disinfectant soap.

"Now what does that all mean…well, it's likely that you will go into labour, maybe tonight, but definitely by tomorrow. However, what we'll do is give you something to help you sleep, comfortably tonight, and I'll reassess you at six in the morning. If you haven't gone into labour by then, I'll have to place some more prostaglandin gel into your cervix to kickstart your labour!" explained Dr Brock. He was now at Maria's right hand side, holding her right hand and looking into her eyes. Occasionally he would look at Jos and Father Khumalo who had rejoined them, so as not to leave them out of the discussion and birth process. Dr Brock always spoke calmly and slowly, so that there was no question of him talking over the heads of his patients.

"How do the prostaglandin's work Dr Brock…I mean what can I expect?" asked Maria.

"Good question my dear. Well the prostaglandin gel will make your cervix softer. It will also cause your womb to start contracting. Those Braxton-Hicks contractions you are now feeling will become more frequent and painful. When you are in established labour, the pain will radiate mostly to your back. This is because your cervix would be dilating" replied Block.

"And for the pain…can I try as much as possible without any analgesia?" asked Maria. They had discussed this aspect of the labour before at length, but Maria wanted to re-affirm her wish and retain some form of control over the birth of her child. She wanted to go through this labour without any drugs for pain relief. She hoped as much as possible to emulate what Mary the Mother of Jesus went through in Jerusalem two Millenniums ago.

"Oh yes my dear! However, if you do change your mind, I have Dr Chamberlain waiting to give you an epidural on request. But let's see how far we can go without one. We'll all give you the support you need Maria". Dr Brock was through now.

"Dr Brock…" it was Maria "I want Father Khumalo to be there at the delivery! He must be the first to receive the baby after you!" she said with firmness in her voice that told Dr Brock that she had clearly given this issue much thought. He turned around to face her, paused as he looked at Jos, and then replied by nodding his head, still smiling.

"That's fine with me!" he concluded and then he left Maria's room.

Dr Brock was met by an anxious crowd of clergy as he left Maria's room. Father James led them. He could sense the tension in them.

"Is The Boy all right…and the mother?" Father James was the first to ask. He tried not to sound too anxious. He went on. "Has she gone into labour?" Dr Brock gestured to them that they should move away from outside Maria's door. He directed them to one of the Boardrooms were there was a log fire burning. It was December in London and an unusually chilly winter. The snow was a foot or so thick outside and the temperature was below zero degrees Celsius.

"Both the mother and The Boy are fine. She hasn't gone into proper labour yet. I'll have to start her labour going tomorrow morning." Dr Brock was brief. Although he appreciated that the extra ordinary concern shown by these men of the cloth, for the labour and baby to be born, his instinct for patient confidentiality was difficult to shake off.

"Nothing must go wrong Dr Brock!" They were all startled by Paulo Galvez's commanding voice and turned to face him. He walked in slowly from the doorway of the huge boardroom. "She will deliver naturally on the 25th of this month…will she not?" he asked. It was more of a command then a question.

"She is perfectly fine. The Boy is in excellent health. He will be born on the 25th of December." Dr Brock answered calmly. He appeared to be the only one in that room who wasn't intimidated by Paulo. Well perhaps him and Father Khumalo.

Brock had noticed that Father Khumalo kept his distance from Paulo Galvez, as if he had the plague. He sensed that Father Khumalo disliked this man intensely and that there was no fear in him at all. He kept a vigilant but non-intrusive eye on Maria. He knew that she trusted him explicitly and as he had just realised, more than Jos her husband.

"Gentlemen I would suggest that you catch some sleep…labour tends to be a very long process" Brock said, smiled courteously and then turned to leave them. This annoyed Galvez.

"Dr Brock…" he said nodding his head waiting for Dr Brock to turn around. "She will deliver the baby through the vagina!" The priests all looked down in embarrassment. How could this man talk with such vulgarity about the mother of the Son of Man? But it was too late for them to voice or show their displeasure. They had already sold their souls to Galvez and the MC.

"Yes by the vagina Mr Galvez…only if all remains well!" Brock then quickly walked away and closed the door behind him. This had visibly upset him. He would not accept being told how to manage his patient by someone whose only contribution to health care was by providing dead bodies that could not be identified.

25th December 1999.

06h00.

"Morning my dear!" said Dr Brock as he walked into Maria's room. He'd managed to dodge the crowd that had kept an all-night vigil in the conference room down the corridor.

"Oh I'm fine…I can feel the contractions are much more frequent now. Sister Lucile said they are now coming once every eight minutes!" Maria was still trying to sound cheerful. She was beginning to feel the pain in her back. She had managed to catch a few hours of sleep, thanks to the sedation and also knowing that Father Khumalo was sleeping on the chair in front of her, below Jesus on the cross, comforted her. She felt safe and secure that with the two of them watching over her, nothing could go wrong!

"Oh…morning Father Khumalo" Brock added as he realised that the father was in the room." I see you're an early riser," he added. Father Khumalo had made himself some tea. He hadn't slept all night. He was only going to sleep once he knew that Maria and the Boy were safe.

"Morning Dr Brock and Merry Christmas!" added Father Khumalo.

"Oh my God…I'd forgotten it was Christmas today!" Brock exclaimed. He'd been so absorbed in all this, that although last night he'd prayed thanking God for another Christmas, when he woke up this morning, he'd forgotten about it.

"Merry Christmas Maria…now you're going bless us all by giving us a Christmas baby. How much more blessings can a old man like me ask for?" he asked with his characteristic smile.

"Morning and Merry Christmas to you…" she just about managed to finish her sentence as another contraction had started. Sister Lucile was at her side with her hand on Maria's tummy, timing the contraction.

"Twenty seconds" she said to Dr Brock "and they are now coming twice every ten minutes…Merry Christmas doctor." she added with a wink. Dr Brock winked back at her affectionately.

"Now it sounds like we're business. I'm sorry Maria but I'll have to do another internal examination to see how far dilated you are" said Dr Brock. Sister Lucile had already set the trolley.

"Good just relax like you did yesterday Maria…there it is, take a deep breath now." he said as he guided his right index and middle finger into Maria's vaginal canal towards her cervix.

"Wait…wait doctor" Maria said moving away slightly "I'm having another contraction!"

"That's all right Maria…we'll wait. There is no rush," Brock said as he stopped advancing his fingers while the contraction went on.

"Finished?" he asked and Maria nodded.

"Wow…we are in business Maria. You've done so well! Your cervix is now five centimetres dilated, that means you're about half way. Remember we need to get to ten centimetres before the baby comes out," said Dr Brock

"Now to help the process a little I'm going to break your fore waters now. That will allow the labour to progress much quicker!"

"Ok…but Dr Brock could I have an epidural first before you break my waters…I can't take the pain anymore?" Maria pleaded.

"No problem my dear…Sr. Lucile would you be so kind and please call Dr Chamberlain for the epidural and also inform Dr Carol Smith to be ready for the baby from now on." said Dr Brock. He took off his gloves and washed his hands. He would rupture the membranes once Chamberlain was through.

Chamberlain had the epidural up and running by 07h15 and Brock had put on his sterile gloves again so that he could rupture the membranes and allow the fore waters to drain out. Maria was now completely relaxed, as she was pain free. The arrival of Chamberlain had alerted the entourage and they had huddled along the corridors. They were tense and nervous. When they saw Chamberlain they thought that the time had arrived, that he was the paediatrician.

"He's the anaesthetist!" Sister Lucile informed them, more to add to their anxiety than to be informative.

"Ah!" was the response as they walked away disappointedly. Sr. Lucile had never seen anything like this. There were at least thirteen clerics from all parts of the world. "All this for one baby…and on Christmas day for that matter when they should have been conducting Mass in their respective parishes?" she asked herself. "Weird!" is all she could think of as she went back into Maria's delivery room to assist Dr Brock with the breaking of the fore waters.

"We'll wait until you have a contraction so that you membranes bulge out…it's easier to break the waters then" he said to Maria with his fingers still in her vaginal canal. She was now six centimetres dilated. He nodded to Sister Lucile. She knew what that meant. She exposed Maria's tummy and started to rub it gently and slowly in a circular motion. She was trying to irritate the uterus. In no time Maria's womb responded and started contracting.

"That's fine" Brock nodded to Sister Lucile. "Ammnio-hook my dear?" he asked Sr. Lucile. She had it waiting and gave it to him. Brock took it into his left hand and with the two fingers of his right hand still stretching her cervix and membranes, he pushed the long plastic instrument into her vagina. It had a hook at the end and he managed to hook the membranes, he pulled at the membranes gently and the fore waters broke. There was a gush of the water that surrounds the baby came out through Maria's vagina and in no time had formed a huge, clear pool between her legs, on the bed.

"There we go now," said Brock with a sense of relief and pride. He allowed more of the water to come out." Now I'm just going to feel your baby's head and feel which way it's positioned.

"Oh…Oh my God!" Brock said it safely, but Sister Lucile knew that there was a big problem. Maria and Jos were a bit slow to catch on, but Father Khumalo sensed it. Something was drastically wrong. He turned around and faced Jesus on the cross and asked softly.

"Please…please don't do this" he pleaded in an almost inaudible whisper. But Maria heard him. She noticed the look of panic in his eyes and that alarmed her. To make things worse, she could hear that the heart sounds from the baby were now much slower. Dr Brock was working quickly and although he'd looked panicky before hand, he now seemed much calmer. But the smile had vanished from his face. He kept his hands in her vagina and asked Sister Lucile for some sterile water. In less than a minute he'd filled up her bladder with water via the catheter tubing that had been placed into her bladder after the epidural. That was routine after an epidural so that the patient doesn't have to go to the toilet to empty their bladder; they wouldn't b able to sense that their bladder was full.

"Ipradol 200 micrograms into the drip set!" Brock said calmly to Sr. Lucile, with his right hand still in the vagina. The Ipradol was to stop the womb from contracting.

"Thanks…Theatre, Chamberlain and Thomas!" he added as Sr. Lucile paged them. The doors to Maria's room were swung open soon there after. It was the theatre staff with a trolley. Only then did Brock start explaining.

"Maria…We have a cord prolapse! Your baby's umbilical cord fell out into the vagina as the water rushed out when we broke the forewaters. It is lying in the vagina, in front of the baby's head and is being pressed by the head. This is blocking the blood supply to your baby and that's why his heart is slowing down. I'm taking you to theatre for a caesarean section now. That's the only way your baby can come out alive!" Brock spoke slowly and firmly and was at the same time helping the theatre staff to lift Maria onto the trolley.

"Please God...please save him, please don't forsake him again!" Maria was crying, her voice a whimper.

"He'll be fine but we must rush!" Brock added as they pushed the trolley. Father Khumalo was holding Maria's right hand and running along with her and the theatre team.

"What's all this?" Father James shouted running after them. The rest of the crowd followed. They knew now that something was not right, that there was a threat to the Son of Man.

"She needs a caesarean section now...Or else the boy will die!" Brock decided to shut them up once and for all. The effect was dramatic. As Maria's trolley disappeared behind the theatre doors, all the clergy were on their knees in prayer. Only Galvez and his troop remained on their feet, dumbfounded.

"Right" Brock nodded to Sr. Lucile. It was time for him to take his hands out of the vagina so that he could start the caesarean section. Sr. Lucile caught that strange and urgent look in his eye. He'd felt that the pulsation's through the baby's cord, which were the result of the baby's heart pumping blood through the cord were now faint and feeble. The heart was slowing down. The baby was preparing to die. He had to take the baby out now.

The instruments had been laid out and Maria's epidural had been increased so that she was totally numb from he chest down. Brock gloved immediately. He didn't even scrub. He figured why scrub and deliver a dead baby?

"Knife!" he shouted this time. He was working on borrowed time. With one stroke he went through the skin and with the next he was into the abdomen looking at Maria's womb which was swollen with child.

"Scissors!" Brock was through the lower part of the uterus and grasped the Boy's head with his right hand and yanked him out of what had been his home for the last nine months, but had suddenly changed into a death trap and a grave.

"Clamps!" he clamped the cord and cut it. The Boy was lifeless. He didn't make a sound. The water that was surrounding him for the last nine months, acting as a cushion and a nourishing bath, had turned green in colour. As Brock pulled the baby out he could see the thick green stool that the Boy had passed, as he became hypoxic, when the blood that was carrying the oxygen from his mother was blocked at the cervix by his head. Some of the thick stool still hung from his anus. It was called meconium and never a good sign.

"Carol!"…Brock shouted as he grabbed the lifeless boy by the legs and handed him over to Dr Thomas.

"I've got him!" the paediatrician responded.

"Is my baby OK?" Maria asked repeatedly.

"He'll make it…He's going to make it!" Sr. Lucile tried to sound positive.

"Size three tube!" Carol asked and pushed the tube into the windpipe of the Boy. She then sucked the thick green meconium that had found itself down the Boy's windpipe. When she thought that she'd cleared it all out, she decided it was time to give him some oxygen.

"Oxygen bag!" and within one fluid motion she had the tube and bad connected than she deflated the bag, pushing some oxygen in to the Boy's lungs.

"Talk to me Carol!" it was Brock who was now closing up.

"Bradycardia of a 100" she replied. His heart was really slow now, for a baby.

"Adrenaline!" Carol squirted the adrenaline in to the tube that was down the boy's windpipe. Then she bagged him, pumping his chest gently and inflating his lungs. Slowly the dusky blue-grey colour of the dead began to fade. His heart picked up to 120 then 130 then 140.

"Oxymeter!" Carol wanted to check how well oxygenated he was before she decided on further management.

"OK!" she said. She could see that the Boy was now beginning to fight against the tube.

"Suction" she asked and proceeded to suck the secretions that had accumulated in his mouth and windpipe. Father Khumalo stood and watched quietly as Carol fought to save the Boy's life.

"Brock!" Carol called.

"Yes?" his heart sunk. He was expecting the worst.

"I'm pulling the tube out!" she concluded.

"Oh no!" Brock broke down for the first time. It had been a long time since he'd lost a baby at birth. Since Maria was on an epidural she was awake and their eyes met. Brock saw that familiar bewildered and frightened look in her eyes. No matter how much he dealt with death, he could never get used to it. It still cut him deep. It hurt. He was closing Maria's skin and his hands were trembling. She noticed the tears rolling down his mask and that. made her panic.

"Oh God no...no...please save your son!" she cried out.

"Don't...give...up yet," Brock said sniffing repeatedly, inbetween the words he tried to articulate with difficulty.

Carol pulled out the tube that was in the Boy's windpipe, hoping that he would start breathing on his own. At first the Boy responded well. He took some deep gulps of air, but he was struggling, as the effort he needed made his ribs stand out. He was recessing heavily and finding it difficult to not only take in air, but also to blow it out. It was as if he was having an asthmatic attack. Father Khumalo saw the bewildered look in the Boy's eyes. It sent a shiver up his spine. He'd seen that look before. It was a look of panic, of things to come that where unavoidable. The Boy could feel all the air around him that he knew he needed to inhale desperately to keep himself alive, but he simply couldn't get enough into his lungs. And the little that he got into him; he was finding it difficult to exhale it once he'd extracted all the oxygen from it. Instinctively Carol asked for another tube. His colour was changing back to the blue-grey shades of death as he failed to keep his body well oxygenated.

"I think he must have aspirated some of the meconium down in to his lungs!" Carol whispered to her assistant. She knew that he would need the tube and the breathing done for him.

"Get the ventilator ready! Set it at thirty breaths per minute and correct the pressures!" she barked the orders out. It was clear that the Boy had meconium aspiration syndrome. He'd inhaled his own excrement and it was now clogging up his lungs.

"More adrenaline!" she demanded as his heart rate was beginning to slow down again. The Boy was connected to the heart machine and the bleeping was clearly slowing down. Carol responded by massaging his heart with her two fingers. In the meantime Brock now knew that things were taking a turn for the worst. He'd finished dressing Maria's wound and nodded to the anaesthetist, who immediately drew some Valium and pushed it into Maria's veins. Brock wanted her sedated slightly as she had now become hysterical as she watched her son struggling for his life. She was trying to get off the theatre table, so that she could reach for her son.

"More adrenaline!" Carol was now desperate. They had been resuscitating the Boy for at least twenty minutes now. She pushed the needle with adrenaline straight into the Boys heart, via his soft ribs and tender skin. His heart responded with a quick flutter, then after thirty seconds or so, it started to slow down again.

"Oh God no!" Carol cried as she looked into the Boys eyes. His pupils were dilated now and were no longer responding to the light from her pen-torch. He was brain dead clinically.

Father Khumalo saw the new look in the Boy's eyes and he understood. The time he'd spent with death in Rwanda and elsewhere, told him that he was again starring at it. His prayers had fallen on deaf ears. His ancestors had failed to pass the message on and now this Boy was going to die.

"Father Khumalo...How is my baby?" Maria asked in a drowsy but distraught voice. The Valium had taken effect. Father Khumalo turned, tears in his eyes, looked at an equally tearful Carol. She looked him in the eye and shook her head in resignation. He frowned at her, as if to ask 'are you sure?'

She nodded slowly. The bleeping sound from the Boy's heart was now beating at the pace of a slow drum as it echoed hauntingly in the theatre. The Boy was dying! Carol and Brock stood next to the Boy on the resuscitation trolley, numb with sorrow and anger. They didn't know what to say. Father Khumalo knew what he had to do. This was where he took over, when life changed hands with death. Slowly he took the leads off the Boy. Carol tried to help him, but her hands were trembling so much that she failed.

"It's all right my daughter...I will do it" Father Khumalo whispered to her. He proceeded to take the tube out of the Boy's windpipe and wiped the thick green secretions off his mouth and cheeks. He stared down his blank, expressionless eyes, looking for some sort of explanation. But he knew he would get none. Instead the Boy took a slow and laboured gasp.

"The Lord giveth and the Lord taketh" he mumbled to himself. God owed no one any explanations. He knew that. So he gently shut the Boy's eyelids as he gasped again. This time with less purpose.

Father Khumalo wrapped the Boy into a warm theatre blanket and kissed the Boy on his forehead and closed his eyes for a moment in prayer. Then he walked over to a frightened Maria.

"Oh God how can you do this to me and your own son?" she broke out. "How can you do this to him?" Even though she'd been sedated, she vented her anger towards God. She was confused. She'd never wanted all this to happen, but she wanted her baby back.

"I want him back...Please God I want him back!" she cried. Father Khumalo had given her the Boy and she cradled the Boy. She felt cheated, robbed and as if a part of her soul had just been surgically removed from her.

"Father Khumalo please tell me why? Tell me why God would do this to his own Son twice...please father?" she pleaded for an answer. Father Khumalo allowed her to vent her anger and grieve for her baby.

"No don't" he commanded softly. The anaesthetist was about to give Maria more Valium. Father Khumalo knew how important it was for her to spend these last moments with her son. She had to accept the reality that he was dying. Cruel as it looked at that very moment, in the end it was in her best interest. It was his experience that those who mourned their loved ones and buried them recovered from the agony much earlier. They reached the insightful acceptance stage much sooner than those who where sheltered from the pain and grief.

"What will you call him my child? He must have a name!" Father John Khumalo asked quietly as he wiped the tears from his blood shot eyes.

"Michael...Father, I want him to be called Michael after my brother" Maria cried out. "And Father...I want his second name to be Mandla!" she added. She had given the boy Father Khumalo's Zulu name. This really touched him. It moved him because he had given up his Zulu name when he'd been christened. And now here was his friend, a good Christian, naming the Son of Man, her dying son that she was prepared to give up her life for, after him. A name he himself had rejected in order that he could embrace Christianity fully. It was the ultimate irony.

Father Khumalo knelt besides Maria's bed and nodded. Then like the man he admired so much, Father John Khumalo blessed the child and baptised him as Michael Mandla Leon. The Boy took one last gasp of air, found the strength within him to open his eyes for the last time to say farewell to the woman that carried him and provided him with a home for the last nine months and was supposed to be his mother. Then his heart stopped. God had taken him back to sit next to him; on his right hand side, were he belonged.

Outside the theatre, the tension and drama that was unfolding proved to be too much for Father James. Things were not going according to plan. The baby would not be born naturally and to make it worse, there was a real chance that he might not make it. He had heard all the crying in theatre. But what frightened him most was the deadly silence that had followed it.

There was a wooden antique chair at the end of the corridor, directly opposite the theatre doors. He decided to rest his weary body there. The wailing and prayers being recited in the background were now a distant buzz. He was tired and the pain in his chest was so sudden that before he could reach out to massage the right side of his chest, he noticed that the light in the corridor had gone. He couldn't lift his hands. He tried to cry for help but the words refused to leave his vocal cords. That burning and crushing pain, if only some one could stop it. It was like his chest was on fire. Then the pain subsided. He felt nothing at all. But the lights didn't come back on. For him, his worst nightmare had just began. The darkness that he'd now developed a fear of had come to take his soul away! He knew instantly that he wouldn't be waking up from this darkness; this madness that had engulfed his mind, body and spirit.

Twenty-two

December 31st 1999, London, UK

Maria was sitting quietly in the church. The black lace just about covered her face. Her eyes were still puffy and swollen from all the crying. It had been a horrific seven days. Her baby boy was gone and even though she prayed hard every night and day, that this was just a dream that would somehow go away, it never did. Father Khumalo had remained by her side all the time. He was determined that no ham would come to his little angel again. She had been used, misused and abused. Then after all that she had carried the Son of Man for nine months within her. She had done her best. She had nourished and protected him, loved him and talked to him every night before his birth. She had really loved the Boy, her son and then in a horrific chain of events she was forced to watch him die even before she could give him her breast. As she sat numbly in church, the pain from her engorged breasts kept reminding her of her loss; swollen from the milk she had so lovingly prepared to nourish the Boy into manhood. But it was not to be. 'What did I do wrong?' she kept asking her self. 'Could it be this happened because at first I hated what they had done t me? That I had wanted to do nothing with this pregnancy?' As these thoughts tormented her, the tears started to roll down her cheeks again, as they had done so continuously for the last seven days.

"Are you alright my child?" Father Khumalo asked Maria.

Maria simply nodded back. He stretched out his right hand and held Maria's left hand in his and gave it a gentle squeeze.

"All this has some explanation my child. Perhaps it was God's plan. You did your part. You carried the child well, but perhaps we, the world, were not ready for him." Father Khumalo had spent the last week counselling and giving spiritual guidance to Maria. This was a difficult time for him too. So many things had happened, so quickly and with such ferocity. He felt sure that he had seen the work and the might of God. That he had been so close to him, so close to his work and his response, frightened him. He felt to small, to impure to have been so close. Father James was dead.

'That was God's punishment!' he thought to himself. The previous day he'd made sure that his body was put on the British Airways flight to Cape Town South Africa. The burial would go ahead without him. His responsibility lay with the Boy and Maria. They had decided that the Boy should be cremated there in London. It was safer that way. It would have been impossible to carry him back to South Africa. Someone would have made an attempt to steal him, even though he was dead. Too many people, too many crazy groups would vandalise his body and deny the Boy a decent burial. Further Maria and him had both decided that this satanic experiment should never ever be done again. So cremation was the best way to destroy all his tissues. There would be nothing left to clone again. After the cremation was over, they would take the ashes to a safe and holy place they had now arranged. His ashes would be sacred there, far from the prying eyes of the public and far from Lucifer's angels.

"I understand Father," Maria answered after wiping her eyes with the tissue that Father Khumalo had just handed her. In the last week she had transformed dramatically. She had aged, matured and it was almost as if she knew that her Boy was watching over her. Although she would cry often, she would cry not the tears of grief. She was past that stage. She had strangely settled quickly into an almost serene inner self-control, of insightful acceptance. She was determined that no one would desecrate her Boy. And she was touched by the fact that she had been given the privileged of having carried him and then as Mary had done two centuries past, gently delivered him into this earth. That she had done that, well that made her cry. It was her that had felt his little nudges in her womb as he played and communicated with her. He was happy then, safe and happy. It was her who had provided him with the warmth of her body, the nourishment in her blood and the love in her heart. And it was her who looked gently into his eyes as the life began to fade. She remembered the power in his eyes, the love in his eyes and as he left her, the sweet faint smile that he gave her. She felt sure that he was thanking her. He knew better, that this was not his time, that man could not decide his destiny. So now when the tears rolled down her cheeks, it was with a strange sense of accomplishment, of gratefulness for the honour that she felt sure no other woman would ever have again for a long time.

"My child, you have done well. Soon we will have completed our duty. Then we must put our next plan into action." Father Khumalo whispered to her, as the ceremony was about to end.

"Don't worry Father." She answered back calmly. The priest went on to recite a prayer about the sins that have been put away by Christ's sacrifice. It was **Hebrews 9,1.**

> "...for then must he have often suffered
> since the foundation of the world;
> but now once in the end of the world
> he hath appeared to put away sin by the sacrifice of himself.
> And it is appointed unto men to once die,
> But after this the judgement:

So Christ was once offered to bear sins of many;
And unto them that look for him
Shall he appear the second time
Without sin unto salvation."

The Priest then crossed over to Maria with the small black box. These were her Son's ashes.

"May the Lord be with you my child. God has a reason for everything. Don't turn away from him because he has taken your son," he added kindly as he placed the box into her hands and held it with her as he talked to her.

"I will always love and trust God father." Maria added." He has been very kind to me." She said this so calmly that even the priest was taken aback for a little while. She and Father Khumalo noticed this. But they made no attempt to explain. He was not privy to what had happened. All these arrangements had been made after Father Khumalo had sent an urgent message to the Vatican. He did that the very day the Boy had died. He'd realised then that the vultures and monsters that were waiting outside the delivery room on that fateful Christmas, were people that were too powerful for him to handle alone. He needed help. And help arrived from the Vatican within two days. They sent a senior delegation led by Cardinal Vincent. He had already instructed the hospital that the boy be cremated the same day. And his orders had been carried out without the knowledge of Galvez and his crew. By the time they'd realised what had happened it was too late. Cardinal Vincenzo and his team of Vatican security had arrived. Surprisingly Galvez and his team didn't offer much resistance. In fact the left even before the Vatican staff had arrived. From then on they were under they care of the Vatican.

That explained why the presiding priest wasn't privy to what had happened. To him this was a sad case of a young mother that had lost her child. She must have been a single mother he thought, as Jos had left with Galvez and his team. That also explained why the church was empty except for a few clergy and security from the Vatican. The only faces that were familiar to Maria were those of her parents and Father Khumalo. Everyone else was Vatican staff.

As she took the ashes, she knelt down with Father Khumalo and they said a short prayer in Zulu. Father Khumalo started the prayer and Maria quickly joined in. The presiding priest frowned again. It was the thanksgiving for the Lord's favour; **A psalm of David.**

"...I will praise thee with my whole heart:
before god will I sing praise unto thee.
I will worship toward thy holy temple,
For thou hast magnified thy word above all thy name..."

Then Maria stood up, turned to Cardinal Vincenzo who was waiting immediately behind her and handed the box to him.

"These are his remains. I now put them in your care and trust." She added.

"They are safe my child...very safe." Cardinal Vincenzo nodded reassuringly to her. He took the box, knelt down and said a short prayer in silence. Then he gently kissed the box. Maria noticed that he had a slight tremor.

"We must leave for Rome immediately Maria and Father Khumalo. You will all be safer there. The forces of evil may not be through yet." He whispered to both of them as he said that and glanced at the dozen or so security men who were all wearing dark suits and shades.

"Yes Cardinal Vincenzo!" Maria answered without hesitation.

"Fine. His Holiness is waiting for us in Rome. His private jet is waiting at Heathrow!"

Bell Residence, Baltimore, USA.

"Who the fuck could have done this?" asked a fuming Galvez.

"I told you we should have been more careful. That Hans must have been working for whoever did this. Shit! What are we going to do now?" Senator Bell was really upset. He had lost almost everything. Hid friends Wilt and O'Neal and the Boy. It all started with Nicky's death. His mind raced back to Nam. He hated the feeling of being stalked by an invisible enemy. This sent a cold shiver up his spine.

"Damn yellow bastards!" he cursed.

"What?" A surprised looking Galvez asked.

"Nothing! Can't you use your damn contacts in the underworld to sort this mess up Galvez?" he shouted.

"We will get revenge Bell. That I can assure you!" Galvez cursed and spat into the fishpond. "I swear upon the memory of my two sons!"

"We have lost everything. We don't even have the boy. This has been a real waste of time and resources Galvez. We will never regain control again!" Bell had every reason to be upset. The FBI had called him in for questioning regarding O'Neal and Wilt's murders. It was common knowledge that they were close acquaintances. The fact that he'd been out of the country had helped a little. But somehow, he felt as if the loop was closing in on him and the MC. It was the worst possible ambush. The enemy was coming from two fronts. It was even possible that there were two enemy camps. And now the FBI! If this leaked to the press this would be the end of his political career. That could not happen. The elections were looming and Bill's two terms were coming to an end. He was looking forward to that. That could only bring more opportunities. Now was the time to consolidate his power base, not weaken it. He made his decision.

"Look Galvez…the FBI are all over me. They are on to us. I don't think it's wise for us to meet…well until the dust settles. I think you should leave the States for a while." Galvez didn't argue. The mention of the FBI was enough to unsettle him. He wasn't prepared to end up behind bars. If they couldn't tie him to the murders they would drum up some drug charge or tax evasion.

"Shit…that tax trick was what got Capone," he whispered to himself. "I understand Bell. We will have to let the second part of our plan take it's course. Maybe this whole thing failed because the timing was all wrong! This year is the real end of the 21st Century. Damn…our timing was fucking off by a year if you ask me!"

"OK then. Let's get plan B into action. And let's pray you get the fucking bastards that killed O'Neal and Wilt!"

"You can bet on that Bell…You can bet your last dollar on that!" Galvez was staring straight ahead of him. He was in a trance. The same zone that he'd entered as he killed Hans. It was death that he wanted to see again.

Moscow, Russia

"Gaspadina Nikoliovic…it's the Kaiser on the line," Uri whispered. Sasha was having his lunch. He knew that he hated being disturbed while he was eating, but this was business, very important business. Sasha was expecting the call. He took a gulp of red wine to wash down the fillet steak.

"Kaiser…I hope the new arrangement s are to your satisfaction!"

"Yes Sasha. Yes indeed. You have done well. You may keep the Billion dollars as arranged. I am satisfied with the alternate arrangements."

"Well that's good to know. I always deliver. And I'm happy this has come to an acceptable conclusion." Sasha put the phone down. He spat on to the floor in disgust and pushed his food of plate on to the floor in a swift motion of anger. Talking to the Kaiser had spoilt his appetite.

"Bastard says he's happy with the alternate arrangements! As if he would have done something about it if he wasn't!" he shouted in anger.

"We should never have gone to bed with the devil. Now my skin is beginning to crawl as if I have worms inside me!"

"It's just business Gaspadina. Business...remember?" Uri was trying to calm his boss. He waited for a minute or two until Sasha had calmed down.

"The Kaiser has received our parcel?" he asked.

"Yes he has. God...what have we done? Uri...we have just sold our souls to the devil." Sasha said this quietly. Uri was taken aback by the sudden remorse that Sasha displayed. Perhaps this time they had gone too far!

Twenty-three

End of February 2000, In the Vatican.

"Why are you so depressed Father Khumalo?" Maria asked. She'd noticed that in the past few days that he'd become a little quiet. And whenever she went to his room at night, she would find him on his hands and knees in prayer. It seemed as if he prayed both day and night, with only a few hours for sleep.

"Yes I am worried my child. The suffering around the world seems to be getting worse. The natural disasters are increasing, not decreasing. Perhaps God has decided to punish us all for what we did!"

"What do you mean Father?"

"You saw the vengeance with which Cyclone Eline has descended on Mozambique and the rest of Southern Africa. I am not sure we will ever recover after this. Hundreds of people have drowned. Over 30000 cattle have died and all the crops have been destroyed. I think what has destroyed me my child, is the site of that lonely girl. You know the one that hung on to a tree for days and gave birth to her child while she clung for both their dear life's, as the raging flood water waited patiently for her to drop her baby as she gave birth."

"Yes I saw that too. But she held on to her baby." Maria had been touched by the site. The helicopters only managed to rescue her after four days.

"How can a people and a continent go through so much. When the floods have stopped, the people are going to die from hunger and disease." Father Khumalo was depressed.

"Let's not despair Father. Surely the international community will respond and help!" Maria answered in earnest.

"I am not so sure my daughter. Remember Rwanda. Almost a million people had to die before the international community stepped in. And now the same thing is happening in Burundi. If it wasn't for Mwalumi Julius Nyerere and our ex-President, Nelson Mandela, the world was prepared to watch again while the people of Burundi were being visited by the devil himself." Father Khumalo continued. "And there are the floods that have submerged half of Queensland in Australia, the freezing temperatures in the East Coast of the States."

"Yes I see what you mean father."

"And just to add more to the injury we're facing and to open up old wounds, decent countries in Europe are electing Neo-Nazis' into power. When will we ever learn?" Father Khumalo was sad. The strain showed. His hair had greyed completely in the last few months. The lines around his eyes were as deep as the rivers that now flooded his homeland. His hair had become as white as the snow that capped the Alps that they had flown over on their way to Rome. And he had lost at least 7 kilograms. Maria had noticed this.

"You must eat more Father. I think God knows that you and I have repented. He needs all the help he can get on earth. You starving yourself is of no help to God Father."

"OK my child. I will eat more." Father Khumalo was trying to brush Maria aside.

"No Father…I am serious. You have been there for me for all these years. I am not going to see you go down into depression again. I need you. We need each other. God need's us. I have a feeling that our work has not ended!"

"Yes my child. I am sorry for having worried you so. Let's go the dining room and get something to eat."

The days had moved slowly at the Vatican. Cardinal Vincenzo kept them informed. They had an audience with his holiness on arrival and now all they could do was wait. Cardinal Vincenzo had sent word to Turin, warning them about the danger the Cloth was possibly in. He had even asked that they consider postponing or cancelling the public viewing that was scheduled for the 29th of August. Perhaps if that was not possible, they could shorten the viewing period to a few weeks, not three months. But the viewing was to go ahead. The agreement then was that Maria and Father Khumalo would stay at the Vatican until the viewing of the Shroud of Turin was over in October 2000. That was the best possible arrangement.

August 2000, Galvez Residence.

"How are you feeling today my angel?" Galvez always greeted her that way. He had kept her at his residence in Bogota, Columbia for the last seven months. She was one of the villager's daughters. She had survived the earthquake in Armenia. He peasant parents were both killed the night the earth opened up and swallowed the city of Armenia. It was the same fiend that had claimed his two boys and his wife. Her name was Christina. She was beautiful, with long black hair that dangled lazily as it rested on the small of her back. Her eyes were green, soft and innocent. She was now 18years old and considered Senor Galvez her saviour. She was willing to do anything for him.

"I'm fine Senor. It's just that I seem to is getting a little tired these days. I think it's because you feed me too much Senor!" she giggled innocently as she rubbed her pregnant belly.

"No Christina…you look lovely and you are going to give birth to a very special baby. It is because you're are special Christina. A very special women indeed!" Galvez was stroking her hair as he said it. He was admiring the beauty and innocence that Christina was and the life that was growing inside her. This time there would be no mistake. E would keep her there in Bogota, under his direct supervision until the Boy was delivered. He smiled as he recalled how he'd managed to do it again, for the second time around. Thanks to Dr Carol Thomas. Yes the very paediatrician that had tried to save the Boys life on that fateful day in London, on Christmas day. The fresh blood she had drawn from the Boy's umbilicus, trying to check how well oxygenated he was before she decided to pull the tube out; well he'd realised the opportunity amid all the chaos that had descended on them that night. When everyone was busy wailing, at a loss of what to do, and shocked by the sudden death of that idiot priest from Cape Town, he had kept his calm. That was what kept him ahead of the pack. It was a survival instinct. He had learnt how to think on his feet. How to see an opportunity when everyone else saw problems. So amid all the chaos, he quietly slipped into the delivery room that night and grabbed the syringe. A syringe that was full of fresh blood cells from the Boy. A perfect tissue sample, with millions of genetic material ready to be cloned. Now that Christina was pregnant, the rest of the blood was hidden, frozen in liquid nitrogen somewhere in Austria. He had friends there, people he could trust. People who understood purity, power and the need for a new Arian messiah. Christina was doing well. There could only be one Messiah, but if his plan failed again, he would do it again and again, until he and Bell got what they wanted.

"Christina…you should try to rest a little more. You don't have to do any of the household chores. There are plenty of servants here to help. All you have to do is ask." Galvez had noticed that she was tidying the room up. For Christina it was the natural thing to do. She had been born in a poor family. They had to work for their daily bread and she wasn't used to this life of luxury, of plenty. It felt almost sinful to her when she thought of those that she had left behind.

"But Senor Galvez, I have to do something," she pleaded innocently.

"Yes my Christina…you are already doing so much for me, for the baby and for the world!"

Kaiser's Residence, September 2000.

"Herr Kaiser…it's time for your morning tea." The Kaiser jerked in surprise. He had been looking at the glass container in front of him intently. This was something he had been doing for the past nine months. He spent at 8 hours a day here, with out fail. He prayed for guidance, wisdom and the strength to complete what he'd promised the Fuhrer before the Fuhrer had shot himself in the bunker. What a terrible night. What a terrible night that was. He couldn't wipe that night out of his memory, no matter how hard he tried. He remembered feeling so ashamed at the acceptance of defeat, of humiliation at the hands of the allies. He managed to escape because the Fuhrer had insisted that he leave early. It was left to him to try again. It was his responsibility to wipe away the shame, to avenge the humiliation. And now…well it seemed that things were finally on track.

"Just give me another minute Adolf," he replied after recollecting his thoughts. Then he turned to look back at the glass container. The Boy's eyes were shut. His skin was grey, a little wrinkled and he looked smaller. He'd shrunk in size and weight. That was to be expected after all he'd been through. But there was no mistaking him though. Even in death he still looked noble, graceful and supreme. The morticians in London had done a good job. Just how Sasha had convinced them not to cremate the Boy…well, he would never know, neither did he care. Sasha had delivered on his promise. Fair enough he would have preferred the Boy alive. But this was the next best solution. If the Cloth of

Turin could be so revered after all these years, then the Boy would be worshiped. He was the real thing, in the flesh. It reminded him of Lenin's body. Ever present, watching over mother Russia. He would wait till the century turned, till the 31st of December 2000. Then he would make his move.

"Damn Russians." He cursed quietly. "Determined characters they are. Fought us well." He was reminiscing about the defeat they suffered in the Second World War. He gathered his thoughts again and fixed his eyes on the Boys face.

"This time we will not fail…for you will be on our side!"

Epilogue

The new Millennium started in January 2001. There are those who feel that it will herald the "Coming of the Son of Man". But if it must be so, they have no right to play God.

The following however are true:

1. The Cloth of Turin is kept in Turin, Italy. It was first photographed in 1898 by Secondo Pia and measures about 14 and a half feet long. A piece of the Cloth is acknowledged to be missing. Historians believe that the piece most likely disappeared during the Crusader wars.

It was put on display for public viewing, only for the third time this century, in the Turin Cathedral for eight weeks, from Saturday August 26 to Sunday October 26, year 2000. It commemorated the Jubilee anniversary of the birth of Jesus. This was be the 5th time that it was publicly displayed since 1898. Red blood cells were said to be isolated and photographed recently. And pollen analysed from the Cloth is said to prove that it was indeed the Cloth that wrapped Jesus Christ.

When it was put on display in 1978, 3 and a half million people viewed it over a 5-week period. i.e. 100000 people each day. More information about the Cloth of Turin may be found on the web site: http://www.shroud.org

2. Dolly the Sheep, was the first mammal to be cloned in 1997.This was achieved by a scientist in Scotland.

3. Scientist in Hawaii succeeded in cloning the first male mammal in May of 1999. It is a mouse called "Fibro"! At the time of publication, Fibro was still alive and well and had fathered two litters. From a scientific perspective, after this hurdle, it should now be possible to clone a human being!

4.The Oberammergau Passion Play takes place every ten years in the village of Oberammergau, in Germany. The first play was performed in 1633 after the plague had decimated the inhabitants of the village. The play is performed every ten years; the last time it was performed was in 1990.The year 2000 saw the last performance of the century and was scheduled for the 8th of June. Details may be found on the web site. (*http://www.gaponline.de/*).

Afterword from the Author

The science of cloning is here to stay. It has become embedded in our minds fore ever. That is the reality. Perhaps this time before we as citizens of the Earth give carte blanche to this science, we should ponder a little longer than we did after Oppenheimer flirted with the science of atoms and nuclei bombs in the 1940s'.

Patrice Matchaba

About the Author

Patrice Matchaba is an Obstetrician and Gynaecologist by training and a graduate of the Harvard Business School, PMD program. This is his third novel.